Bye, Bye Love

Books by K. J. Larsen

The Cat DeLuca Mysteries
Liar, Liar
Sticks and Stones
Some Like it Hot
Bye, Bye Love

Bye, Bye Love

A Cat DeLuca Mystery

K. J. Larsen

Poisoned Pen Press

Copyright © 2015 by K. J. Larsen

First Edition 2015

10 9 8 7 6 5 4 3 2 1

Library of Congress Catalog Card Number: 2014954927

ISBN: 9781464203831   Hardcover
      9781464203855   Trade Paperback

Poisoned Pen Press
6962 E. First Ave., Ste. 103
Scottsdale, AZ 85251
www.poisonedpenpress.com
info@poisonedpenpress.com

Printed in the United States of America

This is dedicated to all the men we've loved.
To the faithful, dogged guys who fell on the sword
and shared our lives.

And to the cheaters. May they never find your bodies.

Acknowledgments

Our heartfelt thanks to Barbara Peters: our incomparable, long-suffering Editor Extraordinaire. We're your biggest fans. And to the amazing cast at Poisoned Pen Press. Nobody does it better.

A big shout-out to our Papa, Amanda Boblet, Alan Mitchell, and everyone who helped make Cat DeLuca's latest adventure possible.

And always to our parents, Harold and Arlene Larsen, and our awesome family. You make us laugh every day. Without you, we could never write comedy.

Chapter One

I was staking out the LeGrande Hotel on Asher and sucking the creamy filling out of a cannoli. My fingers absently drummed out a beat on the steering wheel while I kept an eye on a brunette in the hotel parking lot. Her name is Cookie Allen. Cookie's married to Jerry, a wiry man with a birdlike face and a wild nest of yellow hair. Jerry's an inquisitive kind of guy. He wants to know why his wife reeks of Brut Cologne.

It's not exactly rocket science. Cookie Allen has a lover. She left telltale signs and a big trail of cookie crumbs. A dumbass could figure it out. But not Jerry. He's hired me to spell it out for him.

I'm a great speller.

My name is Cat DeLuca and I'm a Private Dick—though I prefer Jane. I don't investigate for insurance companies or work for ambulance-chasers. I won't find your high school sweetheart. But if you're in Chicagoland and you suspect your partner is stepping out, call me. I kick ass at catching cheaters.

Last week Jerry showed up at my office, his brain in deep freeze. His wife's betrayal was slapping him in the face, but he was swimming in denial. It happens in this business. You know your relationship is in the toilet but you're not ready to go there. So your mind creates an alternative scenario as a coping mechanism. It's a temporary state of insanity.

That's where I come in.

"What do you think is happening with your wife, Jerry?"

His small, birdlike chin quivered. "What do you mean?"

"I dunno. The late nights, unexplained absences. A sudden disinterest in sex and all things you."

"I think it's the change. I hear it affects women that way."

"Your wife is twenty-six years old."

"So?"

"It's not the change."

Jerry scrunched his face, searching for an explanation other than the obvious. I stopped him before he could decide his wife had a part-time job moonlighting for Brut.

"The Brut Factory is in Texas," I said.

"What does that have to do with anything?"

"Just sayin'."

Jerry sighed and gnawed on beakish lips. "I don't wanna make no trouble."

"God, no."

"So what will you do?"

"I'm gonna shadow her."

His eyes flashed alarm. "If Cookie thinks I don't trust her…"

"She won't know I was there. It's what I do".

He dragged out a roll of antacids, popped a handful in his mouth, and chewed furiously.

"Here's the plan. I'll be in the hospital parking lot when your wife's shift ends on Sunday. I'll tail her—"

His eyes widened.

"Not to worry. I'm the queen of discretion. I'll keep a diary of her movements. Make a note of anyone she has contact with."

He nodded staring through me, his brain still on ice.

I wanted to shake him, but I put a hand on his arm and flashed an encouraging smile.

"I got this, Jerry. You're going to be OK. I'm armed with spy-eye binoculars and my super, high-powered camera. I'll snag some steamy 8 by 10 glossies and when I deliver them to you your brain will thaw."

He nodded and then his head did a double take. "Huh?"

"Exactly."

◇◇◇

A horn blared from the street in front of the hotel. Cookie was too busy fidgeting with her hair to notice. She was primping for Brut Boy. I popped the newest Pink album into the CD player, stretched my legs, and waited.

Cookie Allen works as an X-ray tech at Mercy Hospital and I was waiting when her shift ended at 2:30. At 2:31 she bolted out the door and barreled to her car. She gave her face a five-minute touch up and perked up the girls before pulling the red Mazda Miata out of her parking spot. I was on her like sauce on spaghetti. She headed down Twenty-sixth and hit the Dan Ryan toward the west end, hell and gone from her house in Bridgeport.

Her first stop was a dry cleaner's on South Ashland. Cookie dropped off a small bag of clothes, then took a quick spin by Lovers Package. Next stop was Walgreen's for a Snickers bar, some mints, and a copy of *Soap Opera Digest*. And like a cherry on top, a can of whipping cream. I didn't have to be a top-notch detective to know one thing. Some Mama's son was gonna get lucky tonight.

The G in the neon LeGrande Hotel sign sputtered, making it quiver almost hypnotically. I mentally slapped myself and opened my surveillance cooler. It was stocked with Tino's pizza, sausages, and Mama's Mediterranean chicken. As well as her unrivaled cannoli. It will drop you to your knees.

I tossed a sausage to the beagle in the backseat. Inga is my partner at the Pants on Fire Detective Agency. She has soulful brown eyes and an ever-joyful tail. She's fiercely loyal and better company than most people I know.

I poured a cup of coffee and let the steam warm my face. I get what Jerry's going through. My brief marriage to Johnnie Rizzo was a crash course in infidelity. It was like a knife to the gut. Johnnie was a serial cheater, scoring like an Olympic athlete. But then, love can be brutal.

Sometimes you gotta get up, brush yourself off, and take your life back. You go out with your friends and exorcize your lying ex with shameless quantities of tequila and chocolate. You listen to the voice inside you that says you'll create a better life than you ever imagined. Even if it's the tequila talking.

A cool late autumn breeze blew off the lake. I hunched down in my silver Honda Accord and tugged my coat tighter around me. I didn't want to fire up my engine and draw attention to myself. I figured this gig wouldn't last long. The LeGrande is known for renting rooms by the hour. I doubt the sheets change as often as the guests.

Inga kissed my cheek and jumped into the passenger seat to negotiate for more sausages. A beat up blue construction van pulled into the hotel parking lot. Cookie leapt from the car, feet dancing, before Brut Boy killed the engine. Her husband, Jerry, may look like a bird. But her lover was a big burly bear of a guy with dark curly hair exploding from his neckline. Cookie seemed to be exploring a wide spectrum of the animal kingdom.

They ran into each other's arms and held tight for a long time. When they pulled back, they gazed deep in each other's eyes and laughed.

I've been in this business a long time. And I've found people are driven to cheat for a variety of reasons: for the thrill, revenge, self-undoing, conquest, boredom, emptiness, or a sense of loss. Sometimes, it's just for a lack of good sense. Some people cheat because they think they won't get caught. Others just wanna get busted.

I'd probably never know how the affair between Cookie and her bear of a lover began. But I believed she was here today because they were in love. I aimed my camera, knowing I'd hate passing the pics on to Jerry. Cookie's lover wore a wedding ring. I knew Cookie and Jerry didn't have kids. It would be too much to hope her lover's marriage would dissolve so cleanly.

She put an arm around his waist and they drifted my way. I buried my face in the latest *O! Magazine*. The lovers ambled past me and into the hotel, his hand resting on her bum.

I tossed another sausage into the backseat. "Back in a flash, Inga. This won't take long."

I grabbed my flower print handbag with the hidden camcorder and strode to the heavy oak and glass doors. I was locked, loaded, and ready for love.

Or at least ready to expose it on 8 by 10 color glossies.

I paused a moment beneath the quivering neon G and taking a deep, heady breath of Brut, tromped into the hotel behind them.

Chapter Two

The old man puffing on a pipe looked out of place behind the registration desk. He had the rugged, sun-etched face of someone who'd spent his life at sea.

Cookie filled out the registration card and her lover paid for the room in cash. When she was finished, she shoved the card across the smooth surface. He picked it up and looked at it.

"Mr. and Mrs. Smith," he said.

Yeah. That's original.

The man removed one of the keys from a hook behind him and slid it across the desk.

"Room 222. Need a receipt?"

"No," Cookie said hastily.

Shocker.

The front desk clerk palmed the money, not bothering to ring it into the cash register.

I hung around the gumball machine in the lobby until the couple disappeared down the hall.

The old man was packing fresh tobacco in his pipe when I approached the desk. He slid the registration card my way.

"Hourly or overnight rate?"

I didn't ask for the five-minute special.

"One hour."

I checked out the available keys on the wall. "Room 224 please."

His eyes narrowed warily. "You follow Mr. and Mrs. Smith in here? Cuz, lady, I don't want no trouble."

"Ditto." I signed the registration and passed it back.

"Receipt?"

"Yes. Taxes, you know."

He begrudgingly rang up the sale and I dropped the receipt in my bag.

I tossed him a wink. "I'll take that key now."

◇◇◇

The decades had not been kind to the LeGrande Hotel. If there had once been "grandness" here, time had long since stripped it away. And no amount of fresh paint and carpeting would bring it back.

I rode a groaning elevator to the second floor and ambled down a long, threadbare carpet that screamed for a cleaning. My room was smack next to Mr. and Mrs. Smith's tête-à-tête. In passing, I pressed an ear to their door. I could make out a faint murmur. But I couldn't decide if they were breathing hard or talking. I decided to give them a few minutes to tear each other's clothes off.

My key opened the door to a stale-smelling room with a bed and nightstand, a rickety table, two chairs, and a boxy television from the previous century. A mirror hung on the wall over the headboard: a featured bonus for a sleazy flophouse. The bedspread was a mosaic print designed to camouflage dirt and a host of bodily fluids. The thought of seeing this room through a black light made me shudder. I hugged my bag close and steered clear of the furniture. Visions of bedbugs danced in my head.

An adjoining door connected our rooms. I opened my side and heard a definite moan. Enough talk. I tried the knob on the connecting door but 224 was locked from the inside. Plan A would've been too easy.

Plan B was to climb out the window and crawl along the ledge to capture that perfect Kodak moment. I unlocked the window, swung the bag over my shoulder, and heaved. The window opened six inches and stopped. Shit. But I got it. I'd been here five minutes and I already wanted to jump.

I had been hoping to avoid Plan C.

The coast was clear in the hallway. I switched on the video camera hidden in my bag and removed my lock pics from their wallet. Then I scooted to 222, knelt at the door, and did my magic.

With a steadying breath, I twisted the knob, positioning my camera purse for an unobstructed recording of the romp and circumstance. My plan was to enter unnoticed, snag my 8 by 10 glossy, and run like hell. It happens.

But not today.

Cookie was on top. Our eyes met in the mirror.

I positioned my camera purse and gasped, mortified. "I'm so sorry. The guy gave me the wrong key."

Cookie twirled around and snagged a sheet around her.

"I know you."

"No you don't."

"You're following me!"

"Am not."

"You were at Walgreens when I bought the aspirin."

"Was not."

"Liar!"

Psycho woman. My gaze fell to the tube of ForPlay on the night-stand. I moved a bit, positioning the camera bag to pick it up.

"So, how's the aspirin working for you?"

The grizzly guy's face went pale. He shoved Cookie aside and she almost hit the floor.

He choked. "My wife knows?"

"She was following *me*, you idiot. She works for Jerry."

Relief flooded his face.

Cookie smacked him.

I backed up to the door.

"Stop her!" Cookie yelled. "There's a camera in her bag."

He lunged and I ran.

I hauled ass, scooting past the elevator and flying down the stairs. Hot on my heels, Grizzly guy shouted obscenities.

"Potty mouth," I threw back at him.

The guy could run—I had to give him that. His body was a study in hair but he didn't look that scary. God knows he wasn't hiding a weapon.

I hit the ground floor and dashed across the lobby.

The old man moaned behind the desk. "I don't want no police."

"Then don't call them!"

Bare feet slapped the floor behind me. I threw a look over my shoulder. Grizzly man was closing fast, a pillow recklessly covering his groin. I hurled the gumball machine to the ground in passing and flung a coat rack to the floor. Maybe obstruction techniques work for James Bond. But the glass globe didn't break and a gazillion spinning gumballs didn't pitch my pursuer on his face. He vaulted over the coat rack, riding air and swallowing the distance between us.

My heart sank. I wasn't going to make it. I would lose precious seconds at the door and he'd rip the purse from my shoulder and crush it.

Dammit. I love that camera bag.

"Gimme the pictures," he roared and I felt his wheezing breath on my neck.

I hit the brakes and threw my arms up in a show of surrender. I faced him, my heart pounding in my chest.

"You win. You can have the film but I get the camera back."

He hacked a smoker's cough. "You might want to think twice before sticking your nose where it don't belong."

"Yeah, yeah. You sound like my mother."

I plunged a hand in my bag, dragged out my pepper spray, and painted his face with it.

He screeched at an ear-shattering pitch.

"And you, sir, might want to lower that pillow."

I hightailed it out the door to the Silver Bullet and didn't slow down until I landed behind the wheel and cranked the engine.

Inga kissed my cheek. She had sausage breath. I ruffled her neck.

"And that is exactly why I hate Plan C."

Chapter Three

I wanted to wrap up this case and give Jerry a heads-up before Cookie came home. She would almost certainly be in a twit. I hadn't exactly been the queen of discretion as promised. Tonight could be brutal for my client.

I pointed the nose of the Silver Bullet toward my home in Bridgeport. Bridgeport is a tight-knit community and one of Chicago's most vibrant and diverse areas. It's home to a thriving art scene, and nightlife, and a staggering number of DeLucas. The neighbors know you and will tell you your business whether you want them to or not.

My immediate plan was to print up some 8 by 10 glossies and deliver them to my client. I liked Jerry. He was a sweet guy with a rough patch ahead. I was confident he'd make it through and find happiness again.

I was halfway home when "Your Cheatin' Heart" blared from my cell phone. Oh, Hank.

I flipped the lid. "Pants on Fire Detective Agency. We catch liars and cheats."

"Caterina. Is that you?"

"You know it's me, Mama. You dialed this number."

"It doesn't sound like you."

"I'm out of breath. I was, uh, running."

"Good you should run fast. This job you do, this hootchie stalking, it's dangerous."

"I'm not a hootchie stalker, Mama."

"You're not a policeman. You piss people off."

"I'm a private investigator. I'm licensed to piss people off."

Mama gave a soft groan. I knew she was clutching her chest.
"My heart," she choked.

"Take some Tums, Mama. Your heart's fine. The doctor says
it's gas."

"It's not gas. It's an ungrateful daughter who should marry
that nice FBI agent and give her Mama her last dying wish."

"You're not dying from gas, Mama. And you're too young
to make that wish."

"Grandchildren. My dying wish is grandchildren." Mama's
voice was faint. "Is that so much to ask?"

The truth is Mama already has an alarming number of
grandchildren. Thanks in part to my sister Sophie, the walking,
talking baby machine.

"Spasm," she choked.

"Mama, take your Tums."

"Please God, don't take me before I marry the father of my
children."

I took a deep breath and did a full ten-count. "You're already
married, Mama. God got the memo. And on Saturday, you're
getting married *again*."

Mama and Papa were married thirty-five years ago at the
Bridgeport Cook County Courthouse by the Justice of the Peace.
Recently, some loud-mouthed, bitter old church lady told her
God doesn't know you're married if you weren't married in the
church. When Papa came home, Mama was moving his clothes,
shoes, and pillow into the guest room.

The truth is my parents are as happy as any couple I know.
They do what works for them. A long time ago Papa decided to
let Mama be right. And thirty-five years later, Mama still lights
up like Christmas when he enters the room.

My parents' church wedding is scheduled for Saturday. Sophie
and I are bridesmaids. My three brothers are groomsmen. And
a long trail of grandkids will tromp up the aisle with the rings.

"Mama, did you take your Tums? Let me talk to Papa."

"He's not here. He's working on his vows. I haven't seen him this nervous since you kids were born." She gave a giddy laugh.

"I'm sort of tied up right now. Can I help you with something?"

"Tell me where Papa's taking me for our honeymoon."

"Huh?"

"What do I pack? Swimming suit? Sweaters?" She shuddered. "After all these years, I better not be packing the sweaters."

And that is when the truth about Mama's little wedding-charade hit me smack in the face.

"Oh my god, Mama. You hustled Papa."

"*What?*" The shocked indignation was priceless.

"Mmhmm. It's all becoming crystal clear to me. You never believed your first wedding didn't take. But you knew Papa would never go along with renewing your vows. So you made it all about God not recognizing your courthouse marriage."

"My daughter the big detective."

"Uh huh. Spill it."

Mama's voice started with a catch. She knew she was busted. "So sue me. When your Papa and I were married, we didn't have the money for a proper wedding. Tony promised if we went to the judge, I'd have a real church wedding someday. Only every time I brought it up, he changed the subject."

I laughed. "Well he's keeping his promise now."

"I may have to go to Confession."

"I dunno. I think it was genius!"

"It was, wasn't it?" She giggled. "You ordered the cake?"

"And the flowers. And the caterers."

"We don't need caterers. The church ladies will take care of the reception."

"And you'll be in the kitchen supervising. How's the chest pain now?"

Mama made her clicking sound with her mouth. "*Finito.*"

"Good. Don't worry about a thing. I want this day to be perfect for you."

"You want perfect? Perfect is a double wedding. Does your FBI boyfriend have a tux? You can wear Nanna DeLuca's wedding dress."

"*Seriously?* She's a foot shorter than I am."

"So you show some leg. You should give your FBI boyfriend ideas. You can start making babies on your honeymoon."

"OK, Mama. Now I have gas."

◇◇◇

I disconnected the call and made another one.

"Tony DeLuca."

"Where are you, Papa? Mama said you're working on your vows."

"I'm at your house. Come home and write my vows."

"I can't write your vows, Papa."

"Of course you can. Does the President write his own speeches?"

"Nice try."

Papa sucked a breath and I knew he was clutching his scar. My family are experts in dishing out the guilt. Papa's career with the Chicago PD was cut short a few years ago when he was shot in the caboose on the mean streets of Chicago. Now he's a real Chicago hero. He rides on the back of a convertible in every Bridgeport parade. He works as a liaison between the Chicago Police Department and the schools. He visits schools, sharing his brave, inspiring story with kids all over the city. He talks about guns and alternatives to violence.

The details of the shooting are apparently too hideous for children to hear. The bullet Papa took defending the good people of Chicago was a regrettable misfire from a rookie cop whose future with the force is forever cemented in traffic duty. He's the loneliest guy at the Ninth Precinct.

The school kids love Papa. They giggle when he pulls the back of his trousers down just far enough to see his scar. And then the teacher serves cupcakes.

One day, Papa flashed his scar at a Catholic school. A nun gasped and crossed herself. She said the scar was a perfect image of the Mother Mary. Father Timothy blessed Papa's whole right cheek with holy water.

"OK, Papa, read me what you've got."

"Let me see." He rustled some pages and cleared his throat. "I, Tony DeLuca..."

"That's a strong start. Go on."

"That's it."

"*Seriously?* That's what you got? Your wedding is Saturday."

"No, my wedding was thirty-five years ago." He groaned. "I got nothin', Caterina. You gotta help me out here. I can't take this any longer. I can't sleep. Your Mama booted me to the guest room. I'm a *guest* in my own house."

"Pull it together, Papa. It's just 'til Saturday."

"I haven't touched your Mama for a—"

"Whoa. Way too much info."

"Men have needs, Kitten. It's not natural for a man to—"

"La la la la." I held the cell away from my head and waited a moment for the rant to stop. When I thought it was safe, I moved the phone to my ear again.

"—your Mama is too delicious, I—"

I hand smacked my head. "Enough! I surrender. I'll help with your vows."

He chuckled. "*Grazie.*"

"I'll be home when I can. Maybe you can make a list of things you like about Mama and your life together. And nix on the delicious parts. We'll put it all together when I get there. I'm just wrapping up a case."

"A case?" Papa's voice piqued with uncharacteristic interest. "Who's doing who?"

"I'm going to pretend you didn't say that. Sleeping in the guest room is making you creepy."

He laughed. "I knew you'd come through with my vows."

"Whatever. Mama wants to know what she should pack for the honeymoon. She's hoping for something tropical."

"I don't think so. Your Mama likes Wisconsin."

"Wisconsin? *Seriously?*"

"I thought we'd drive up north and find a cozy cabin. Like we did when you kids were young."

My hands clenched. He hadn't even made a reservation. It's just as well his neck wasn't in reach.

"Forget Wisconsin, Papa. This is your *honeymoon*. Mama wants you to blow her away."

"There's wind in Wisconsin."

"She wants *tropical*. She wants a cruise. When I get home we'll make online reservations. And it won't cost more than the Viking barbeque monstrosity you bought yourself a few years ago."

He winced. *"Madre di dio!"*

I laughed. "Buck up, Papa. When Mama's happy, everybody's happy."

I wasn't quite ready to deal with Papa yet. Rather than print my 8 by 10 glossies at home, I took a quick detour to the FedEx on West Thirty-Fifth.

I parked and gave Jerry a call. My client was on his way home from work and stuck on Stevenson. I could hear him cursing the potato truck that had lost its load. This would take a while. It was not Jerry's day.

I figured I'd still get to him before Cookie did. I didn't expect her anytime soon. It would take her a while to figure out a story to spin for her husband.

Good luck with that.

First, I printed a dozen 8 by 10 glossies in vivid Technicolor and put them in a large white envelope. This is the hardest part of my job. Even if a client is prepared for the worst, it's brutal to see your partner with another lover. And this birdlike guy was more fragile than most.

I had no doubt that Jerry would get through this. I also knew that nothing I could say would help. As much as I try, I've never found a kind way to break bad news to my clients. And I didn't think one would pop into my consciousness now.

Inga and I still had a little time to kill while Jerry broke through the potato blockade. We swung by a little neighborhood park that was once crumbling concrete and a vacant lot.

Chicago is greening up by converting many of these lots into beautiful shared spaces all over the city.

Inga made fast friends with an English bulldog named Jackson. He was three times her size but my partner didn't know it. A few quick butt-sniffs and they were besties. It should be so easy for humans.

We made it to Jerry's in perfect time. He pulled into his driveway behind us, left his car, and made a face.

"I'll never eat another potato. Those things are vicious."

I smiled.

He stared at the envelope in my hand. "You have something for me."

"Yeah."

His eyes flashed panic and I thought the flight instinct had kicked in. For a moment I wondered if I had a runner. Instead, he breathed deeply and dragged his feet to the front door. His hands were shaking badly. I took the key from him, unlocked the door, and pushed him inside.

He blew a sigh. "It's bad, isn't it?"

"You don't have to do this, Jerry. I'll take the pictures and go home if you wish."

"No. Don't go." He raked his fingers through the yellow nest on his head. "I need to do this. Maybe I should grab a beer first."

I nodded. "Only if you don't have anything stronger."

Chapter Four

Papa's jet-black Cadillac was parked in my driveway when I pulled in front of the Bridgeport brick bungalow I call home. He wasn't alone. The shiny yellow Corvette belonging to my former-client-turned-assistant, Cleo Jones, was also there. Cleo recently inherited the car and all her cheating husband's earthly possessions after someone put a slug in Walter's chest. In fact, she was standing over him when the cops stumbled on Walter's very dead body.

Cleo was a shoe-in for the murder. The cops dragged her to jail, and her YouTube video went viral. She was crucified by the press. An old woman pummeled her with tomatoes at the supermarket. For a while, I was the only person in Chicago who believed Cleo Jones wasn't guilty. Not for lack of motive so much as for opportunity. Cleo's only defense was that someone beat her to it.

I hauled the surveillance cooler up to the porch and opened the front door. A black, hairy dog bounded from the kitchen, body-slammed Inga, and bounced circles around me. Inga threw back her head and howled.

Beau is Cleo's Tibetan Terrier and Inga's best friend. They have weekly sleepovers and Mama takes them on playdates. If Beau appears bigger than Inga, it's all fluff and hair. There's a lot of brushing involved and Cleo's dog brush is attached to her hip. It works for her, but I prefer the wash-and-go beagle.

I dragged the cooler to the kitchen. Cleo was at the stove, her spiraled auburn, pink-tipped tresses corralled in a clip on top of her head. She stirred something dark and decadent and chocolate. I decided it was icing for the chocolate fudge cake still warm from the oven.

Cleo is a master chef with a true passion for cooking. Uncle Joey offered to finance a chic Chicago restaurant with her. Six months ago she would have jumped at the chance. After working at the Pants On Fire Detective Agency, she discovered she likes shooting people more.

Papa hunched at the kitchen table, besieged by piles of scribbled notes and papers. An hour ago, he had three words.

"Are all those papers for your vows?"

He nodded miserably.

"Papa, you don't have to say that much."

Cleo pulled the pan from the burner and added a splash of Grand Marnier. "Don't worry about it. I finished the vows for him."

A note of hysteria squeaked out of me. "No way."

"He just has to work on presentation." She waved a chocolaty wooden spoon at the table. "Second pile on his left. A real showstopper. If he delivers it right, there won't be a dry eye in the house."

I wanted to beat the woman over her head with that chocolate covered spoon, but threw her a look instead. I gave Papa a hug. "This isn't a performance. I'll help you organize your thoughts, but the words will be yours."

Papa pulled his fingers through his thinning hair.

I scooped a few pages from the second pile and scanned the vows Cleo wrote for Papa. "What's this about *shared power?*"

"I like the sound of that," Papa said.

I wondered if he liked the sound of spending the rest of his life in the guest room.

I pivoted, hands on my hips, to face Cleo. "Don't mess with my parents' perfectly dysfunctional relationship, girlfriend. You're the last person to coach anyone's marriage."

"Me? What about you? Your marriage to Johnnie Rizzo was a bust."

"At least I didn't shoot his ass on his way out the door."

"Only because you lack passion."

Papa slugged down his wine and grabbed the bottle.

"Passion? Seriously? Passion? I'm talking marbles here. Or rather, your lack of them. A modicum of sanity would do you wonders."

She sniffed. "I'm an impassioned woman, Cat. I'm a lot like your mom."

"You're nothing like Mama. She doesn't shoot people."

Papa dumped the rest of the wine in his glass. "To be fair, Caterina, we never gave your Mama a gun."

◇◇◇

I tossed a salad and heated up Mama's spinach and ricotta cannelloni. I added a few pieces of Mediterranean chicken from my surveillance cooler. Papa opened another bottle of wine and made reservations for their honeymoon. He decided on a two-week cruise. They would leave from Miami on the *Norwegian Pearl*. Their first port of call would be in Cartagena before traveling through the Panama Canal. After that, they would continue on to Costa Rica, the Banana Coast, Belize, and Costa Maya. Papa dragged out his Visa, clutching his scar. I kissed his cheek. "Put it away. The honeymoon is a wedding gift from your five kids."

He grinned. The scar didn't seem to bother him much after that.

"Now, for the vows." I topped off his wine and, with pen in hand, said, "How did you feel the first time you saw Mama?"

He smiled. "*O mio dio.* Your mama took my breath away. She was the most beautiful—"

Just then Papa's cell phone rang. He put it on speaker. "Where are you, Papa? You don't call. I don't know if you've had supper."

"I'm with Caterina at her house," Papa said.

Mama made a disapproving clicking noise with her mouth. "What did Caterina feed you? My daughter hardly cooks. She's thirty for God's sake. It's no wonder she's not married and has no children."

"I heard that, Mama."

Mama blew a dismissive sound. "What? So now it's a secret?"

"Oh, please."

"I can't sleep, Caterina. Your biological clock keeps me up all night. Tick tock. Tick tock. My heart can't take it."

"Kill me now."

Papa said, "Caterina served a delicious dinner. We had your cannelloni and the Mediterranean chicken that you brought over yesterday. And Cleo made a chocolate cream cake."

"Hi, Mama!" Cleo sang.

"Cleo?" Mama said warmly. "Caterina, you should be more like your partner. *She* can cook."

"*Assistant*," I corrected her. "And Cleo doesn't have kids either."

Cleo glared and I shrugged.

Mama sniffed. "That's cruel, Caterina. Your partner has a medical condition that makes her infertile."

I rolled my eyes. She has a medical condition all right. It's called the pill.

Mama softened her voice. "Tony, when are you coming home? Practice your vows tomorrow. You know I can't sleep when you're not here."

Papa's brows lifted. "Can I sleep in our room, tonight?"

"Not in front of the children, Tony. The wedding is Saturday."

Papa muttered something under his breath that would almost certainly come up at Confession.

She laughed softly. "Papa. It's not that bad, is it?"

I jabbed Papa's ribs before he could answer. "Caterina's picking on me. I'm on my way."

He disconnected the call. "What was that about?"

Papa didn't get it. This was Mama's moment. And in my book, he owed her. For thirty-five years she put the needs of her husband and five kids before her own. Just the thought of labor and diapers and colic and PTA meetings and raising teenagers is a scream for therapy. For every night that Papa had a cold one at Mickey's bar while Mama nursed a sick kid or ironed his uniform, I say he owes her.

"You're giving Mama the wedding and honeymoon she's always dreamed of. Until then, you're in the guest room. Deal with it. Suck it up, and learn your damn vows."

His eyes widened. "Caterina, I've never seen you like this. You're scary-bossy like your Mama."

"My work here is done."

Cleo sent Papa home with half of the rich, sensual chocolate cake, a sparkling bottle of champagne from my personal stash, and a bouquet of fresh flowers from my coffee table.

"What are you doing?" I asked.

"Just giving your papa a little boost."

"What boost?"

"Chocolate, flowers, and champagne. A passionate woman like your mama just might drag her man to bed with her."

"Eeeuw."

Cleo topped our wineglasses and sighed. "I love weddings." Wine splashed on her monumental ta-ta's. Her double D's were always getting in the way. She blew another sigh. "You know, Walter's been gone a long time."

"Not that long."

"If Frankie asked me—"

"Don't say it."

"—to marry him—"

"Enough booze for you, girlfriend." I pried the bottle from her vice-like grip.

I understand Cleo and Frankie are dating. But no amount of alcohol should make a woman want to marry my crazy, unbalanced cousin.

OK. So they're both crazy. And trigger-happy. Their eyes glaze over whenever they fondle a weapon. It's a dangerous combination.

"Face it, Cat. Frankie and I are made for each other."

"Made to kill each other, maybe."

Cleo gave me the evil eye. Or tried to. Mostly her eyeballs crossed. "What are you saying?"

"You're dating a nut, Cleo. And the jury is still out on you."

"That's cold. I love Frankie."

"And I'm almost happy for you. But he's just as hotheaded as you are."

She grinned as if that was a good thing.

"I don't know how Frankie handles relationship problems. But I remember what happened when Walter cheated on you."

She waved a hand, blowing me off. "Walter was a fool. It's not like he didn't know I'd have to shoot him."

"OK. The jury just came back."

"It's the last thing I said in my vows. I said, 'Walter Jones, I marry you and I give you fair warning. Keep your pants zipped or keep your ass covered. You belong to me now.'"

"Wow."

"Powerful stuff, right? There wasn't a dry eye at my wedding."

"Wow," I said again.

She sighed happily. "I'm such a romantic."

◇◇◇

After a while, I wandered to my office and started tackling e-mails and phone messages before checking my Facebook page. When I trotted out again, Cleo was passed out on the couch with two dogs, an empty bottle of wine, and a tub of popcorn. I didn't bother to wake her and ask if she wanted to go for a run. My assistant avoids exercise at all costs. To be fair, Cleo and Beau have joined us on occasion. They run as far as the closest bakery.

A hard, sideways rain pummeled the streets of Chicago, but it didn't trump the fat slice of cake I had for supper. I tugged on my Nikes, pulled my mahogany hair into a ponytail, slipped on a pink rain slicker, and dangled a leash in Inga's face.

"Come on, girl. We're going for a run."

The beagle opened one eye just enough to take in the wet misery beating at the windows. She squeezed it tight again.

"*Seriously?*" I said and popped the leash on her. I pulled up my hoodie and I dragged her ass out the door.

The night was quiet and traffic light. Our feet pounded the wet sidewalk. We passed a few neighbors walking in the rain with their dogs.

The rain eased to a drizzle and stopped soon after we reached the park. The city felt washed and clean and we had the park pretty much to ourselves. We passed a couple diehard runners. A

Chicago Parks employee messed with something in his van. And two soggy, teenage lovers groped each other on a park bench.

Inga led the way. We ran the perimeter of the park and were about three-quarters of the way around our loop when she picked up a scent. Without warning, she stopped dead in her tracks right in front of me. My arms flailed. I dropped the leash, stumbled, and vaulted over her, narrowly averting a crash. When I recovered my balance, she was gone.

My partner was hot on a trail. Mumbling a few choice words, I tore after her through a tangle of shrubbery, following her ear-shattering bay. Oh yeah, beagles don't bark. They scream.

My foot caught on an immovable object, no amount of arm flailing could save me. This time I crashed and burned. The landing was alarmingly lumpy. I was sprawled over something big and wet. I hoped it was Bridgeport's first beached whale. But I wouldn't be so lucky.

In one terrible moment, I knew what Inga had got a whiff of. I smelled it too. Blood.

Chapter Five

A terrified scream welled in my throat and I teetered on the brink of hysteria. I was primed for the plunge. And then, in one sanity-saving moment, my mind nudged me back with a distraction. I had a mental image of blueberries. Big, fat, juicy blueberries.

I thought, if I'd eaten a few blueberries like my anorexic Aunt Linda instead of a big fat slice of Cleo's cake, I wouldn't have had to run in the rain. And if I hadn't run in the rain, I wouldn't be straddling a dead body right now.

I knew, sure as hell, my Aunt Linda wasn't.

I swallowed the blood curdling scream and shot off the body like it was a hot bed of coals. The white tip of Inga's tail wagged happily in the dark. She was showing off. Like she was all that.

I get it. She's a partner in a topnotch detective agency. She found a dead body. It's a lot bigger trophy than nailing a cheater with his pants down. She actually thought she was getting sausages for this.

Think again, princess.

I steadied myself with a slow breath and dragged a flashlight from my pocket.

The victim was on his back, the front of his jacket bloody. I looked down. Some of the sticky red blood had transferred to my pink slicker. The body was unnaturally contorted. He didn't free-fall into these bushes. He had to have been dragged here.

The ground was soft from the recent rain and Inga's and my footprints danced all over the place. I winced. Captain Bob was gonna be pissed. He's not a big fan of the Pants On Fire Detective Agency, and that's before we botch his crime scene.

I moved the flashlight up the black and white Spats shoes, over the black pants, past the bulging white shirt under a gray trench coat, to the victim's face. My knees went rubbery and a black wave swept across my vision.

In my defense, I don't faint at the sight of death. I'm a professional, dammit. OK. So Captain Bob says I'm a hootchie stalker. But I come from a family of Chicago cops. And the Pants On Fire Detective Agency has investigated a few homicides. It's not as if I haven't stared death in the face without throwing up.

But this guy's face was gone. I tried to run, but only got a few steps away. My stomach lurched and I tossed my chocolate Italian cream cake.

That alone is a crime.

I wanted to keep running all the way home and make an anonymous call to 911. But I'd already deposited my DNA all over the crime scene. So I pulled up my big girl panties and wobbled back to the body.

I crouched down beside him, carefully diverting the flashlight from the no-face. I touched the vic's wrist, checking for the pulse that couldn't be there. His skin was gray and clammy.

There wasn't a wedding ring, on the calloused, working man's hand. I made out a few fresh cuts on his fingers but couldn't know if they were defensive wounds or marks from a barroom brawl.

I sucked up my courage and dragged my cell from my pocket. I would have to call it in. Rising, my gaze glimpsed paper in his jacket pocket. Taking a tissue from my pocket, I wrestled the envelope from his jacket and read the hastily scrawled name.

Joe DeLuca.

Uncle Joey? I peered inside the envelope. There were a helluva lot of Ben Franklins in there. Maybe forty or fifty. I couldn't breathe.

I had no idea who this dead guy was. Or how he knew Uncle Joey. It's possible he rented one of Joey's properties. But I was savvy enough to know that if a cop's name is on an envelope of cash in a homicide victim's pocket, it's gonna raise a red flag. And every red flag at the Chicago PD has Internal Affairs written all over it.

Of course all cops don't take bribes. But no one is so squeaky clean—and sufficiently insane—to tempt IA's bloodthirsty scrutiny. Least of all my Uncle Joey, with his bright red Ferrari.

I jammed the envelope into a pocket. I squatted down again and wrestled a hand under No-Face's bottom. He had been a big guy. His body would have been cumbersome to move in life. In death he was cement. But I was on a mission for Uncle Joey. And we DeLucas stick together.

I gave three heaves and a groan. I couldn't feel my hand anymore. But the wallet was in it.

The dead guy had some cash on him, about three hundred bucks. Sort of rules out a robbery. There was an ATM card. An organ donor card. And a driver's license.

His name was Bernard Love, and he looked better with eyes. The license said they were blue. I guess he could forget about donating them.

Inga growled. I felt, rather than heard, that the three of us weren't alone any longer. Fear gripped me and my heart pounded in my chest.

I darted my flashlight into the night. The park employee I had seen earlier emerged from the shadows. I blew a huge sigh of relief. Then I decided I'd better explain myself fast. If he thought I was the killer, he could clobber me with a shovel.

"This man has no face. I was calling the cops."

Inga growled more urgently.

The smile didn't reach his eyes. "That won't be necessary. The cops are on their way."

He checked his wrist.

"Wow. Nice Rolex."

My gaze traveled down the Chicago Parks Department uniform. His pant legs were too short. The better to see his expensive designer shoes.

The name on the uniform was Juan Gonzalez.

Seriously? This guy was a poster boy for Hitler's master race. I didn't have to be a hotshot detective to wonder if he knew a taco from an enchilada.

I backed away, forcing a smile that felt like wood. "OK then. I'm done here. Looks like you got this."

"Stick around." It wasn't a request.

He stepped toward me and Inga lunged for his leg. He yelped in pain. I dropped No-Face's wallet and grappled for the taser in my pocket.

It wasn't a fair fight. I'm not saying his taser was bigger or that he was quicker to the draw. When he approached me, his taser was in his hand. I never got mine out.

Fifty thousand volts ripped through me. My body became rigid and I couldn't move. It felt like being violently kicked with each jolting pulse.

My attacker's teeth clenched and his lips pulled back in a sneer. He dashed a hand into his wheelbarrow and pulled out a nasty smelling rag. He stuffed it in my face and everything went black.

Chapter Six

A warm, wet tongue brought me back. My eyes swam and I held Inga against me. I managed to sit up and examine her body with my hands. She whimpered when I touched her right shoulder. That monster had kicked my partner. Thankfully, she was OK. I promised her I'd hunt him down and deliver his body to Alpo.

I was a mess of death and dirt. Something on that filthy rag gave me a raging headache. My skull felt as if it was in a vise.

I staggered to my feet and looked around me. Then I rubbed my eyes and looked again.

Holy crap.

I called Rocco.

My brother's voice was hushed. "Yo, Sis. I'll have to call you back. I'm waiting for Captain Bob."

"Well, it's sort of important."

"What's happened?"

"I found a body."

"Are you OK?"

"Yes. But I'm not eating cake for a long time."

"My god, Cat. Do you need a doctor?"

"I'm pretty sure I saw the killer."

"Who is he?"

"Some asshole with a Rolex. He's dog food, Rocco."

"Wait. What? Tell me where you are."

"The park by my house. My partner ID'ed him for you. She chomped his right leg."

I could make out Captain Bob's voice, calling Rocco into his office.

"Rocco, don't tell Bob—"

Rocco said, "Captain, I'm putting Cat on speaker."

Crap.

"She's found a body."

"Of course she has," Bob snapped after an explosion of expletives. "Your sister is the poster girl for murder in Bridgeport."

"That hurts, Bob" I said.

"I'll call dispatch," Rocco said.

"Wait. There's something I have to tell you about the body."

"When I get there."

"But—"

Captain Bob growled. "I'm coming too, goddammit. We'll take my car."

"Sir, your wife will be waiting at the restaurant."

He growled and I could almost hear his face twitch. "When your sister's involved, it's best to stay on top of the damage control."

"Again. Not nice, Bob."

Rocco's voice was choppy. He was running now. "Don't let anyone compromise the crime scene."

A little late for that.

Bob yelled, "We're on our way. Stay with the body."

"Yeah. About the body. There's something you should—hello?"

They were gone.

Awkward.

I plopped down on the curb and waited for Chicago's Finest. Not to disappoint, they came with sirens screaming in a parade flashing blue lights, with Captain Bob leading the way.

He hopped from the car barking orders.

"O'Malley and Hall, secure the crime scene. Pacelli, set up lights. I want four officers to sweep the park. If there are witnesses, bring them back here."

Apparently I looked worse than I thought. And I thought I looked like shit. Rocco dashed over, his face pinched with worry.

"My god, Cat, you're bleeding. I'm taking you to the hospital."

I stared at my slicker. "This isn't my blood. "It's the vic's."

Rocco's voice was wary. "How did—"

The captain stomped over and his gaze fell on my jacket. "I need a medic here," he yelled.

I guess Bob loves me after all.

"It's not her blood," Rocco said.

The captain's bushy brows shot up. This couldn't be good. And it wasn't.

"Inga and I were out for a run. She broke away and discovered the body." I patted her neck. "She's the real hero here."

"Where's the body?"

I led the way into the bushes. O'Malley and Hall tromped behind us with an adequate supply of red and yellow crime scene barrier tape, evidence markers, and weapon recovery kits.

Everybody whipped their flashlights around.

Rocco said, "Something stinks back here."

"Yeah, I threw up. Watch your step."

"Nasty," Rocco said.

"The man had no face. I think someone shot it off."

Bob growled. "I'm missing more than a face here. Where's the body?"

"I tried to tell you on the phone. The killer took it. He stole a van, impersonated a Mexican, and took off with the body. After he tased and knocked me out, of course."

"Of course he did." Bob's face twitched.

"Set me up with a sketch artist. I'd recognize his Rolex and designer shoes anywhere. And Inga left marks from her choppers on his leg. That's how they got Ted Bundy."

Bob opened his mouth to say something. He closed it again and stomped back to his car instead.

I chased after him. "Hey! Where are you going? This is a crime scene. It needs to be processed. There's forensic evidence on the ground, for God's sake."

"What can you tell us about the body?" Rocco followed.

"Six feet tall. two hundred pounds. Brown hair. Blue eyes. Square chin. A mole on his right cheek."

"That's a lot of detail for a guy with no face."

"I'm going with the driver's license here. It expires this year. But that's not going to be a problem."

"And you didn't think it was important to mention a license? Did you *think* to get a name?"

"I'm not an idiot. His name is—er *was*—Bernard Love."

Bob leaned against his car, turned to me, and blew out air. "Is it a cry for help, Caterina. Is that what this is?" He tapped his right temple. "You haven't been right up here since you were hit in the head last spring by an exploding building."

"It wasn't a building, Bob. It was a Vacancy sign."

"It took," somebody sneered.

"Look, we're on the same side here," I said. "I like to think we're partners in law enforcement."

"Partners!!?" Bob's face contorted.

"Now that was rude. We've solved some critical cases together. I'm not one to toot my horn but I'm a valuable detective. You might consider working with me more often."

He choked on a laugh.

"That's just ungrateful. And at least I found a body for you."

"What body? There's no body."

"OK, so I lost it. No one's perfect. But the vic will show up again. There's still a crime scene to process." I did a palms-up in front of my coat. "This isn't chicken blood on me, for God's sake. How do you explain this blood on my slicker?"

"To be honest, I'm afraid to." He removed my hand from his arm and stomped to his car. "What's telling is a decided lack of blood at the crime scene. Puke, yes. Blood, no. How do you explain that?"

"Uh, give me a minute."

"We'll leave it like this. You found a body. And you lost it. Don't tell me about it. Tell a doctor."

He stood beside his car and radioed the cops swarming the park. "False alarm, officers. There is no body. Repeat. No body. Return to what you were doing."

"What is this?" someone demanded. "A joke?"

"Yeah. A bad one." Bob cast an evil eye on me. "I'm late. My wife's pissed. I swear, Caterina, if you pull a prank like this again, I'll have you arrested." He turned to my brother. "You coming, Rocco?"

"Sorry, Captain. If Cat says there was a body, I believe her."

I threw him a grateful look.

The captain made those facial twitches I seem to bring out in him. He climbed in his car and burned rubber driving away. I winced and watched his taillights disappear.

The men and women in Bob's parade marched past me to their cars. Some snickered. Some were pissed. They barreled off as if they had something more important to do. I wasn't impressed. I come from a family of cops. I knew they were getting donuts.

My brother put an arm around my shoulder. Rocco is my best friend. He's bossy and overly protective at times. But when I find myself in trouble, his is the first number I think to call.

"Thanks for believing me"

He shrugged.

"Bob didn't."

"The captain doesn't like surprises. He wants a body to hang around until the cops get there."

"How predictable. So now what are we going to do?"

"We're going to find a body to show the captain. Even if we steal one from the morgue."

I smiled.

"No. I'm serious."

Rocco dragged out his cell and jabbed a number with his finger. He hit speaker. His partner answered.

"Jackson."

"Yo. I need help processing a crime scene."

Jackson groaned. "I'm on a date. The woman is a masseuse."

"You're a lucky guy."

"Not tonight, apparently."

"Sorry, man. I need you on this one. If we don't come up with some compelling shit, the captain will boot me down to traffic duty. That means you have to break in a new partner. You could get my Cousin Frankie."

"All right. You're scaring me. Whadya do to piss off the captain?"

"It was Cat. She—"

"Say no more."

I groaned. "I heard that, Jackson."

He laughed. "It's OK, sweetheart. I can use the overtime. There's a sweet Harley on Craigslist."

"Oh," Rocco said. "About that bike—"

"Yeah?"

"Did I mention you won't get paid?"

Rocco shoved the phone in his pocket before his partner could object.

"Now let's get you out of that jacket."

I followed Rocco to his trunk and he removed a large evidence bag, some antiseptic and wipes, and a clean coat. I emptied my pockets and Rocco bagged the pink slicker. I cleaned my hands and face and tugged on my brother's big coat. Then we joined Inga in the car and Rocco cranked up the heat while we waited for Jackson.

I handed Rocco the envelope I found in Bernie Love's pocket.

He glanced at the name scrawled on the envelope. *Joey DeLuca.* He looked inside and whistled.

"What's this?"

"Some serious cash. It was in the vic's pocket."

"Jeezus." Rocco slapped the envelope against the steering wheel. "This could be cause for an immediate suspension and an Internal Affairs nightmare. Joey has resources I don't even want to know about."

"That's what I was thinking."

"I suppose there could be another Joey DeLuca."

"Keep telling yourself that."

A car pulled in behind us. Headlights flashed.

"Jackson's here," Rocco said. He stuffed the envelope in my hand. "Talk to Uncle Joey. If this investigation leads back to him, he'll want to get his shit in order."

I chewed a lip. There might not be enough order for all of Uncle Joey's shit.

Chapter Seven

"Watch where you step," Rocco said. "Cat tossed her cookies back here."

Jackson beamed his flashlight over the ground and grinned. "Cannelloni? And something chocolate. You eat a lot for a skinny girl."

"The guy had no face." I said, as if that explained everything.

I moved the beam of my own flashlight to the scene of the crime.

"Here. This is where I found him. On his back. Two hundred pounds of Big Macs and beer."

Jackson said, "One guy didn't move the body. He had to have help."

"Does a wheelbarrow count? The guy was wearing a Chicago Parks Department uniform that said *Juan Gonzalez*. The pants were too short. And the shirt didn't fit."

"He should speak to his union rep."

"Juan was blue eyed and blond. He wore a Rolex. And black designer dress shoes."

"So he was an imposter."

"If he wasn't, I want to work for the city," I said.

Rocco gave a short laugh. "No you don't," he said scratching his head thoughtfully. "The question is, how does someone wheel a body around a public park without the neighbors lighting up the 911 switchboard?"

I thought a moment. "He stole a city van. Inga and I passed a Chicago Parks vehicle on our run. It didn't ring any bells. I guess it worked for the neighbors too."

Rocco moved his light around. "Where's the blood? You shoot a guy's face off, there's a lot of blood. We're looking for another scene."

Jackson nodded grimly. "We find the primary, we'll have Captain Bob's attention. You might dodge traffic duty after all."

The guys spread out and widened their search. I zipped back to Rocco's car. This was a job for the Pants On Fire Detective Agency.

I snapped the leash on Inga. "Find the crime scene, partner."

Inga howled and dragged me into the park, nose to the ground. We blazed past Chicago's Finest, bolting headlong toward a stand of maples. The last leaves had fallen from their branches. I held Inga back from the soft bed of yellow and red leaves that covered the ground. She sniffed, her feet danced, and she howled bloody murder.

That's my partner. I scratched her ears and she licked her lips. That's beagle for "sausage."

Bernie Love had been killed here. Rolex Man dragged his body to the bushes and came back with a van.

"Over here!" I called.

I found a long branch and poked around a clump of leaves, exposing a dark, gooey glob. Blood. The killer had made a hasty, half-assed attempt to kick leaves over the carnage. It could have worked, I suppose. The snows would come and cloak the ground. Any trace of the horrific crime could melt with the snow before the real Juan Gonzalez came around to mow next spring.

The guys flashed their lights on the glob.

"I'll call it in. We need a forensic investigator out here." Jackson said.

Rocco grimaced. "The captain isn't going to like this. Cat made him look like an asshat."

"He didn't need a lot of help," I said.

"Don't you have to be somewhere? Somewhere other than with the captain?"

Jackson chuckled. "I'll drive her home."

I kissed my brother's cheek. "Tell Bob I'll stop by tomorrow. I'm sure he'll want to thank me personally."

"Yeah, I'm not seeing that happening any time soon. When you see Uncle Joey, have him call me. We need to talk about that envelope. I want to keep it on the down-low until we get a handle on this."

"Envelope? What envelope?" Jackson said.

"I'll explain when we stop for a beer."

"You're not as cute as my masseuse. But if you're buying..."

"Cat's definitely buying." Rocco cocked his head at me. "My partner and I need drinks and dinner at Mickey's."

"Tell Mickey to put it on my tab. Come on, Inga. Let's get out of here before the big bad captain gets back."

I turned and my foot kicked something. I shined my flashlight around the ground and picked up a metallic reflection. My heart jumped.

"It's a phone," I said. "It could belong to the killer."

"It could belong to anyone in Bridgeport," Jackson said.

I made a face. "Killjoy."

Rocco dragged two plastic gloves from his pocket. He scooped up the phone with a gloved hand. I held my flashlight on it, as he examined it.

"It's your basic Verizon cell. No Internet. Not enough bells and whistles for a kid."

Rocco flipped it open. "OK. Let's see what number was dialed last."

He pushed redial.

"Put it on speaker," I said leaning in.

The phone was picked up on the first ring. As if someone were waiting for it.

A familiar, gravelly voice answered. "Hey, Bernie. You heading out now?"

I gaped at the phone and then at my brother.

"Bernie? Are you there?"

Rocco's jaw tightened and he dropped the cell in his pocket.

"Go see Uncle Joey. I wanna know what the hell he's gotten himself into this time."

◇◇◇

Jackson hustled Inga and me to his car and hauled us home before Captain Bob blazed in with his posse.

Beau met us at the door. Cleo had ditched the couch. I followed a trail of popcorn to the guest room where she snored softly. Inga took care of the popcorn; I picked up the empty wine bottle and dropped it in the recycling bin.

I needed a long hot shower with absurd quantities of antiseptic soap. I'd been sprawled out on a corpse. I had dead guy germs on me. I scrubbed vigorously until my skin was pink. I dressed in a pullover lavender sweater with a pair of Levi's, blow-dried and finger-combed my hair. I told Inga to stay with Beau and was walking out the door when my cell phone played "Just Breathe" by Pearl Jam.

It was Chance.

I wrestled my bag for the phone. "Hey."

"Babe," Chance said. "My mom called. They're flying in Tuesday. They want to have dinner with us."

"Us? As in you and me?"

"Yes."

Whew.

"And your parents, of course. Oh, and your mama's bringing Father Timothy."

"Of course she is."

"Your mom's making the reservations."

I groaned.

Chance is an only child. God help me. Since we started dating, his mom's been on a mission to meet me and my interfering, dysfunctional family.

Don't get me wrong. I love my family and I wouldn't trade them for a bunch of people who don't make me crazy. However, Chance's parents are ex-hippies. They're anti-gun, tree-hugging vegans. Which is great. My parents however, are hippie-hating, gun-toting, carnivores. I may not be psychic but even I can see this huge freaking train wreck headed for Bridgeport.

I had sworn our parents would never meet. I'd been successful avoiding their trips to Chicago, until now. Last month, a near-disastrous meeting between the parents was diverted when Mr. Savino was hospitalized with a rather terrifying burst appendix. It renewed my faith in God.

I coughed and choked a bit.

"Cat, what's wrong?"

"Sick," I croaked in a hoarse whisper. "Dying here."

"I suppose you're contagious," he said dryly.

"God yes. Call your parents. They shouldn't be here."

"You don't know my mother. She'll come to the hospital."

"I'm in quarantine."

"She'll wear a mask."

"Dammit."

"You can't get out of this, babe. It's happening. My parents and your parents are meeting."

"Fine," I snapped recovering my voice.

"Love you, babe."

"Yeah, whatever. Maybe somebody will lose another body part."

He laughed. "I'm almost finished here. I'll bring Thai food if you're hungry."

"I am hungry," I admitted. "I tossed my cookies in the park. Inga and I were running. I fell on a dead guy. With no face."

"My god, DeLucky. Are you OK?"

"I'm fine."

"Who was the vic? Have they identified him?"

"Well, there's a teensy bit of a problem with that. The body kind of disappeared."

"Kind of? What happened to it?"

I jammed my hand deep in my bag, found my Dr. Pepper Lip Smacker and smeared my lips.

"Body snatchers. But we have a likely identification on the vic. A guy named Bernard Love. He goes by Bernie."

"Uh huh."

"Uncle Joey knows the guy. I'm heading over there now to talk to him."

"Would you like me to come with you?"

"I'll probably be late." I said quickly. "And besides, you have court in the morning."

There were too many questions about the envelope marked for Uncle Joey in Bernie Love's pocket. The last thing I needed at this point was to involve the FBI, even if he was my boyfriend.

"You can trust me, DeLucky. What are you holding back?"

"Me? Hold back?"

"I'm a trained agent. And I know you. You're voice does the slightest lilt when you lie. You're digging for your Dr. Pepper Lip Smacker, aren't you?"

It's true. Smacker is my tell. I slather it on my lips whenever I lie.

"Nope," I said double smacking my mouth.

He gave up. "Okay, babe. Be careful. And call me if you change your mind."

"I'll tell you everything tomorrow."

I crossed my fingers just in case.

Chapter Eight

I stepped onto the porch and locked the door behind me. Next door, a curtain moved and Mrs. Pickins' binoculars follow me to my car. I waved to the neighborhood snoop, slipped into the Silver Bullet, and headed to Uncle Joey's.

Joey's house is bigger and badder than you might expect for a public servant. You could say the same about his Ferrari. To my knowledge, Joey has never won the lottery. But when other people make that assumption, I don't correct them.

I like to think my uncle is a complex person with amazing entrepreneurial skills. He sees the world differently than most people. Moral norms are fuzzy, gray areas to Joey. This can be a problem in law enforcement.

I'm not saying my uncle's a dirty cop. And I'm not saying he wouldn't fix a parking ticket. Or make evidence disappear. Uncle Joey has friends in low places. I don't ask him about them. He doesn't bring his business home with him. Just their money.

It was a little after nine when I pulled up to Joey's. Sunday is poker night for my uncle, and girls' night out for Aunt Linda. Linda's Mustang was gone, and my uncle's poker buddies had crammed their cars in the circular driveway. Except Tino.

Tino runs the best deli in south Chicago. He makes Inga's sausages and just about everything in my refrigerator that doesn't come from Mama. He has a secret past. I'm pretty sure he was a government spy in his former life. I don't know if he has enemies or if old habits die hard, but he keeps an eye peeled over his shoulder. And he parks his bulletproof Buick on the street, tires turned out for a rubber-burning escape.

I cut the engine and stomped toward the front door. A dark form jumped from the shadows and I gave a bloodcurdling scream. He stepped into the light and shot an impish grin.

I swallowed my heart back into my chest. "Do you have a death wish, Doug?"

Doug Schuchard is a self-absorbed forty-something man with a round face, soft body, and the emotional maturity of an adolescent. Doug's an ex-cop. He worked some cases with Joey before ditching the force for a position as union treasurer. Sometimes they still hang out.

Doug's eyes raked me over, looking me up and down. He pinched his fingers. "Va va voom."

I smacked his arm as the front door ripped open and four guys brandishing guns fought each other to get out the door first. The youngest and unquestionably hottest guy with the biggest gun won the push-fest. He rocketed off the porch and wrestled Doug to the ground.

Max is ex-Special Forces. He's six delicious feet of hard muscle and hotness. He played my bodyguard last spring when my life got a little crazy.

Max growled. "Did he hurt you?"

I shook my head.

"Get this Neanderthal off me," Doug sputtered. "Tell him who I am."

I squinted my eyes and checked out the guy on the grass.

"I never saw this man before in my life."

Joey chuckled and put away his gun. "Max, you're sitting on Doug Schuchard. He's here to play poker. And he's late."

Max stood and brushed himself off. "No hard feelings," he said giving Doug a hand and helping him to his feet.

I flashed a smile. "Doug, this is Max. He can kill with his bare hands."

Joey slapped Doug's shoulder. "Come into my man cave. You need a drink."

Doug threw Max a withering look and stromped into the house behind Joey.

"Well played," Booker winked. He kissed my cheek and sauntered to the door.

Booker and Joey are partners in the Ninth Precinct. They've been chasing Bridgeport's bad guys since I can remember. Their sons, BJ and Joey Jr., are in their first year at Cambridge. They've been friends since the second grade. They're both super smart and a little geeky. I've long suspected there's more to their relationship than just buds. The thought doesn't seem to have crossed Uncle Joey's mind. I'm not entirely sure he's accepted the fact that his one hundred forty-pound computer-genius son who loves musicals will never play football. I hope when he finally figures it out, there's a paper bag, and defibrillator close by.

Tino hugged me and I squeezed the deli-man back. My arms barely made it around his middle. He's put away a lot of pasta since his 007 days.

"You screamed. What happened out here, Caterina?"

I forced an unconvincing smile. "It's been a rough night. You know Doug. He was goofing around and startled me."

Max searched my face. "You're not a screamer. There's something wrong."

"Not really," I lied and piled on the Dr. Pepper Lip Smacker.

Max, in all his hotness, shot up a brow. I was off my game and he knew it. He took a step toward me, and I could feel his breath on my hair. For a moment, I couldn't breathe.

I've never had a thing with Max and sometimes I think that's a crying shame. The man is a Nordic god. But I'm in a relationship with Chance Savino and I don't cross that line. Chance is smokin' hot. His cobalt baby blues make me go all gumby inside. And he puts up with my shit. The guy is decent and kind in ways that surprise me.

"The truth," Max said.

I feigned surprise. "What?" And then I made a face and the words spilled out on their own. "We were in the park. My partner got kicked. I got tased. And Captain Bob blames me for losing the body."

"The body?" Tino said.

"The one I crashed on."

"Anyone we know?" Max asked.

I sighed. "He might be a friend of Joey's."

Tino hooked my arm in his and we took the steps together.

"Come inside, Caterina. I'll pour you a nice glass of wine and you'll tell us all about it. And then Max will kick some ass."

◇◇◇

Last winter Uncle Joey had Ken Millani add a man cave to his house. The added room oozes testosterone. It's a shrine to Joey's high school football trophies, his sports memorabilia, and all things male. It's a mini sports bar with a pool table, darts, and live games playing on multiple screens. There's even a TV above the toilet so the guys can take a leak without missing a play.

My Aunt Linda hates it. She says the testosterone is thick enough in there to grow hair on her back.

Joey put a glass of Bertagna white burgundy in my hand and I took a big gulp.

"Have you heard from BJ?" I asked Booker.

"Every Friday night," he said. "He calls his mom for money."

I laughed. "How do the boys like Harvard?"

"What's not to like? They're in college. That means girls, beer, and pizza every night."

Doug knuckle-punched Booker. "Those kids have more smarts than both their papas put together."

"That's not exactly a high bar," Tino joked and topped my glass.

Doug shuffled cards. "Who's in?"

"Hold on a sec. Cat has something to tell us," Max said.

Joey's gaze narrowed with concern. "What's going on, Caterina?"

"If you prefer, we could talk alone in the kitchen."

Joey shrugged, arms open, hands out front. "I got no secrets from these guys."

OK then.

I drained the rest of the wine from my glass, took the bottle from Tino's hand, and filled it up again.

"It's bad," Tino said.

I slapped the envelope with Joey's name on it down on the table. Then I sat and told them all how bad it was.

◇◇◇

Before tonight, I'd seen Uncle Joey tear up three times in my life. Once, when his daughter was stillborn, the umbilical cord wrapped around her neck. The second time was the day his sister passed. And third was the night he pulled a child from a raging house fire. He had been too late to save her.

The death of Bernie Love was number four.

Joey dashed a fist across his eyes and tossed back his beer. He plunked six bourbon glasses on the bar. Pulled out his best single malt Scotch and poured doubles.

Tino passed the glasses around the table and we raised them in the air. "To Bernie." Glasses clinked.

"To the smartest guy I ever knew," Booker said. "Bernie cooked the books for the Provenza family fortune."

"*The* Provenzas?" I blinked.

Doug chuckled. "Wish I'd known Bernie. He cudda cooked up some of that gravy for me."

Tino threw him a *you're an idiot* look.

Joey stared at his glass. "No way Bernie saw it coming. If somebody got to him, they had to grab him from behind. Bernie grew up on the streets. He was a tough guy. Given half a chance, he could take care of himself."

"You gotta be tough to work for Nick Provenza." Booker said. "Provenza associates with some shady characters. It's the nature of his business."

"So how did Bernie come to work for this guy?" Max said.

"Bernie's father ran numbers for Old Man Provenza," Joey said. "When Bernie was fifteen, his dad died. He quit school and Old Man Provenza took him on—gave him odd jobs so he could take care of his mother and sister. He didn't sweep floors very long though." Joey gave a crooked smile. "Bernie was a freaking genius with numbers.""

"I bet," Doug chortled.

"The old man soon discovered Bernie could do anything with money. Invest it, hide it, launder it, multiply it. He made Bernie his bookkeeper. After he died, Bernie kept the books for the son."

Booker gave a sad smile and rubbed his thumbs over his fingertips. "Bernie had the goddam Midas touch. Hell, Provenza has more investments and hidden overseas accounts than he knows about."

Tino picked the envelope off the table and rifled through the crisp, new hundred-dollar bills. He whistled and tossed me a smile.

"You did good snagging this envelope, Cat. Internal Affairs would be all over Joey's ass."

Doug downed another shot. "That would require a body," he hooted, "and Cat took care of that. Joey should be safe enough."

I kicked him under the table cuz he's an idiot.

"Who did that?" Doug demanded.

I made little finger circles around my ear.

Max frowned and wrinkled his forehead. "What was the money for?"

Joey shrugged and splashed more Scotch in our glasses. "Maybe he wanted to thank me. Bernie said he wanted to disappear for a while. I helped him. He needed a new identity and a passport and they had to be foolproof. I hooked him up with a guy. And I took care of some loose ends so he could get away."

Booker heaved a sigh. "He almost made it out. His flight was late tonight and Joey was gonna drive him to the airport."

Emboldened by booze, Doug's voice was menacing. "Some bastard killed your friend, Joey. We're gonna find who he is. We're gonna hunt him down. And we're gonna make him pay."

Joey tossed back his Scotch. "Shit. I already know who killed Bernie. What we gotta do is prove it."

Chapter Nine

An odd sound saved me from the monsters chasing my dreams. I opened an eye and gasped. One was here in my bedroom.

I rubbed my eyes and opened them again. "Mama?"

She made that disapproving clicking noise with her mouth. That was the sound that woke me.

"What are you doing here?"

She wagged a hanger with one hand and made an elaborate show of bending over and picking up the jeans I wore last night from the floor.

This woman has no boundaries.

She sighed loudly, shook the pants out, and hung them in my closet.

I sat up in bed. My head reeled and my cotton mouth tasted nasty. Old Scotch. I tugged my covers close and pulled my legs up under my chin. I hated that I felt compelled to explain myself to the clothes police.

"I'm on a case. I worked late last night."

I decided it wasn't a total lie.

Last night. The memories came back, pictures spinning in my head.

Running with Inga in the rain. Crashing through the brush. Diving on a dead man. Being dissed by Captain Bob. And leaving Uncle Joey's with a thirty-seven-dollar hole in my pocket.

I suck at poker.

I hardly remembered driving home. I almost remembered dropping my clothes on the floor and slipping into a Minnie Mouse nightshirt. And I didn't remember my head hitting the pillow at all.

I sniffed and the copper smell of blood still lingered in my nostrils. Or maybe it was all in my head.

"Your sister didn't sleep in. And she was up all night. Her kids have the flu."

"All twenty?"

Mama let that slide. "Sophia was making chicken broth when I called at seven.

"Yes, Mama, Sophie's an inspiration to women everywhere."

That was a total lie.

Mama moved her finger back and forth like the pendulum on a clock. "Tick tock."

"Don't start."

My biological clock screamed from Mama's mouth. "Tick tock. If you let this nice FBI agent get away—"

"Enough with the tick tock already."

Mama smiled and plopped beside me on the bed. "Now, that you're awake, what did Papa say?"

"That's why you're here at the butt-crack of dawn?"

"Well? Did you ask where he's taking me for our honeymoon?"

"I did."

"And?"

"Not Wisconsin."

She heaved a sigh of relief. "Thank the saints."

She should've thanked me.

"Your Papa thinks stuffed animal heads are romantic."

"Not this time. Papa wanted to go all out."

She giggled like a school girl. "Where are we going? How should I pack?"

"He said it's a surprise. But I got this much from him. *Dress tropical.*"

Mama made a little jump and clapped. "If it's sunny and warm, we might just stay all winter."

"God yes."

"But," she sighed regretfully, "my children need me here."

"God no. I mean, we'll be fine."

"You need me."

"Trust me. You'll still hear my biological clock on the other side of the world."

Mama shook her head. "You're the child that keeps me awake at night. At your age you should have a family of your own. Not stalking some hootchie all night."

"I'm working on a murder, Mama. It happened last night right here in Bridgeport."

"Do we know this dead person?"

"Uncle Joey knew him."

Mama crossed herself.

"The Pants On Fire Detective Agency was first on the scene. The Chicago PD is depending on us to identify one of the guys involved. And bring him to justice."

Her hand gripped her chest. "This is dangerous, no? These are not nice men."

"I know, Mama. It's not nice to kill people."

"This is not your business. You're not the police. This is much too dangerous."

"I'm a trained professional."

"You're a snoop."

"I'm working closely with the Ninth Precinct on this case. In a consulting capacity, of course."

Her eyes widened and she looked hopeful. This was something she could tell the women at church.

"Is this true?"

I made a little cross over my heart with my finger.

"So this is good with Captain Bob?"

"Bob honestly couldn't find the words to thank me."

"My little girl, a consultant with the Chicago Police!" Mama mulled the words over, pleased. "This is good. We tell this at dinner tomorrow night. The Savinos should know what kind of girl their boy is marrying."

"You're the one getting married, Mama. Not me. And it's about flippin' time."

She winked. "And if you change your mind about the double wedding, I had Grandma DeLuca's wedding dress cleaned. You might want to stuff your bra with something though. Your grandmother had huge *tettes*."

"My boobs are fine, Mama. And they're not going near that dress."

She flashed an indulgent smile like she didn't believe me. "You and your FBI man can talk to Father Timothy tomorrow night. He'll be with us at the steakhouse when we meet the Savinos."

"Not the Steak House," I implored her. "You have to change the dinner to Indian or Thai or someplace with lots of vegetables."

"You know vegetables give your Papa gas."

"Mama, I told you already. Chance's parents are vegetarians. They don't eat meat."

She waved a dismissive hand. "Don't be silly, Caterina. Everyone eats meat."

Cleo poked her head in the doorway. She looked way too cheery for a woman who should have a brutal hangover.

"Crazy people don't eat meat," she said.

Mama gave me the eye. "Everybody knows that."

"Don't encourage her, Cleo."

"Breakfast is ready," Cleo said taking Mama's arm. "I cut up some melon. Popovers are hot from the oven. And we have Mama's best-ever chokecherry jam."

Mama beamed.

"And we got bacon. Lots of crispy bacon," Cleo said. "Ain't no crazy people here, Mama."

Right.

Cleo and Mama scooted to the kitchen laughing.

"You don't want to get into a crazy contest that you're sure to win," I hollered.

I kicked off the comforter, slapped bunny slippers on my feet, and padded down the hall behind them.

◇◇◇

When Mama hit the road to shop for beachwear, Cleo and I carried our coffees to the living room and sat by the fire. I told her about the body in the park, Rolex Man, and the snickers I got from Captain Bob and his Ninth Precinct.

Her eyes got big as saucers. "You crashed on a stiff?"

"Pretty much."

She wagged a scolding finger at me. I shuddered. She was turning into my mother.

"It's insane to go running at night alone," she said. "Why didn't you wake me to go with you?"

"Because you wouldn't have come."

"Exactly. Because it's insane."

I told her the rest of it. About the poker party and what Uncle Joey told us about Bernie Love.

"Bernie wanted to retire. He's worked for the Provenza family since he was a kid. He told his boss to find a replacement—someone Bernie could teach to take over the books. But no one can do what Bernie did. When you manage the books for a guy like Provenza, you know all the family secrets. It's all locked in that super brain of his. Retirement might not be an option."

Cleo grunted. "Sounds a little paranoid to me."

"Maybe. As long as Bernie was on the inside, he's one of the family. But if he's outside the life and protection of the organization, he's a potential target for anyone coming after the family's financial interests."

Cleo looked skeptical. "Was anyone coming?"

"Joey didn't think so. But if the Feds or IRS start poking around the family business, they'll be all over Bernie. Joey says Bernie was fiercely loyal and he'd never give the Provenzas up. Maybe someone wasn't willing to take that chance."

"You mean—"

"Yep. Uncle Joey says the boss put a hit out on Bernie. He was killed hours before his escape to Costa Rica where no one could find him."

"This is a job for the Pants On Fire Detective Agency." She dragged a gun from the waistband of her jeans. It was, in a word, large. Like a small cannon. "We're gonna get this Provenza guy. And his dog-kicking partner."

"I was hoping you'd say that."

"Damn straight. Frank gave me this little pocket rocket. Do you like it?"

She rubbed her hand along the long, gleaming barrel in a way that almost made me uncomfortable.

"Whoa, girlfriend. Leave it in your pants."

She tucked the gun away. "What's the plan?"

"I'm heading to the Ninth Precinct to look through the mug books. If Rolex Man's ugly mug is there, we'll have a name. And he's all ours."

She nodded. "I'll stop by Provenza's house and talk to the staff. See what kind of dirt I can dig up on the family."

"They're not just going to let you in."

"You worry about your mugshot. I got a plan."

"A plan? You're not gonna shoot your way in, are you? I'm pretty sure their security has bigger guns."

She frowned. "Really? Cuz we can swing by my house."

I groaned and Cleo laughed. "I'm joking, girlfriend. I still got a few slick tricks up my sleeve. I got a plan."

"Will I be bailing you out of jail again?"

"No."

"Good."

"But I might pack a toothbrush just in case. They got some shitty brushes in that jail. No respect for a person's oral health."

"I've got a plan too. It's called lunch. So don't get popped. I'll be waiting at Tino's."

Chapter Ten

Captain Bob was sitting at his desk, fingers steepled, when I poked my head in the door.

His face did that twitchy spasmy thing. "Go away."

I wiggled a white donut bag.

"Are those lemon crèmes?"

"You know they are."

Bob is a hard-boiled cop who loves donuts. He lives for lemon crèmes. But when some of the numbers from his last physical were bad, Bob's wife put him on a high fiber/no donut diet.

He gaped at the bag and his eyes went glassy. "My wife is brutal. The woman has spies everywhere. Every donut shop in Bridgeport has blacklisted me."

I plopped his donuts and hot coffee on the table and pulled up a chair. "So, that's why you're so cranky."

"Shut up."

He bit into a lemon crème and groaned with pleasure. I let him finish. When every last bite was gone, he licked a splat of lemon from his fingers. His lips were powdery white.

"Thanks for the donuts, Cat." He said, focusing on his computer screen. "Shut the door on your way out."

"Not so fast, Bobby-boy. I think somebody owes me an apology."

"Oh really." His voice dropped to a growl. "For what?"

"Last night."

"Bullshit."

"I reported a bloody murder and you thought I was crazy. That hurts, Bob. That really hurts."

"I was going with the evidence. Or lack, thereof. There was no body."

"You know, this is Chicago. People steal stuff."

"This wasn't a car, Cat." Captain Bob dragged another donut out of the bag. "Besides, there are past mental issues that caused me to question your, um, sanity."

"*Seriously?* I had a concussion seven months ago, not a psychotic break. I'm over it."

"Of course you are."

My eyes shot to the donuts on the desk. He shoved them in a drawer.

"I think we should team up on this one," I said.

"Hah!" Bob took a swallow of his coffee. "There aren't enough donuts in Bridgeport."

"Keep an open mind. I'm your star witness. I got a good, hard look at this guy. If he didn't pull the trigger, he knows who did. You need me."

"I need you to go away."

"Not a chance. At least let me look through your mug books. If the perp's in there, I'll find him. If he's not, get me a sketch artist."

"I know I'm gonna regret this." The captain kicked his chair back. "I'll get someone to help you. If you can find a photo of this ass-wipe, we'll take it from there."

"I can help you catch this guy."

"Maybe. If you were on my team. But, you're not."

That's the moment I decided to go rogue.

OK, I know it was childish and dumb as hell. But Captain Bob refused to treat me with the professional respect I deserve. I mean, who did he think he was? My mother?

I decided I would solve the murder of Bernie Love by myself. I'd hunt this Rolex Man down and prop his head on a platter. The next time I strutted into Bob's office, I wouldn't be waggling a bag of lemon crèmes.

"You're just a concerned citizen here. Nothing more. Do we have a deal?"

I crossed my fingers behind my back. "Deal."

And that was the biggest lie of all.

◇◇◇

I followed Captain Bob into the buzz of the bull pen. Our ears were assailed by the hum of several conversations mixing together and interspersed with the clacking of keyboards and ringing of phones. If you closed your eyes, you might mistake the sounds for a public television pledge drive.

I caught Tommy's eye across the room and waved. Tommy is Leo's partner and a rookie from Wisconsin. Veteran cops are notoriously tough on rookies. But Tommy skirted most of the hazing when he unwittingly took a bullet for me. Well, not a bullet exactly. More accurately, a bomb. The rookie became an instant hero. He won the old guard over at the Ninth with a little shrapnel and a few broken ribs. Now they include him when they stop at Mickey's for a beer. Papa invites him to barbeque suppers with his burnt chicken and Mama's pasta salads and Italian Cream Cake. But he hasn't earned a seat at Uncle Joey's poker game yet.

We both cheated death that week. For Tommy, it was his very first day as one of Chicago's Finest. For me, it was the week I ran into an exploding building. Not my best move.

A smartass voice from the back of the room shot out, "911 Emergency. A woman's no-good husband is ganting around. P.I. Hot Pants DeLuca on the scene."

A snicker rippled through the bull pen. A smile tugged the edges of Captain Bob's mouth.

Booker's voice boomed from the back. "All right, give it a rest."

Joey's partner pushed his way to the joker and smacked the back of his head. "Cat, don't listen to this fool. He couldn't light a spark in his own pants—let alone someone else's."

The joker grinned. "My pants see plenty. They're smokin' hot."

Booker waved a hand in front of his face. "That's not smoke."

"OK, back to work," Captain Bob barked over the laughter.

The room quieted to its usual dull roar and Bob gestured to Tommy. The rookie shot over.

"Yes, Captain," he said, grinning at me.

"Take Caterina to an empty desk and bring her the mug books. She says she saw a guy in the park last night. If he's not a park employee, he could be a person of interest."

As usual, Captain Bob minimized my contribution to our partnership.

Booker appeared behind the captain. "Park employees don't pull weeds after dark. This guy wore a Rolex. There's no way he worked for the city."

Captain Bob brow shot up. "Joey has a Rolex."

"He moonlights." Booker hung an arm around my shoulder. "I'll take it from here, Tommy. I'll fix Cat up with the mug books and bring her a cup of cop shop coffee."

"I'll pass on the sludge." I said.

"I got this," Tommy protested.

Bob shrugged. "I thought Booker had more sense. If he wants it, it's his."

"The douche-bag killed my partner's friend," Booker said. "Assaulted his niece. And kicked her dog. I owe it to Joey to bring him in."

"In tiny little pieces," I suggested.

Tommy said, "Did this guy hurt you?"

"I'm fine. But my partner bit him. The teeth-marks on his legs will convict him."

Captain Bob rolled his eyes.

"Ted Bundy," I said. "Thanks anyway, Tommy."

"Maybe we can have a beer later. Unless you got somebody to stalk."

"Just you, Tommy. Be at Mickey's at seven."

◇◇◇

Booker put me in a stark, windowless room, buried in mug books. He stuck his head in the door from time to time. The first time he brought a cup of the cop shop's nasty-ass coffee,

I made him take it away. The next time he brought a bottle of water and a package of crackers and cheese from the vending machine. I kissed his cheek. The third time he opened the door, I was walking out.

I needed air and a brisk walk. Poring over mug shots was depressing. I was seeing some of these guys on the worst day of their life. There weren't a lot of cheesy smiles. I saw dazed, drunken faces with deer-in-headlight eyes. I saw typical angry bad boys. Then there were some who didn't give a damn and guys who appeared genuinely scared. I saw a good number of arrogant jerks. And more than a few sociopaths with feral eyes as cold as ice.

Booker caught me at the door. "Running away?"

"Definitely."

He fell in step. "Me too."

I welcomed the company. We stepped out into the crisp, morning air and walked south on Halsted. Mama had taken Inga to the vet. She was a little sore after the Rolex monster kicked her last night. Mama gave me a thorough tongue-lashing for endangering her favorite granddog. She gathered up Inga's sleepover pillow and favorite chew toys and my traitorous girl bounced happily out the door. She didn't look back. I wasn't expecting to see either of them anytime soon.

I hooked my arm in Booker's and dragged him to one of Bridgeport's hidden gems. Jackalope Coffee and Tea House is tucked away at the end of a dead-end street. It's Bridgeport's version of Cheers, a place where everybody knows your name. When I'm stuck on a case I grab my laptop and drop in for a cupcake, latte, or wild berry smoothie. Their amazing Day of the Dead artwork inspires me.

Booker had the Unicorn sandwich and I sipped on a spicy chai latte in a brightly colored mug. I ordered a big bowl of chicken gumbo soup and a strawberry scone to go for Joey. My uncle loves to eat but Linda hates to cook. And he can barely manage a microwave. Joey's friends and family feed him. He keeps a foot in Mama's kitchen.

Mama might adore Joey but she's not crazy about his wife. She doesn't trust anyone who turns down her lasagna. She says Linda is too thin. And she refuses to believe there's a connection between her sister-in-law's fabulous figure and her grueling workouts at the gym. Mostly, Mama suspects Linda is puking up her cannoli.

Booker dug his cell phone out and showed me a selfie of his son BJ and Joey Jr. having pizza and giant-sized sodas in their messy dorm room.

"Look at those boys," Booker grinned. "They're killin' the ladies,"

"They're definitely knockouts. And brilliant." I smiled. "Wherever did they get it from?"

"Joey and I think their mamas were doing the computer salesman. That guy was brainy. And a smooth talker."

I laughed. "I don't know about the salesman. But I remember your kids had new computers every year."

The coffee shop door opened and a gorgelicious hottie in Spandex and running shoes trotted in with his English sheepdog. They placed an order to go at the counter. Booker caught me gawking.

"Nice eyes?" he deadpanned.

"Dunno. The face was a little hairy."

"Nice try, kid. You were checking out the guy in the sprayed-on Spandex. Not the dog."

"Oh," I said all innocent like. "Did he have eyes?"

Booker dumped extra sugar in his coffee and stirred. "BJ is acing his classes at Harvard."

"You must be proud."

Booker shrugged. "He might be enjoying this college thing too much. He wants to be an oral maxillofacial surgeon. I don't even know what that means. He says the word and all I hear is cha-ching. Do you have any idea how much that's gonna cost me?"

"BJ should be eligible for some scholarships and grants."

"I gotta think of something."

Booker's brow furrowed. He had two more kids at home. They'd be heading to college in a few years.

"My youngest says she's gonna be an environmental biologist and save the Oregon Spotted Frog. A goddam *frog*," He made a face. "That's what I get for sending her to camp last summer."

I laughed. "Marcy's a great kid."

"My kids' got big dreams. You'd think at least one of 'em would wanna be a cop like the old man."

"When Papa went to work, he told the twins he was going to save the world."

"And they became cops. They believed him. Why didn't I think of that?"

"Yeah. Well the twins aren't that bright."

Our server dropped a brown paper bag with Uncle Joey's chicken gumbo and our bill on the table. I slapped a card in his hand before Booker could pull out his wallet.

"I don't have to worry about tuition. Inga's already smarter than I am. Even without college. This is on me."

"In that case, I'll take another bowl of that chicken gumbo and a raspberry almond puff of doom. To go."

The server trotted off and Booker smiled broadly. "If there's one thing my partner hates, it's eating alone."

Back in my windowless room at the Ninth, I found two more mug books on the crowded table. And a note from Tommy.

Found these in the back. Night shift leaves their crap around. See you tonight. T

I picked up one of Tommy's books and leafed through the pages. Same shit, different pile. I made myself comfortable and got to work. Halfway through Tommy's second book, I felt the hair rise on the back of my neck. For a moment I couldn't breathe. My gaze narrowed on a photo. And Rolex Man glared back at me. He was a burley guy with short dark hair and no neck. Someone had carved a thin scar along his left cheekbone and down his jaw with a knife. He probably had it coming.

Toby Smoak. I jotted down his name, date of birth, and booking ID and stuffed the paper in my pocket.

My lip curled when I said his name. Ain't karma a bitch?

I grabbed my bag and bolted out the door. I was scampering down the hall toward the exit when Booker called my name.

I winced and turned around. He was walking toward me, the open mug book in his hand.

Crap! I'd been so pumped, I left the book open on the table.

"You found something," he said. "On this page."

"Not really." I slathered Dr. Pepper Lipsmacker all over my lying mouth.

"Show me. Who is he?"

"Here's the thing. This mug shot thing isn't working for me."

He pushed the open book in my face. "Which one."

I squinted at the photos. "I can't be sure. It was dark. It may have been foggy."

"What are you pulling, Cat? These are not guys you want to mess with."

I exaggerated a sigh. "I tried, Booker. I looked at *hundreds* of photos. But you know how men are. After a while, you all look alike."

Chapter Eleven

Bernie lived on a block of wood-frame houses with painted shutters and pampered yards. I parked in front of the one with cheery yellow police tape across the porch. There were potted flowers and a cool, iron bird sculpture on the stoop. If Bernie was home, I would've asked where he got it.

I left a message on Cleo's voice mail to call me. I had the name of the killer. Or at least his cleaner.

I slipped on plastic gloves, held my head high, and strode purposefully up the steps. When you B&E, you gotta act as if you own the place. Regrettably, the integrity of my arrival was compromised when I botched my lateral side kick. I thrust a leg over the police barrier and the yellow tape stuck to my shoe like a stream of toilet paper.

I did a total bad-ass kickboxing move but the tape was a stickler. I reached down and ripped it off my shoe. Then I pried it off my gloves and threw the whole crumpled mess on the porch. I used my picks to turn the dead bolt and then the doorknob lock. I darted inside and closed the door behind me. Smooth.

Bernie's living room was a wash of earth-tones and masculine mahogany woods and leather. I wandered from room to room searching for a glimpse of the bookkeeper's life, when he had a face.

I concluded that Bernie lived alone but sometimes he had company. The guest bathroom was well-stocked with new toothbrushes and women's toiletries. He wore expensive, tailored clothes and preferred natural fabrics. He had golf clubs and he liked soft, fuzzy sweaters. He owned three robes and three pair of slippers. He was a boxer guy. And he didn't wear pajamas.

Bernie's refrigerator was a tribute to cheese. He drank Peroni beer and Chianti. There was a whole pizza from Tino's Deli that should have been last night's supper. I helped myself to a Greek yogurt and a handful of strawberries, and washed them down with a cold mineral water.

Bernie had books in every room. He'd been reading Hemingway's *A Moveable Feast* when he died. The book was beside his bed, open to the last chapter. I read it in school a long time ago. I can't remember the ending but it had to be better than the one Bernie got.

Bernie liked history and crime fiction. But birds were his passion. Entire bookshelves were devoted to birds and photographing them. He'd traveled all over the world to capture the pictures displayed on his walls.

Frankly, I didn't get this guy. There was a decided disconnect between the bird whisperer and the man who made a career hiding a very bad man's money. For some reason Bernie aligned himself with a killer thirty-some years ago. What I did get was why he wanted out.

I wandered into his office, plopped onto a plush leather desk chair, and spun around a few times. Rocco and Jackson took the hard drive with them before they plastered police tape across the door. The keyboard, monitor, and printer were fluff without it.

I snooped through the desk drawers. Paper clips, pens, and paper for the printer. I emptied the waste basket on the desk. I smoothed out the crumpled papers one by one and tossed them back in the can. The last item on the desk was a lottery ticket from last night's drawing. Not a winner, apparently. I found a sandwich baggie in the kitchen, tucked the ticket inside and zipped.

I drummed my fingers on the desk. Uncle Joey said Bernie suspected his boss was after him. I needed something to back that up. If my find was convincing enough, a judge could sign off on a search warrant for Provenza. And just maybe, it would make enough noise to spook Toby Smoak out from under his rock.

Outside, I heard a car door close. There was the quick patter of running footsteps. A shadowy figure skulked past the big bay window. I scooted to the far side of the curtain, and carefully nudged it aside. The skulker was one of Chicago's boys in blue. He pushed in tight against the side of the house. He was crouched low and his backside turned my way like a moon.

I'd know those buns anywhere. They belonged to my cousin, Frankie DeLuca.

Busted.

I'd been made breaking the police tape and manipulating the locks on the front door. Somebody ratted me out. Some busybody, tattletale neighbor called the cops. The first responder was here. Frankie. More cops were on the way. I know how this works. He was supposed to wait for backup. But not my crazola Cousin Frankie. He barreled up the porch steps like a superhero with no powers.

Frankie burst through the front door as I slipped out the back. I followed the sidewalk around the house to the front and slid into my car. The front door was open. I could see Frankie darting about looking for something to shoot.

I punched a number on my cell. "Frankie, I'm outside in my car. You can stop searching the house."

Frankie's whisper was ragged and tense. "Not now, Cuz. I've got a situation here. I'll call you back."

"Wait. I can see you in the window. Wave to me."

"Yeah, right."

"Seriously. I'm outside Bernie Love's house."

"Stand down, Cat. A dangerous woman is on the loose. A neighbor called it in. She's tall. He said she was hot."

"Really?" I looked around. "Which neighbor?"

"He said there's something wrong with her feet. I'm thinking a limp."

"I don't limp. It was sticky police tape."

"*Geesh*, Cat. It's not all about you."

"Whatever. Wise up, Frankie. The perp's gone. She's in my car."

He yelped. "She *stole* your car? You couldn't outrun a cripple?"

The sirens screamed louder. I pulled the Silver Bullet away from the curb and blew a sigh.

"Goodbye, Einstein. If you're hungry, there's a pizza in the fridge."

◇◇◇

I was tooling to Tino's Deli for some spy chitchat when my phone blared "We Are Family." It was Rocco.

"Yo. Cat."

"Hi, Bro. Did Bernie's body show up?"

"No one's seen it since you lost it."

"You're hilarious."

"Booker says you ID'ed the guy in the park. I thought you might want to tell me who he is."

I rummaged for my Lip Smacker. "Oh puh-leeze. You know how Booker is."

"Yeah. He's damn smart when it comes to reading people. What's going on, Sis?"

I popped the top off the Dr. Pepper and smothered my lips. "Nuthin'."

"Let me guess. Captain Bob ticked you off. He said you're not a real detective and you're gonna prove him wrong."

"You don't know that."

"I'm a real detective. Like you."

To my brother's credit, his voice didn't smile.

"I knew you'd understand. Bob has disrespected the Pants On Fire Detective Agency for the last time. I hope he chokes on his donuts."

"I don't understand. This is way up on the Stupid Idea List, and you've had some whoppers. Give me a name."

"I got this."

"No. You don't. This is police matter. These guys are dangerous."

"Oh yeah?" I dug my heels in even more. "Maybe they don't know who they're messin' with."

"They're messing with a dead woman."

I gave a snort. "Where is your faith in me?"

There was a long sigh on the other end of the phone. "Where are you?"

"On my way to Tino's. Uhm, by the way, have you heard anything about Cleo lately?"

"Like what?"

"Like is she wearing silver bracelets?"

"Dammit, Cat, what are the two of you up to now?" He took a deep, breath and silently counted to ten. I know cuz I counted with him. "No. Cleo hasn't been arrested. *Yet,*" he added for good measure.

"Good. Then I'm meeting her for lunch."

"We'll join you."

Ten minutes later, I pulled into the deli parking lot. My booty vibrated. It was Chance.

"Babe. Mom just called. She wanted to confirm we're on for tomorrow night."

"I hope you told her of my untimely demise."

"Give it up, Cat. Our parents are meeting. It'll be fine."

"You sound way too cheery."

"What can I say. I'm an optimist. My glass is half-full."

"And my parents are half-crazy."

"All parents are crazy. I think having kids makes you a little nuts."

"Yeah? Well my folks had five."

He chuckled. "My parents didn't need five. They did enough drugs in the seventies. Don't worry, DeLucky. We'll have dinner and everyone will get along."

"What about Father Timothy?"

"Keep filling his wineglass. A sober priest can be one hell of a buzz-kill."

I laughed. "Gotcha."

"One more thing, DeLucky."

"Yeah?"

"You were going to tell me about last night."

"It was a freaking nightmare."

"Catch me up tonight. Be careful. And don't take any chances. If there's anything you need…"

"I thought you'd never ask. I've got two names. Toby Smoak and Nick Provenza. I'll e-mail the particulars."

"I'm guessing these guys have something to do with what happened in the park last night."

"Bingo."

"The word is the cops still don't have a body."

"I know. Awkward, right? Some jerk stole the body."

"It happens."

"Thank you very much. Captain Bob acted all huffy, like I was the only one to ever lose a dead guy. But it happens, right?"

"Not really. I was kidding. But I want to hear everything tonight. I should make it around nine. I'll get takeout. Thai? Falafels? Sushi?"

"Surprise me."

"Red or white?"

"Just you. I have both. If you're early, swing by Mickey's. I'm meeting Tommy for a beer."

"I will."

"And about those names—"

"Let me guess. This is between us."

"You know me so well."

"Hmm." Savino sounded distracted for a moment. "Was there anything else you wanted to tell me, DeLucky?"

"Uh, nope. Not off the top of my head."

"Really? I just got a text from Cleo. Frankie said a one-legged woman stole your car."

Seriously?

"Cat? Are you there?"

"Arrrrrgh!"

I tossed the phone on the passenger seat and grabbed my bag with the lottery ticket. Then I stomped into Tino's Deli, muttering under my potty-mouth breath.

Chapter Twelve

Tino's Deli hummed with the late lunch crowd. The line drifted from the counter and the staff buzzed like bees on steroids. Tino plated two orders of broccoli and shrimp linguini and barked for a server. I caught his eye and pointed to the same.

"I'll have that," I mouthed.

Tino signaled for one of his staff to take over for him. He joined me with the two plates and a broad smile.

"For you and Cleo." He held out his hands and I greedily scooped the plates in mine. I took a deep breath of the linguini and my eyes rolled back in my head.

"OMG," I breathed and kissed his cheek. "Tino, you're a prince."

He laughed. "Your partner wanted—"

"Assistant," I corrected him.

He smiled. "The audacious Ms. Jones ordered Caesar salads. But you should eat well when you're on a case. You never know when you'll have another chance."

"Is that what they taught you in spy school?"

He winked. "The only spy here was your mama. She came by for pepperoni and smoked pork chops this morning."

"Pork chops? Maybe I'll drop by later."

"If you do, you'll eat pepperoni. The pork chops are for Inga."

"Of course they are." I made a face. "In my next life, I'm coming back as my parents' granddog."

Tino laughed. "The chops and pepperoni were a cover story. Your mama wanted to know where Tony's taking her for their honeymoon."

I groaned. "She woke me cleaning my bedroom. The woman is obsessed. What did you tell her?"

He smiled wickedly. "I might have said she'd look lovely in a bikini."

I didn't ask how he knew about the cruise when Papa just got the tickets last night. Tino knows stuff. I've given up wondering how.

The deli door jangled and a burst of cool air swept the room. My head spun around as an older couple hobbled inside.

"Expecting someone?" Tino asked.

"My brother and Jackson."

"Ah," Tino smiled. "I know just what to make."

He excused himself and helped the couple find a table. I waited for him to return.

"I found one of your pizzas in Bernie's fridge this morning. Did he drop by yesterday?"

"No. Bernie was on the down-low. His boss thought he was out of town. If my pizza was in his fridge, someone delivered it to him. What was on the pizza?"

"Hmm. Meatballs. Fresh tomatoes. Oregano. Peppers."

"And Kalamata olives. My South Chicago Special."

"No olives on this one. Capers."

Tino's brow lifted. "Booker bought that pizza yesterday afternoon. It's odd he didn't mention it last night."

"Booker would've been one of the last guys to see Bernie alive."

Tino put his palms together. "And now, Caterina, you have something to tell me."

"Do I?"

"The guy in the park. You have a name."

"Oh. That."

He smiled. "What is it?"

I smiled back. "Toby Smoak."

Tino's eyes flickered.

"You know him."

He shrugged. "I know he's a lowlife shylock. Made a name for himself collecting debts for South Chicago loan sharks."

"Nice guy."

"His mistake was 'collecting' from a guy whose uncle was a judge. Smoak did a stretch in Joliet for breaking the nephew's legs."

"Well, he's on Provenza's payroll now."

"Maybe. I'll ask around and let you know."

"I'm gonna find Toby Smoak. I'm gonna tie him to Provenza. And I don't need the captain's help."

"Take Max with you."

"Thanks, but I got this."

"Just until we know what we're dealing with. Toby Smoak was one sadistic son of a bitch, and that was before he was sent away to prison. You can implicate him in a murder. You're not bulletproof."

"Max isn't bulletproof either."

Tino smiled. "He's a hell of a lot scarier than Provenza's soldiers."

He shuffled behind the counter again, barking at a server to bring salads and a basket of crunchy bread to our table.

My eyes swept through the room and found Cleo. She sat in the back, her head buried in one of her steamy romances. There were only a few dozen customers at Tino's. But I could pick Cleo Jones out in a parade. Her pink-tipped hair is a dead giveaway. But it's her magnetic energy and brass-ball chutzpa that suck me in.

Cleo glanced up and her lips broke into a smile. She popped out of her seat and captured a plate of linguini with juicy, buttery shrimp.

"God, I love that guy," she said.

"I told him we're taking Smoak down."

"Damn straight."

"He wants Max with us."

"Why?"

"I think he doesn't want Toby Smoak to blow my face off."

"I got your face, girlfriend."

She flashed her coat open exposing the Glock in her shoulder holster. Then she hiked up her skirt to show off the .22 in her garter holster. She started unbuttoning her blouse and I threw up my hands.

"Gotcha."

Geesh.

She frowned. "Who the hell is Toby Smoak?"

"Rolex Man."

Her face shone with unabashed admiration. "You found him?"

"Oh yeah, baby."

"Damn, girl. You got Captain Bob eating some serious crow."

"Well, not exactly."

"So where is this Smoak? Does Bobby got a SWAT team surrounding his rat hole?"

"The SWAT team is you and me. And Max, if Tino has his way."

"Huh? I'm feeling like I missed something here."

I climbed back on my soap box. "Captain Bob was a jerk. He has dissed the Pants On Fire Detective Agency for the last time."

She feigned shock. "Bob? No! Go on."

"We're doin' this on our own. Without Bob and without the Ninth. It's you and me. And Inga if Mama lets me have her back."

"Oh yeah. You're a force to be reckoned with."

"Here's the plan. We bring Smoak in. And we take Provenza down. And when we're finished, Captain Bob will have to admit he's a dumbass."

"Must have taken you hours to come up with that plan." Cleo said as she twisted her fork around the linguini, stabbed a juicy, garlicky shrimp and stuffed it all in her mouth.

"Did you not hear the part about Bob disrespecting us?"

Cleo blubbered some mumbo jumbo with her mouth full. I didn't get a word of it. I waited for her to swallow.

"Say what?" I asked.

"So this is your plan." She took a long swill of lemon water. "We snag this Smoak guy. We rearrange his face and choke him with his Rolex. And then we take him to the captain."

"That's the plan."

"OK. But nix on taking down Provenza. He walks."

"Who are you, and what have you done with Cleo?" I looked for signs of some alien abduction.

She started to stab shrimp again. I resisted the urge to wrestle the fork from her and clamped a hand over hers instead.

"You got the wrong guy," she said. "Bernie's boss didn't do it."

"Provenza got to you," I said incredulously. "You went to his house and he got to you."

"That's the meanest thing you've ever said. I'm a damn good detective, Cat DeLuca. I'm *practically* your partner."

She challenged me with a glare but I know when to keep my mouth shut. I mentally superglued my lips and gnawed on my tongue.

She snorted. "You didn't ask what I learned on my mission to the Provenza residence."

Frankly I'd been relieved and somewhat surprised that Cleo wasn't wearing a blue Cook County jumpsuit. That was, in itself, a spectacular success.

"My bad. What do you have to tell me?"

"Two things. First, boss man is innocent. Provenza wasn't involved in Bernie's untimely demise."

"That's a load of bull pucky."

"I'm not finished."

"Sorry. What's the second thing?"

"Let go of my hand before I shoot you."

Chapter Thirteen

A bell jingled and the deli door opened with authority. Rocco tromped in and Jackson swaggered behind him. Both are gorgeous, muscled guys but Jackson is Samoan. He's got thick curly black hair and a bleached white smile. His shirts are tailored to show off six-pack abs. Jackson's a nice guy. He takes his mom to dinner every Sunday. The other six, he tries to get a date. Sometimes he gets lucky.

My brother Rocco is no slouch. He's got the casual guy look. That mostly means he prefers blue jeans and a sweater and forgets to comb his hair. Women turn their heads when he walks in a room but Rocco's out of the game and doesn't seem to notice. He's crazy about Maria and he's way too smart to be stupid.

I gave Cleo the QT sign.

"What's up with you today?" she said. "Your craziac is showing. Hell, it's a big-ass neon sign."

I glared as I spoke without moving my lips. "Just, follow my lead for once. And don't tell them anything."

She made a scoffing snort. "Like that's gonna happen. Rocco needs to know Provenza is not our guy."

"Is so," I said all ventriloquist like.

"What's wrong with your mouth?" Jackson asked, pulling up a chair.

Rocco chuckled and sat beside me. "She thinks she's keeping secrets."

"Got that right," Cleo muttered.

He leaned over and gave me a hug. "How ya holdin' up, Sis?"

"She had a rough night," Cleo volunteered. "She dreamed Mama was in her bedroom, hanging up clothes and ranting that the room was a disaster."

I shuddered. "It was a freakin' nightmare."

"She's revisiting her childhood," Rocco said. "When we were kids, my room was always neater than Cat's."

"Only cuz Mama cleaned it for you. And she did the twins' room. There's a word for that."

"Su-weet," Jackson said.

"Sexist," I countered.

Rocco commandeered my lunch. "Mmmm," he said making yummy noises. "You should eat this while it's warm."

He chomped away and I went to work on a breadstick and salad. We talked about Mama's church wedding and I told Rocco about Papa's honeymoon cruise. The guys were getting fitted for their tuxes tomorrow and my brother wasn't digging it.

"Who wears a freakin' powder-blue tuxedo?" he demanded.

"That would be you," Cleo said.

Rocco winced.

"Be nice," I said. "Mama's having the wedding she planned thirty-five years ago. Powder-blue tuxes with a matching blue ruffled shirt. It was a big hit in the eighties."

"So were mullets and parachute pants. We should learn from our mistakes."

I laughed. "Papa's wearing a white tuxedo and powder-blue shirt. Mama says he looks like an Italian Don Johnson."

"You might as well get into it," Jackson said. "I'm going as Al Pacino."

"You don't look at all like Pacino. I bet you don't know very much about him."

"I know he's a tough guy. And he didn't wear powder-blue pants." Jackson grinned. "I can do Al Pacino."

Mama had asked the guests to dress "retro eighties" for the wedding. There would be big hair and shoulder pads as far as the eye could see.

"Frankie's gonna dress like Indiana Jones. Including the whip." Cleo gave a little shiver of excitement.

"Damn," Jackson said. "I see him more as Rain Man."

Tino appeared with a bright smile and two steaming plates of chicken scallopini in a light tomato and wine sauce.

Rocco's face lit up. "My favorite!" he said and shoved my linguini back to me.

I looked down at my plate. He'd saved the broccoli for me.

"Thank you. Lunch is on me," Tino said.

"Wow," Cleo said. "What did we do?"

"You're getting justice for Bernie. He was one of the good guys."

"We're on it," Jackson said, greedily digging in.

A server with long legs and red hair brought the guys Cokes and extra breadsticks. Jackson flashed his bleached smile with a spot of spinach in his teeth. She sashayed away and Jackson twisted around in his chair, craning his neck to check out her bootie.

"Smooth, Popeye," I said.

"How's the investigation coming?" Tino said.

"We're waiting on the blood analysis from the crime scene," Jackson said. "It'll be several days. Forensics is backed up."

We got a hit on the stolen city parks van Cat saw last night," Rocco said. "The port authority called it in. It had been abandoned on South Ewing near Calumet Harbor."

My hopes of Bernie Love's body turning up again took a long, wet dive.

"Forensics said the van was wiped clean," Jackson said. "The back smelled like bleach."

Tino snorted. "Sounds like Bernie's swimming with the fishes."

"Bye bye, Love," Cleo said.

I looked at Tino. "You might want your lunch money back. We'll find Rolex. But unless he gives up Provenza and signs a confession, we got squat."

Tino's eyes hardened but his voice was soft. "Sometimes, the blind lady of justice needs a helping hand."

Cleo chewed a corner of her mouth. "What's that supposed to mean?"

"It means the fish are still hungry," I said. "And Provenza will make tasty bait."

Jackson put up his hands. "I didn't hear that."

My brother did. But if there's one thing you can say about the DeLucas, we know how to keep our big mouths shut.

"Uh, hello!" Cleo said. "Bernie's boss didn't do it."

"You might be right," Jackson grunted. "We interviewed Provenza at his restaurant, the Tapas Spoon, this morning. When we told him we believe Bernie is dead, he totally lost it."

Rocco nodded. "I gotta agree. I've been doing this a long time. Provenza seemed genuinely shocked."

"Give him an Oscar," I spat. "He's a liar."

Jackson shrugged. "Provenza has a solid alibi for last night. It was his wife's birthday. She had a birthday party at Palermo's. There were fifty guests that can vouch for his whereabouts."

"All part of his plan," I said.

"You'll figure it out," Tino said.

"We put an APB out on Bernie's car. A Volvo late model sedan. It's missing. Joey said the car was at the house Sunday afternoon."

I switched gears a bit. "Did you guys find anything of interest at Bernie's house? Like on his computer?"

Jackson shook his head incredulously. "You broke into Bernie's?"

"I'm a hotshot detective. It's what I do."

"Did you miss the *Do Not Cross* police tape all over the door?"

"Um yeah. You might want to replace that," I said. "Frankie claimed some one-legged woman made a mess of the tape."

Rocco hid a smile. "The computer forensics has Bernie's hard drive. I'll let you know what the investigator learns."

"Thanks, bro."

Jackson said, "You know how it works Cat. It's a two-way street. What do you have for us?"

"You can run some prints." I opened my purse and dragged out the plastic baggie with last night's lottery ticket. "This ticket was in the trash can in Bernie's office."

Jackson stuffed a bite in his mouth. "You never bought a losing lottery ticket?"

"Weekly," Tino said.

"Here's the thing," I said. "The numbers were drawn *after* Bernie was killed."

Rocco's nodded slowly. "Someone was in Bernie's house last night."

I smiled, "We should know who that is."

Jackson flashed a winning smile. "Nice work, Sherlock. And now we'd like that name you found in the mug book."

"Good God. Is there anyone Booker doesn't blab to?"

Tino disappeared to the kitchen laughing.

Cleo's eyes bulged and she fairly danced in her chair. The woman cannot keep a secret. I half-expected her head to spin around and Rolex's name spew from her mouth.

I resorted to sign language. I looked at Cleo hard, locked my lips, and threw away the key. She booted me a good one under the table. I kicked her back.

Jackson's radio crackled and the dispatcher's nasally voice announced a 10-14 in progress a few blocks away on Aberdeen.

I was momentarily saved. A big goofy grin hijacked my face. Sometimes a burglary can be downright cheery.

"We gotta jam." Jackson grabbed the end of the breadsticks and flagged the leggy redhead to pack up their meals.

He tossed a generous tip on the table. "We'll be back for these. I'd like extra breadsticks and your phone number in mine."

She scooted away giggling.

"Does that ever work?" I asked.

"You'd be surprised," Rocco said. "Women are into Jackson, until they get to know him."

His partner stabbed his heart with his fist.

"Be careful out there," I said. "Go and save the world."

Rocco pushed away from the table and whispered in my ear. "This isn't over, Sister. I need that name."

"Yeah, yeah."

Chapter Fourteen

Cleo parked across the street from the Tapas Spoon where Rocco and Jackson had interviewed Bernie's boss earlier that morning. Provenza must have put on a good show to bamboozle the boys. It would take more than a few crocodile tears to convince me otherwise.

Cleo pushed her car seat back and filed her nails. "We're wastin' time, girlfriend. Provenza's not our guy."

"And you say this because—"

"I was at his house. I got the facts from Gabbie."

"Gabbie's the wife?"

"Sharon's the wife. Gabbie's the chef. You know what they say. The kitchen staff knows all the gossip."

"Nobody says that."

'I'm pretty sure they do. Gabbie's been with the family twenty years. She never wants to leave."

"Maybe that's because she doesn't want to get shot in the face."

"You're a comedian."

"How did you get inside the kitchen anyway?"

"I wore a boxy red singing telegram hat and carried a big box of chocolates. I told the guy at the gate it was National Staff week and I had a delivery and song for the employees from Mr. Provenza."

"He confiscated the chocolates at the gate, didn't he?"

She nodded bitterly. "I hope he gets acne. He didn't even want to hear the song."

"You climbed the fence."

"Sort of. It's kind of a long story. I don't want to bore you with the details."

"Well, did anyone see you?"

"Just Gabbie. But she stopped screaming when I showed her my gun. We're good now."

Geesh.

"Anyway, Gabbie says Bernie was a frequent dinner guest at the Provenzas. And he spent Christmas and Thanksgiving with them. He took the boys on photo shoots at Lincoln Park Bird Sanctuary."

"What's your point, Sherlock?"

"The kids call him Uncle Bernie. Nick couldn't have whacked him. He was family, for godsake."

"This coming from a woman who chased her husband down with a shotgun."

The restaurant door opened and Provenza stepped outside hugging a phone to his ear. He was followed by a muscle guy with car keys who beeped a buttery yellow Lexus sedan and opened the back door for his boss. The driver slid behind the wheel and merged into traffic. Cleo kicked the Camry in gear and we followed them.

He made a stop at Marty's Steakhouse on West Kinzie. The restaurant was on the list of Provenza's businesses Chance e-mailed earlier. The beefy driver parked at a fire hydrant and Provenza went inside. The driver wore a dark suit and dark shades. He was like the Men In Black. He smoked Camels without a filter and ground the little butts on the curb before tossing them in the street. A Traffic Management guy came by and began scribbling in his little book. The driver jammed a beefy hand deep in his pocket and extracted something so amazing, both the ticket and the traffic cop disappeared. My Uncle Joey is magical too. He makes all my tickets vanish and my hand doesn't touch my pocket.

I did a quick google search. Marty's Steakhouse got five stars on the Hot List in *Chicago Magazine*. The website boasts a photo of a grinning Provenza beside Mark Wahlberg and the cast from *Transformers 4*. Customer comments confirm Marty's has a loyal fan base. I wondered where they'll get their beef when Provenza takes his meals in Joliet.

Cleo filed the nails on both hands and was slipping off a shoe when Provenza exited the restaurant and climbed into the backseat.

We were on the road again.

Our next stop was Leo's Metropolitan Florist. There wasn't a parking spot or fire hydrant in front of this place. The ever resourceful driver let Provenza out in front of the florist, walked to the front of the car, and lifted the hood. Traffic slowed to a crawl as cars made their way around the Lexus blocking the lane.

"*Seriously?*" I said. "He can't drive around the block?"

"I like this guy," Cleo said with unabashed admiration.

A passing truck offered a tow but the man in black shouted, "Help is on the way!" and waved him on. Provenza returned with a big bouquet of blue iris, white traditional daisies, and yellow lilies. The driver dropped the hood and opened the door for him

"Now we see who the flowers are for," I said.

"I bet they're for a lover. Sexy secretary? Unscrupulous maid?" Cleo grinned. "It's employee appreciation day, you know."

"Only in your universe. It could be an employee, but probably not a lover. The bouquet is bright with bold colors but there's nothing soft going on. It's not whimsical or romantic. No yin, all yang."

Cleo nodded. "There aren't any roses. Roses scream sex."

Cleo skillfully tailed the creamy yellow Lexus across Chicagoland, keeping a buffer of three or four cars between us. I had to give her credit. Surveillance is a challenge for Cleo. God knows she's sneaky enough. But she lacks the subtlety gene. Her preferred approach would be to rear end Provenza's car and demand a conversation.

Provenza's driver turned off East 67th street and drove through the Oak Woods Cemetery gates and followed the narrow winding road.

"Keep driving," I said. Cleo breezed past the entrance, made a U-ey when she could and found a place to pull off the road with a good view of the cemetery. Provenza walked away from the car, flowers in hand. He climbed up a knoll and we lost him after that. His driver stood outside the car, fishing in his pocket for a smoke.

I didn't know who Provenza was visiting, but it was a twenty-minute chat. He returned to the car, and it was another twenty before the Lexus rolled out the gate.

I took the wheel while Cleo texted Frankie, and sucked on a bag of M&Ms. The Lexus drove north on Minerva avenue, passed by the Flying Squirrel Park on Marquette and made a surprising right turn on to a residential side street. I slowed the Camry to a crawl and a chill ran down my spine.

Something wasn't right. It's not that six figure cars *can't* drive down streets where people might struggle to make ends meet. It's just that they don't.

Cleo's furious fingers stopped texting and she glanced up at the road. "Where'd they go? You're letting them get away."

"I have a bad feeling about this."

"Buck up and drive already. We're losing them."

A car honked behind me and I checked my rear view mirror. Two suits gave me the finger. I was holding up traffic.

Cleo hung out her window. "Douche-bags!"

I negotiated the turn and Cleo gave a startled gasp. My stomach clenched tight.

The Lexus was parked halfway down the block in the middle of the narrow street. Outside the car, leaning against the trunk, was Nicolas Provenza. He was spinning a yo-yo.

Our eyes locked. His shot daggers.

"Abort! Abort!" Cleo shrieked.

I stomped the brake and threw the car into reverse. I waved a frantic hand to the suits behind me.

"Go back!"

The driver bared his teeth in a mirthless grin and nudged forward.

"Holy crap," I said.

"Ambush!" Cleo screeched and hit the floor. Her body doesn't fold well. Her knees were on the floor but the pink tips of her hair poked up over the dash.

I tugged at her sleeve. "Pull up your big girl panties, Cleo, and sit in your seat."

She smacked me. "No! He's probably after me. Uh, you might want to say I went on a really long vacation. I know you'll think of something. Go with your gut. Your gut is good."

I smacked her back. "You wanna tell me what happened at Provenza's house that might have slipped your mind earlier?"

"Nothing, really."

"Really?"

"It was just a minor misunderstanding really. You know, some people got no sense of humor."

"Yeah. You want to go tell it to the guy with the yo yo? Or should I?"

The Camry gave a vicious jolt as the car behind us rammed our bumper.

"That jerk dented my car!" Cleo said savagely.

"Well I would suggest you stop kissing that carpet over there, and go get his insurance information."

Chapter Fifteen

Cleo cursed under her breath. I threw the Camry in drive, and crept toward a cold-blooded murderer. I didn't get this guy. Uncle Joey said Bernie was honest and fiercely loyal. The cook claimed he was a family friend. I mean, how horrible can a guy who's crazy about birds possibly be?

Perhaps I should've been scared or at least embarrassed that I, super sleuth and stalker, had been busted on a tail. I wasn't. I was too mad at myself for making this stupid turn. And for waiting outside the cemetery while Provenza sat in his car and got his soldiers in place.

I locked eyes on the dark daggers and shot a few back of my own.

"Go ahead," I muttered. "Make my day."

"You tell em, girl," Cleo cheered me on from the floor.

I edged the Camry forward and braked maybe twenty feet from the Lexus. Climbing out of the car, I squared my shoulders and counted ten steps. Provenza pocketed the yo-yo and signaled his driver to wait in the car. He met me halfway.

He was stocky and barrel-chested and the sun reflected off his bald head like glass. His hands clenched and unclenched.

"Your big fat car is blocking the street," I said.

"You're following me."

He had me there. I shrugged.

"It's a bad idea."

I made a scoffing sound. "Killing people is a bad idea. Stalking is," I searched for a word, "annoying at best."

His eyebrows arched and then dropped to a flat line. He was looking for signs of cray cray. He made a quick assessment.

"You're insane," he said.

I slapped a card in his hand.

"Pants on Fire Detective Agency. We catch liars and cheats."

He paused and choked. "My wife sent you?"

"Not yet." I made a mental note to send her a business card. "We also catch *murderers*."

He looked at the card again. "It doesn't say that."

"It's implied. Mr. Provenza, we're investigating the death of your bookkeeper, Bernie Love. I'm working closely with the Ninth Precinct."

"Right," he said super sneery like.

"And my fully qualified staff."

That would be Cleo, cowering on the floor mat. And Inga, who doubles as a beagle.

"I'll need to verify this collaboration with Bob. Er, Captain Maxfield."

Just my luck. "You and Bobby are friends."

"Golf buddies."

He produced a cell phone and scrolled down with his finger. I was busted. There weren't enough lemon crèmes in Bridgeport to save me from Captain Bob's impending nuclear meltdown.

Nick found Bob's number and his finger was poised to Send when he paused thoughtfully and looked me in the eye.

"A member of my security team sent me a photo. I intended to ask Bob to look at it. It occurs to me that you may be the one to help me with the identification."

The smile didn't reach his chilling eyes. His finger scanned the screen until he found what he was looking for. Then he shoved it in my face.

I gaped. The woman was Cleo. She was escaping back over the fence that surrounds the Provenza estate. Somehow she'd neglected to mention that she was chased off the property. A guard's hairy hand grappled at her skirt as she hurled herself over the fence.

I squinted and studied the photo. "I've never seen that woman before in my life."

He pinched the bridge of his nose between his eyes. "Look again at the pink hair. She bears a remarkable resemblance to the photo on Cleo Jones' driver's license. Do you remember her? The car you're driving is registered to Ms. Jones."

I stared at the photo again, scrunching my nose uncertainly.

His voice was ice. "Should I instruct my driver to escort the woman cowering in the car to join us. Maybe then we'll see if it helps jog your memory."

I caught my breath in mock surprise. "My god, that's Cleo Jones. I can see the pink tips now. I didn't recognize her at first from that angle. Thankfully, I hadn't looked up her skirt before."

He clamped his mouth into a tight line.

"And I'm sorry I've seen it now. That scarlet red thong is disturbing. I can only hope there weren't children in the yard."

"The guards were disturbed as well. My men won't make the same mistake again. Intruders are a serious threat to my family. They will be shot."

"In the face like Bernie?"

A flicker of pain crossed his face and then it was gone. "Do you understand?"

"Okay then. Thanks for the heads up. And now if you'll have your driver move out of my way."

"Just one thing more."

I tapped my foot. "What?"

He looked me in the eye. "Bernie knew a Joey DeLuca. Is he your father?"

"Uncle." I stomped back toward the Camry. Cleo's pink tipped spiked hair poked above dash.

"Tell me, Caterina," he called after me. "How does a public servant like Joey afford a new Ferrari?"

I answered without looking back. "You should know, Mr. Provenza. You had the same bookkeeper."

I waved to the glaring suits who had smashed Cleo's bumper and slid behind the wheel.

Cleo whispered from the floor. "What did Provenza say? Did he mention me at all?"

"He did mention something about shooting you next time he saw you."

She shuddered. "Oh god. Did you tell him I'm on his side? Does he know I think he's innocent?"

"That's our secret, Cleo. I didn't want him to think you're a complete dumb ass."

I cranked the engine and we rounded the block in a three-car parade. Provenza and his suits made a left turn on East 63rd, continuing on toward Bridgeport. I made a right and retraced the route to the cemetery. I picked up speed and Cleo began a tentative, wide-eyed climb back up to her seat.

"Are they gone?" she whispered.

"Nope." I pushed her head down again.

Chapter Sixteen

Beneath a blue Chicago sky, Cleo and I stood over the bones of Andrew Michael Love. We didn't have much trouble figuring out whose ghost Nicky Provenza had visited earlier. Several graves had fresh flowers. But only one included a brilliant spray of blue irises.

"Andrew Michael Love," I read. *"Beloved Husband, Father, Friend."* I did the math. He was forty-four when he died.

"Who the hell is Andrew Love," Cleo demanded.

"It's gotta be Bernie's dad. He was the Provenza family chauffer when Nicky was growing up."

"Ah, yes. Candy Andy," she said airily.

Cleo spent twenty minutes with the cook and suddenly she's an expert on all things Provenza.

"Candy Andy?"

Cleo tossed her head back. "That's what the kids called Bernie's dad. Andy kept a few lollypops or tootsie rolls in his pocket for the kids. They were crazy about him."

"I bet."

"Gabby—that's the cook—"

"I knew that."

"Gabby says the Provenza kids saw more of Andy than their own dad. He drove the kids to school and gymnastics and soccer practice. He went to their games on his days off."

I wondered about Andy's son, Bernie, and how much time he had with his papa.

"Nicky took Andy's death hard," she said. "Andy was helping him put his first car together when he suffered a heart attack."

I thought about that. Nick Provenza had a close bond with the family chauffer while growing up. He was still visiting his grave after all these years.

Cleo waggled a finger at the gravestone and threw me a broad, triumphant smile. "And there, Cat DeLuca, is your proof. Nicky Provenza didn't kill his bookkeeper. He couldn't have."

"What proof?"

"The flowers are the proof. Nick couldn't possibly have done the dirty deed. If he had, he wouldn't have come here."

"I'm not feeling it."

She exaggerated a sigh like I was dense. "*Hello!* Nobody kills a man's son and brings flowers. Why would he do that? It's like sayin', *Hey, Andy! I got you some company.*"

"That's your proof? He brought *flowers?*"

"No jury would convict him."

"You're delirious. Maybe the flowers are saying, *Sorry, Andy. I hope you recognize your son without a face.*"

"Not even close. Here's what happened. Rocco and Jackson go to Tapas Spoon and tell Nick that Bernie pegged out. Nick's shattered. He's overcome with grief."

"Really? Cuz he wasn't all choked up when he ambushed us. Mostly he was pissed at his guards for not shooting you."

She swallowed hard. "He had to be out of his mind with grief."

"You are going with that. Whatever."

She popped a piece of bubblegum in her mouth and chewed thoughtfully. "Nicky needed to say goodbye. He stopped at the florist and bought flowers for Bernie. He threw in a few tootsie rolls for Candy Andy and drives to the cemetery."

I peered closely at the bouquet and spied the Tootsie rolls stuffed inside. Nice touch.

"A totally insane theory. Why would Nick put flowers for Bernie on his father's grave?"

Cleo threw me a look like I was the crazy one. "Because Nick figures Bernie's right here hanging out with his dad. And that's precisely why these flowers prove Nick Provenza is innocent."

She zipped out her camera phone and captured the image. Presumably for Nick's defense. I was at a loss for words.

"Bernie's still here if you want to say something to him," she said.

"Oh, I do."

"Go ahead. What do you want to say?"

I cleared my throat and spoke into the flowers. "You're a dumb ass, Cleo."

◇◇◇

We drove across Chicago in search of Rolex Man's apartment. A smoking hot FBI agent had e-mailed me an address and I retrieved it from my smartphone.

According to the Illinois Department of Corrections, Tony Smoak lived in an apartment a few blocks off Foster Avenue in the Albany Park neighborhood. Cleo punched the address in her GPS and found a hideous red wig in her trunk for me to wear. The cherry red hair concealed some of my face and Cleo was confident Toby wouldn't recognize me. I said she'd have to leave her guns in the car. I suspected she wanted to get close enough to Toby to shoot him.

I was familiar with Albany Park. A few months ago I had a case at North Park College and Max invited himself to tag along. Mostly because his favorite restaurant is across the street from the college. Tre Kronor boasts some of Chicago's best Swedish fare. We brought dinner home every night and washed it down with Carlsberg beer and Aquavit. Max is a good Dane. A Scandinavian diet, rich in cream and butter, adds muscle mass to Max's gorgeous hotness. I, however, after a week in culinary Valhalla, had to shake five pounds of *princesstarta* off my ass.

The Magellan directed us to the address the Illinois Department of Corrections provided for Toby Smoak. Cleo drove until the mechanical female voice said *You have arrived*. We got out of the car and looked around.

I peered over the bridge. "There it is. Toby's Smoak lives smack in the middle of the Chicago river."

Cleo hissed. "I hate this guy. Maybe he'll drown."

"The river's not deep enough."

"It is if I hold his head down." She popped a big piece of bubblegum in her mouth. "You'd think the Department of Corrections could get his address right. Aren't they supposed to send a parole officer over?"

"Maybe they're ignoring him, hoping he was rehabilitated."

"What did he do anyway?"

"He broke legs. He was a loan enforcer until he broke the legs of a guy whose uncle was a judge."

Cleo grinned. "Maybe he was rehabilitated. He didn't break Bernie's legs."

My phone blared the James Bond theme and I flipped the lid.

"Hey, Tino," I said.

"Caterina. How's it going?"

"Not great. Unless he's a river rat, our lead on Toby Smoak was a bust."

"I might have something for you. I asked Ronnie to locate Toby Smoaks. He doesn't have a home address yet but he will."

"You rock, Tino."

Ronnie is Tino's go-to guy. I don't know what his business is called and I doubt you'd find it in the yellow pages. Ronnie does investigations for the ex-spy. He has a quiet, steady demeanor and a knack for making troubles disappear by the sheer charm of brute strength.

"Ronnie says Smoak hangs out at the Whiskey Run on the Lower West Side. You might find him there."

"I've seen the place. It's a biker bar," I said. "Tough crowd."

"Not as tough as we are," Cleo blabbed into the phone.

I stared at her.

"I'll call Max and have him meet you there," Tino said.

Cleo blew a hot pink bubble. "Cat doesn't need Max. She has me. I'm her partner, her back up, and her extra muscle."

"Lies, lies, so many lies." I shook my head.

Tino grunted. "Don't do anything stupid, Cat. If you see Smoak, don't try to bring him in. Just call me."

"Gotcha," I said.

"Like that's gonna happen," Cleo mouthed.

"I heard that," Tino said.

She laughed. "What are you, spy man. A freakin' wizard?"

I punched her arm.

"Ouch!"

"Cleo's just messing around, Tino, we'll call."

"She's a goddam loose cannon. She's gonna get you seriously hurt, or worse, if you don't get your assistant under control," he said grumpily and disconnected.

"Assistant! Hah!" Cleo loosened two shirt buttons and hiked up her pencil skirt right there on the street. Then she gave me a critical once over.

I was wearing my J Brand Skinny Jeans, boots, and a low scoop-neck pullover exposing a creamy silk camisole beneath my sweater.

"Lose the pullover," she said, all bossy like she's the fashion police. "We're goin' to a bad-ass biker bar."

"I like this sweater, and it's cold out."

She made a lemon-sucking face. "My sister, the nun, has that sweater. It's boring."

"Jennifer Anniston wore this sweater on *The View*."

"She wasn't in a biker bar. The jeans and that sexy under-thing you're wearing scream biker bitch."

Walking into a biker bar in my underwear wasn't my idea of a good time. But it was, in the grand scheme of things, small stuff and not worth a fracas over. With Cleo, you learn to choose your battles.

"OK," I relented. "I'll wrap my sweater around my shoulders if you leave your arsenal in the car."

"Dammit."

I tugged off my sweater and gave a little shiver. Cleo adjusted my camisole and drew a slow whistle. "Now, you look like my sister the ho."

"Oh, yay." I clapped my hands.

Chapter Seventeen

A dozen bikes were corralled outside the Whiskey Run when we pulled up to the bar.

"Next time I'll borrow my neighbor's Harley." Cleo said. "We'll wear leather and get those little bugs in our teeth."

"You really know how to show a girl a good time."

She grinned. "You can ride bitch."

"I didn't know you rode."

She shrugged. "How hard can it be?"

Cleo led the way. I have to say the woman knows how to make an entrance. She paused in the doorway and her eyes devoured the room. She made a yummy noise in her throat.

"Mmm. Sausage fest."

The bar smelled of booze, cigarettes, and leather. I checked out the sausage and didn't see a lot of *yummy*. The other thing I didn't see was Toby Smoak. But it was early yet and a man's gotta make a living. So many faces to shoot, so little time.

We sat at the bar and Cleo loosened yet another button on her shirt. The woman's got some double whammy sweater stretchers. If she leaned forward, the girls would almost certainly make a break for it.

The bartender slapped down a couple coasters. He was pushing fifty and his remaining hair was banded in a ponytail. I guessed his missing front teeth had kissed the floor in a bar fight. He grinned at Cleo's chest and the girls perked up and winked back. Cleo doesn't share a lot of genes with her sister the nun.

"What's your pleasure, ladies," he said.

Cleo put her elbows on the bar and leaned forward.

"Down," I murmured to the girls.

"We'll start with two blue motorcycles," Cleo said all sultry.

He nodded to the girls and walked away. I smacked her with an elbow.

"What are you doing?"

"Don't be daft. If Toby's a regular, this guy knows him. I'm feeling him out, reeling him in."

"Get a room. And what's a blue motorcycle? Who drinks that?"

"Biker babes."

"And you know this, how?"

"Remember the salesman from Toledo who helped me get over Walter? He rode a chopper. He knows all about us biker chicks." She smiled wickedly. "Wanna know what else he taught me?"

"No! And I'm not riding on the back of your neighbor's Harley."

"Bahk! Bahk!" She made little chicken noises.

Here's the thing. Cleo drives a car like a suicidal maniac. I make my peace with God every time she's behind the wheel. And that's with three thousand pounds of steel around me and a seatbelt. But I refuse to make my peace with God on the back of a motorcycle. It's a conversation I'd rather not have with the big guy face to face.

The bartender plunked our drinks on the bar, eyes all over Cleo. "Wanna run a tab?"

I slapped a Jackson on the table. "No thanks."

Surveillance is a drink and dash business. I learned a long time ago to pay as I go or keep my money on the table. You never know when you might have to shoot off the barstool and hit the floor running.

There were only a few other women in the bar and one was serving drinks. The barmaid was crowding fifty and her body was a tribute to piercings and body art. Her arms were tattooed with skulls and crossbones and words like *Die Trying* and *Road Warrior*. A full color likeness of herself on a Harley Davidson was tattooed across her back. She was a large woman with an easy smile and a lot of canvas to work with. She screamed drink orders from across the room and picked them up at the bar.

I'm not a big fan of blue food coloring but the drink was tasty. It was, however, a little strong on a day I intended to stuff an apple in Toby's mouth and drag him into Captain Bob's office. I shoved my blue drink over to Cleo and ordered a Perone instead.

The bartender brought me a Budweiser and a bowl of pretzels.

"We ain't got no Perone beer here," he said.

"What else do you have?"

"Budweiser."

"Perfect."

The barmaid collapsed on a stool beside me. She kicked off her shoes and rubbed her feet.

"Hardwood floors are a bitch on the trotters."

Cleo made a sympathetic clucking sound. She was still channeling a chicken.

"I waitressed in a titty bar and all I got was bad tips and aching feet." Cleo gave a self-deprecating smile. "And a no-good husband. He broke my heart."

"Bastard."

"He's dead now."

"Karma's a bitch."

Cleo sighed. "All I got was a house, a Corvette, and a bunch of ill-gotten money."

"And they say money can't buy happiness."

Cleo smiled. "They lie,"

The bartender poured the woman a drink and she shot him a grateful smile. He called out to the sausages. "We're giving Ellie a break, guys. Order your drinks at the bar."

"Nice place to work," I said.

"Wanna job?" Ellie said.

A half dozen guys gathered around the bar to place their orders and check out the estrogen in the room. Cleo ate up the attention. She was clearly not raised with three brothers and a hundred boy cousins. They were invading my bubble. I wanted my nun-sweater back.

Ellie tossed back her head and emptied her glass. "I haven't seen you girls in here before. Unless you come in after my shift."

"We've been in a few times," Cleo said breezily. "Cat got hammered last time we were here. Her boyfriend had just dumped her—"

The guy drinking Jack Daniels breathed in my face. "Asshole. Want me to hurt him?"

"Hurt Cleo," I said.

"This girl was a mess," Cleo raved on. "I think we all know what she was looking for."

There was a sudden surge of testosterone in the room. I couldn't breathe.

Jack Daniels slung an arm around my shoulder. "Bartender! Bring this woman a double shot of Tennessee Honey."

I shook his arm off. "Please don't."

"Make that two," Cleo said.

Some guy gave a course laugh. "I got her honey right here."

"I don't think so. I seen yours. It ain't no double," somebody snickered.

"I'll kill her," I said.

The bartender ogled Cleo's chest. "There's no shame in a woman admitting she has needs."

"Damn straight," she cooed. *Blink blink.*

I willed myself to not go for her throat. "You're fired," I said. "Just throwin' it out there."

Ellie patted my knee. "You're among friends here. We don't judge."

Cleo laughed giddily. "There was a guy Cat liked the last time we were here."

"What was his name?"

I butted in before she blabbed that we had sex in the bathroom. "He left before I could talk to him." I looked thoughtful and bit a pretzel. "I think people called him, uh, was it Coby? Or Cody?

The bartender shook his head. "Not here."

I twirled a finger in the red wig. "Uh, maybe it was Stokes."

"Nope."

"Or, could it be, uh, Toby?"

Ellie clapped her hands. "That's it! Toby Smoak!"

"Goddam lucky dog," Jack Daniels grumbled.

The bar door opened and the bartender whistled. "Speak of the devil, ladies."

The sea of testosterone parted. I spun the barstool around and stared across the room into cold, dead eyes. His gaze locked mine and his mouth curled. An icy chill pierced through me. Toby Smoak was almost certainly the creepiest guy I'd ever encountered.

Ellie called out, "Hey, Tob. There's a lady here to see you."

"Lucky bastard," somebody laughed.

"Cat DeLuca," Smoak said and his growl was low and menacing. "You're one dumb ass crazy bitch, to show up here."

I couldn't have been more stunned if he slapped me. How did this psychopath know my name?

"Not cool," the bartender said. "Ain't no way to talk to a lady."

"She's no lady," Smoak snarled. "She's working with the cops."

"Bitch!" Ellie screamed.

Jack Daniels looked crushed. "It was a lie?"

"Not all of it," Cleo said. "Cat really is a lush."

Jack Daniels beamed at me.

I slid off the stool and stood there, legs slightly apart, looking fierce. I faced the guy who tased me in the park. I wanted to bring him to his knees with a stun gun. But instead I said, "I'm taking you in, Toby Smoak, for the murder of Bernie Love."

"She's insane," Toby said.

I shrugged. "Captain Bob won't argue with you."

Toby pivoted and darted out the door. I tore after him. Three men with cue sticks beat me to the door. They blocked my way.

A bike fired up outside and Toby Smoak made his escape. He was in the wind.

"Are you a goddam cop?" one of them asked.

"No."

"She's a liar!" Ellie shrieked behind me.

Something struck the back of my head and my legs jello-ed. I crumbled to the ground and looked up. Ellie was holding a serving platter and my red wig.

I sat on my bum and cradled my head. "Dammit, Ellie, you said you didn't judge."

"What did Toby ever do to you?" she spat.

"He kicked her dog," Cleo said.

Ellie sniffed. "Toby doesn't need this right now. He lost his wife a few weeks back. She up and disappeared. No one can find her."

"Try digging up his back yard."

The door police returned to their game. Jack Daniels sauntered over from the bar and handed me the double shot of Tennessee Honey he'd ordered.

"If you ever get over Stokes, sweetheart, I'll be here."

I opened my mouth to say something and tossed the drink down my throat instead.

Cleo helped me to my feet. "Now aren't you glad we didn't bring Max. It would be downright embarrassing for him to see you like this."

Chapter Eighteen

"That was a knee-slapper, what you said back there about firing me," Cleo said when she dropped me off at my house.

"Yes it was."

"I mean, you were kidding. Right?"

"Was I?"

She chuckled.

I threw her my mean look. "You said I was a jilted lover on the prowl, hanging out in a biker dive, desperate to get laid."

"And this offended you, how?"

I threw the hideous wig at her.

"It was off the cuff. I improvised.'

"If you kept your mouth shut, we would've had Smoak when he walked through the door. We could've trailed him home and I would've drug his tased ass to Captain Bob's office."

She shook her head. "Not happenin'. Your cover was blown, girlfriend. Maybe it's your green eyes. I dunno but he made you. Red hair and all."

I glared at her. "My cover was blown because he knew my name."

"Well, he's on to you, girlfriend. Since he knows your name. He probably knows where you live."

"Provenza told him."

She snorted. "Provenza isn't our guy. He doesn't know Smoak."

It was my turn to snort.

Cleo gave me her best bitch stare. "That asshole is comin' for you," she said ominously. "You saw him in the park. He's gotta shut you up."

"Would you shut up."

I closed my eyes and massaged my head. It had been petty and stupid of me to not let Rocco bring Smoak in. If Smoak was behind bars, he couldn't fixate on the one person who can connect him to Bernie Love's corpse.

I knew I had to call my brother. But not tonight. Today was Rocco and Maria's youngest daughter's birthday and they were taking the girls to Rodger's and Hammerstein's *Cinderella—The Musical*. If I told Rocco about Toby Smoak tonight, he'd be all over it. Preoccupied, making calls from the Palace Theater's lobby. I thought of the birthdays Papa missed when I was growing up. It's tough on a kid.

I dragged out my cell and Cleo frowned. "What are you doing?"

"It's time to call Tino."

She slapped the phone shut. "Forget Tino, girlfriend. I got mad skills."

She whipped a rhinestone studded pistol from under her short skirt and spun it on her finger like a wild-west gangster.

"I'm a dead woman," I said.

◇◇◇

I waved to Cleo from the porch and inserted my key in the lock. It hadn't been easy to convince her I wouldn't need her gun slinging skills tonight. I'd be surrounded by law enforcement. At seven I was meeting a cop at a cop bar. And I fully intended be in a hot FBI agent's very skilled hands all night.

Cleo finally agreed to go home and have dinner with Frankie. I stepped inside my house and breathed the deep soothing essence of lemon-oil and lavender. While I was away the blessed Merry Maids had done their magic. Everything sparkled. There were fresh flowers on the table and clean sheets on the bed. Rosie, the merriest maid of all, left a loaf of ginger pear bread on the kitchen counter she'd made especially for me. It's the one thing I do to spoil myself. If my finances go south someday, I'll ax new shoes, Jackalope Coffee, and White Sox season tickets before losing Rosie and her team of clean.

I showered and dressed in my favorite black lace fit-and-flare dress. Then I chilled a bottle of Italian white, placed scented candles around the house, and popped Savino's favorite Eric Clapton CD in the player. I poked my head in a bag of goodies I purchased while following Cookie around the love store and selected a black lace chemise and a piña colada warming massage oil. Chance was coming over tonight and I wanted everything to be perfect.

I still had a little time before meeting Tommy so I lit a fire and hunkered down with Chance's file on Bernie's boss. Provenza's record was squeaky clean, without so much as a traffic ticket. Which didn't necessarily mean he doesn't speed. He could have a really cool uncle who makes his tickets go away.

There was a familiar rap at the door and Uncle Joey let himself in. He sniffed the air. "What's for dinner? Linda went to Vegas to stay with her sister."

"Is Kathy all right?"

"Maybe she has a sniffle. The other sisters have major surgery and Linda sends flowers. Kathy sneezes and my wife's right there, wiping her nose in a casino."

I laughed.

"Linda kicks ass at blackjack." He sniffed the air again. "It smells like flowers in here. Seriously, what's for dinner?"

I laughed. "How about Mickey's. Tommy's meeting us there at seven."

He tapped his stomach. "Good. I'm starved."

I drummed the stack of papers on my lap. "I asked Chance to dig up Provenza's bio and financials. There aren't any surprises yet, but it makes for interesting reading."

Joey's mouth twisted. "Does it say he blows people's faces off?"

I smiled. "That detail was overlooked in the report. Here's a *Tribune* article titled 'Chicago's New Philanthropists.' Nick and Sharon Provenza are mentioned for their work with at risk youth."

"Stop. You're making me cry."

I waved another page. "Nick went to Yale where his double major was in History and Philosophy. He might've been anticipating a career as a college professor or historian. I'm guessing running the family business wasn't his big dream back then."

Uncle Joey held my coat while I slipped it on. "Boo hoo. So daddy Provenza pressured him into taking over the family business."

"Not necessarily. The career switch could've been his choice. But a degree in business or marketing would've served him better."

"Do you have a point?"

"I'm guessing Nick Provenza is a liberal arts right-brained kind of guy. He gave Bernie categorical control over his books because he's clueless with corporate finances. It's over his head or maybe the math doesn't interest him."

"Bernie used to say his boss didn't know where all his money was stashed. Bernie gave him a brief overview of the money situation from time to time but Nick wasn't interested in the details. He trusted his bookkeeper a hundred percent. Bernie made his boss freaking rich. And he never stole a dime."

"He was a class act."

"Damn straight."

"Joey, I get why Provenza didn't want Bernie to retire. You can't replace a guy like Bernie. What I don't get, is why Provenza would off him. It doesn't make sense."

Joey shrugged. "He got paranoid and thought Bernie went to the other side."

"What other side? Provenza isn't on any FBI watch lists for criminal activity or rubbing elbows with the mob. He's a successful business man who lies to the IRS and hides money in the Caymans. It's a common practice among those in his income bracket."

"Nick Provenza's a snake. Wait 'til you meet him. He'll—"

He stopped abruptly.

"What?"

"You talked to Provenza," he said incredulously. "He schmoozed you over to his side."

"Stop with the *sides*," I laughed. "I was waiting until dinner to tell you about my day. I saw the guy but he wasn't trying to win me over. He asked about you though. Said something about your Ferrari."

"He knows I'm onto him," Joey smirked with satisfaction.

He tossed his keys to me. "Let's see watcha got," he said.

I grinned like a kid in a candy store. Joey doesn't usually surrender the wheel easily. DeLuca men have control issues.

Mickey's is five minutes from home but I gunned the gas and took the twenty-minute scenic route. When I screeched up to Mickey's, a parking spot opened in front of the bar and I whipped in without having to back up or adjust my wheels. My uncle couldn't help himself. He was impressed.

"You can leave this baby with me when you and Linda go to Hawaii next month," I said.

Joey barked a laugh. "I wouldn't leave my keys with Joey Jr. In fact, he's never driven this car."

"That's because he's eighteen, a relatively inexperienced driver, and you have an obsessive, dysfunctional relationship with this car."

"I let you drive it. Didn't I?"

I smiled. "Because you want something. I'm waiting to find out what."

Joey looked offended. "Can't an uncle let his favorite niece take a spin in his Ferrari?

"Spill it."

He shrugged. "I'm bringing down Provenza for killing Bernie."

"You have a plan. And I'm in it."

"Yes. But you have total deniability."

I searched his face. His eyes were dark, brooding circles and I knew he hadn't slept. He'd been blindsided by the death of a close friend. Grief and exhaustion can be a dangerous combination. Especially for a man like Joey who makes up the rules as he goes.

"We're gonna get the guys who killed Bernie," I said. "But we're gonna do it right. If Provenza is our man—"

"He is."

"Then we'll get the evidence to convict him. You can arrest him and testify at the trial that Bernie feared his boss would kill him. Suffering the public humiliation of a murder rap and living with what he did to Bernie is the sweeter revenge."

"What if the evidence is there but Provenza was too smart for us. I mean, the Prosecuting Attorney can't touch him cuz he covered his tracks and alibied out."

I kissed my uncle's cheek. "Then we can talk about deniability."

◇◇◇

We pushed through Mickey's heavy oak door and Joey gave a deep throated laugh. Standing on a table, his glass raised in a dramatic pose, was Doug Schuchard. His voice caught in his throat.

"Corey Corcino wouldn't pay into the office football pool because he said he was the unluckiest guy in the world."

"I guess he proved that when he fell out a window," someone snickered.

"It was a freak accident," a voice growled. "Corey was fiddling with the satellite dish outside his window when he fell."

"He was a good kid," somebody sniffed.

"Corey's parents live in California," Doug said. "His dad's on disability and his mom has failing health. She was hospitalized for shock but she's home now."

Mickey held up a donation jar. "There's a jar on the bar for donations to help the family with transporting and funeral expenses."

Someone shouted from the back. "Give generously. Mickey has offered to match what we can squeeze in this jar."

Mickey faked a growl. "And everybody drink up so I can pay for this." He grabbed the jar off the bar and carried it around to the tables.

"Dig deep, men," Joey called behind me. "The next round's on me."

"Make mine a double," Doug called and clambered down from the table.

Mickey came by with the jar. I gave him a hug and dropped some money inside. A picture had been taped to the jar of Corey and his black German Shepherd. I didn't know Corey but he had honest brown eyes and an easy smile. He looked like someone I would have liked to know. And he was a dog-person. Need I say more?

"Corey's dog is gorgeous. Where is she now?"

"Dixie's at the shelter. She's a great girl. I'd take her in a heartbeat if my kid wasn't allergic."

"I bet she misses Corey."

He nodded. "She went everywhere with him. They had something special."

Joey, Booker, and Doug sat at a front window table and I joined them. The server brought a few pitchers of Perone, an extra glass for Tommy, and double shots of Crown Royal. I kept my promise to Joey and ran down my day while Doug finished off shots. Doug got cheerier as I went along and totally cracked up when I told about Provenza's ambush. When I got to the part about the tattooed biker bitch bonking me over the head, he almost lost it.

"Stop!" he gasped. "I'm laughing so hard I'm gonna piss my pants."

"A blow to the head isn't funny, asshole," Booker said.

"I know. I know," he gasped for air. "Not funny at all."

"Whatever," I said and gave Booker a *let it go* look. Grief is a process and people manage it differently. Doug's approach seemed to involve a lot of alcohol and stupidity.

"What am I missing?" Tommy said behind me.

"Doug's being Doug," I said and patted the seat beside me. "If you don't mind, we'll have a beer with everybody before we get our own table."

"Woo woo woo," Doug said, cracking up with the emotional maturity of a twelve-year-old.

"Doug's been drinking all day," Joey said quietly. "He's dealing with his loss."

That sent Doug into raucous peals of laughter.

My head started pounding and I rose to my feet. "Let's find that table now, Tommy. We'll catch these guys later."

Tommy didn't budge. He was staring out the window.

"Hey, Joey. What's that guy doing by the Fire Dragon?"

We followed Tommy's gaze outside where a guy leaned against the Ferrari. He pulled a cell phone from an inside pocket and his wrist, beneath the street light, glittered gold. Oh yeah. Rolex Man.

He stared through the window and our eyes locked. A dark smile tugged the sides of his mouth. He thought he was a real badass.

But he didn't know Cat DeLuca.

My phone vibrated and I checked the screen. *Unknown number.*

"Who's that guy?" Joey demanded.

"The monster who kicked my partner."

I raised the phone to my ear. "What?"

"Boom," Toby Smoak said.

A chilling awareness pierced through me. I sprang from my seat. "No!" I shouted.

Everything happened in slow motion. The rookie, Tommy, pushed past me, leading the charge. He wrestled a gun from his holster.

"Whoa," I said. "You can't shoot him."

"Ha!"

Our server gaped at Tommy's gun and reached for the sky. A middle-aged couple screamed coming through the door.

We exploded onto the sidewalk and raked the street with our eyes. Smoak was gone. Joey and Booker burst through the door, hot on our tail.

"Where'd he go?" Joey shouted.

BOOM! The explosion was deafening. In an instant, Joey's red Ferrari was reduced to a sucking, sweltering fireball. The explosion lit the block and flaming car parts shot into the night. Joey's license plate broke free and soared spinning through the air, landing at Joey's feet. The metal plate smoked and the edges seared red but I could easily make out the letters. FYRDRGN.

Chapter Nineteen

The bar emptied onto the street. Guns drawn, cops shouted and darted about, looking for someone to shoot. Only Doug Schuchard remained inside. I studied him through the window; laughing to himself and slamming another shot of whiskey. He was working on a drunken stupor.

"Provenza!" Joey roared. "You really wanna mess with me? I'll effin kill you!"

If I'd had a tranquilizer, I would've stabbed him with it. I needed to take him down a notch before he did something crazy.

"We don't know Provenza was involved. Smoak could be acting alone," I said in a soothing voice. "He saw me driving the Ferrari and he was scaring me off."

"An extraordinary coincidence, don't you think?" Joey said bitterly. "Provenza asks about my Ferrari and suddenly it's a goddam inferno."

"Cat's got a point, man," Booker said. "If Provenza was sending you a message, you would've got the call. Not Cat."

"Uh, you don't wanna go off halfcocked," Tommy said and took a step back before Joey could cuff the rookie.

My phone buzzed again. *Unknown.* This time I put it on speaker and pressed Talk.

Joey snatched the cell from my hand. "You blew up my Ferrari, asshole. I'm coming for you."

"It's a message. Tell the bitch to back off. Or next time she'll be in it."

Joey's voice was terrifyingly calm. "Here's a message for you and your boss. Dead men don't scare me."

He tossed the phone back. I caught it and tucked it away. Sirens blared in the distance. Fire trucks were descending.

Joey held out a hand. "Your keys, Booker. I'll drive."

They tromped off to Booker's car and Tommy and I chased after them.

Joey called over his shoulder. "Go home, Cat. This isn't your fight."

"The hell it's not. Go home, Tommy. This can't be legal. You don't want to jeopardize your career."

I felt his breath on my shoulder.

"You think I'm missing this?"

Joey slid behind the wheel. Booker rode shotgun and Tommy and I scooted into the back before the partners could protest. Joey stared once more at the smoldering Firedragon before burning rubber.

I didn't ask my uncle where we were going. I just knew he was driving the wrong way to shoot Provenza. That was good enough for me.

No one said a word until Joey pulled in front of Bernie's house. It was Tommy who broke the silence.

"Where are we?"

"Bernie's house," I said. "We're breaking in."

"Cool," Tommy said.

Parking hadn't been an issue when I was here this morning. But it was evening now. People were home and cars lined up and down the street. Joey found a fireplug, parked, and killed the engine. He propped a Police Business Parking Permit in the window. Like the one I stole last year from Rocco.

"Caterina," he said. "Open the door."

I charged up the steps and beat off the sticky yellow police tape. My set of picks were in my bag, back at the bar. I remembered Bernie's iron bird sculpture on the stoop and I hoisted it in my hands. I breathed my apologies to Bernie and muttered two quick Hail Mary's to save Father Timothy time. Then I broke a glass door pane and we were inside.

I pushed the door open and gasped.

The neat, orderly home I'd walked through this morning had been thoroughly tossed. The violence was unnerving. The perps could've used a knife and sledgehammer. Cushions were cut and walls gaped holes. Drawers were emptied. Books swept from their shelves. A couple brainless morons had turned the place inside out and upside down. They'd hit every room.

"Holy shit," Tommy said.

Booker grunted. "Whatever they were looking for, they didn't find it."

"Why do you say that?" Tommy said.

"Because if they had, they would've stopped. But these guys kept going. They trashed room after room and they didn't quit."

"What do they want?" Tommy looked from room to room.

"They want the same thing that we're here for," I said.

We both looked at Uncle Joey. He smiled.

"Bernie kept two books for Nick Provenza. The fictional copy is at Bernie's office. It's a work of art. It's satisfied the IRS for almost three decades while omitting the bulk of Provenza's assets."

"And Bernie's real ledger is here," I said.

"It's here all right."

Joey moved through the house to Bernie's bedroom. "It was Provenza's idea to keep the second book at Bernie's house," he said. "He said it was safer if the ledgers weren't together."

Tommy frowned. "Maybe the boss didn't do it. I mean, why put a hit out on your bookkeeper before you have the ledger in your hand."

"Cuz Provenza's an asshole," Joey growled. "And you're a rookie, Tom. You're not a detective."

I didn't say I was a detective and I'd wondered the same thing.

Joey opened the bedroom closet door, pulled up the carpet, and exposed a small safe embedded in the floor.

"Once Bernie was out of the country with his new identity, I was to get this to Provenza. He gave a twisted smile. "Bernie almost made it. He was so close."

"Horse shoes and hand grenades," I said.

Joey reached into the hidden safe and pulled out a black leather book. He handed it to me and I opened it greedily.

There were columns of numbers and abbreviated words. It could be written in code.

I flipped the pages. "What is this?"

Uncle Joey took the worn ledger in his hand and flashed a grin. "This is Nicolas Provenza buying me a new Ferrari."

Booker muttered under his breath. "I'd like to put some cash on my kids' education."

Joey needed ten minutes and a cool little black book to spend four-hundred eighty thousand smackeroos. The fierce red F12 Berlinetta had dramatic, swooping lines and does zero to sixty in three seconds. It helped that Joey knew exactly every detail he wanted; the Ferrari Official website is his home page.

Joey cleared out Bernie's safe and stuffed all Bernie's files and folders and personal records and documents in a box. There appeared to be various investment and advisory projects he was working on when he died.

"There's a lot here to sort through here," Joey said. "But nothing that won't keep." He scooted us back to the car and drove me home. I stepped outside and Tommy gave a chuckle.

"We never got that drink. But tonight was the most fun I've had in this town."

"I'll take a rain check," I smiled.

"That boy needs to get out more," Joey muttered under his breath. He hoisted the box of goodies from Bernie's safe and walked with me to the door.

"You and Savino should take a nice romantic trip to Italy this winter. Cruise the Almafi coast. Explore Pompeii, the Piazza del Campo…"

I laughed. "Compliments of Nick Provenza?"

He shrugged. "Why not? He's not seeing that money, Caterina. He killed Bernie."

"*If* he killed Bernie. Let's be sure first."

He kissed my cheek. "Hide this box where no one can find it. And don't let anyone know you have it."

I took the box. "Like Nonna DeLuca used to say. It's as safe as if it was in God's pocket."

◇◇◇

I placed the box in the secret compartment, behind my pantry that hid the spirits during the Prohibition. It had been an intense twenty-four hours and I was exhausted. I missed my running partner and I wasn't motivated to go out alone. Last night hadn't worked out well for either of us.

I imagined Inga would be having a late night snack of warm milk and Mama's lamb stew. My stomach rumbled at the thought. I was hungry but I mostly wanted to crawl into bed and sleep. I lit the candles instead and two forgotten oil lamps I discovered in the attic when I moved in. Then I turned on Eric Clapton and had just poured a glass of wine when Chance called.

"Hey, babe."

"Cat, thank God. You're OK?"

"Of course."

He expelled air. "I just got a report of a car bombing in Bridgeport at Mickey's. You said you were meeting Tommy."

"We were there with Joey. It was the Fire Dragon that blew."

He winced. "The Ferrari?"

"I know, huh? That's a bomber with no soul."

"Joey better have some kick-ass insurance."

"A brand new upgraded model is already on the way. I'll tell you about it when you get here."

"There's a lot to tell. I haven't heard about last night at the park."

"As it turns out, it's all one story."

He digested that. "You mean the guy in the park and the bomber are -"

"You got it, my FBI Agent in Charge. They're one and the same." I grimaced. "Thanks to Toby Smoak stealing my body, now Captain Bob thinks I'm incompetent."

"Yeah, like that's never happened before."

I ignored that. "I'm looking in the refrigerator. Will you be here soon or should I go for a cold slice of pizza."

"I'm almost there and the Thai is hot. I got phad Thai and Panang curry and even got those spring rolls you like."

"It's so hot when you feed me."

"Anything else?"

I opened the freezer door. "We're out of Ben and Jerry's."

"Preference?"

"Something chocolate."

"Whipping cream?"

"Definitely. And, uhm, maybe a little extra for the ice-cream."

Chance brought Ben and Jerry's Chocolate Therapy ice-cream and a dozen yellow roses. I remembered what Cleo said about roses and swallowed a smile. We were on the same page.

We ate on the couch by the fire and I told my story. I just didn't tell him everything.

I told about running at the park last night and crash landing on the corpse of Bernie Love. I told him Bernie worked for Provenza and how Bernie almost made a new life for himself in Costa Rica. I told him about Cleo dropping from Provenza's wall onto the estate and talking to Gabbie, the cook. And I said the address he gave me for Toby Smoak is in the middle of the Chicago River.

I totally skipped my humiliating ambush on a narrow side street and seeing the image of Cleo's hoo-haa on Provenza's cell phone. My eyes still ached.

I also neglected to share those last humiliating moments at the biker bar. The part when I was flat on my back, staring up at tattoo biker babe and her dodgy serving tray. I'm thankful she wasn't wearing a skirt.

If I bleeped other stuff it was cuz I don't want Savino to think the Pants On Fire cast are idiots. And I didn't want him to over-react and think I was in danger from Toby Smoak. Savino can be as interfering and bossy as the DeLuca men. I could handle the river rat myself.

We snuggled on the couch in front of the fire. Chance talked about his day. A critical witness in a federal case had fled to

Nevada. Jury selection was in process and the court case was scheduled to begin in a few days. Someone got to the runaway witness. And there would be no case without him

I listened to the soothing tremor of his voice. I let the music run over me and the wine lull me to a slight euphoric state. I could feel my neck and shoulder muscles relax and the tension leave my body. I leaned into Chance, resting my head on his shoulder. The next thing I knew he was carrying me to bed.

I was done. Put-a-fork-in-me finished. The last thirty hours had been rough. There was the faceless body at the park. The explosion at Mickey's. A biker bitch clonked me over the head and when I closed my eyes, Toby Smoak lurked in the shadows.

Savino put me on the bed. I awoke enough to pull my clothes off and slip into a Minnie Mouse tee. The sexy teddy from Cookie's love store would wait for another day.

I lay my head on my pillow and stared into Chance's deep cobalt blue eyes.

He kissed my nose. And then my cheeks. I was as fun as a corpse.

"You're ruined," he said. "You've had a rough couple days."

"Hmm," I said sleepily. "Unless you have a secret fantasy to have sex with a dead woman…"

He smiled. "Not even a little bit."

"Then this isn't your lucky night."

"It's OK." He wrapped his arms around me and I felt his warm breath in my hair. "Tonight this is enough."

Without meaning to, my breathing slowed and deepened until my breath matched Savino's.

"DeLucky," he said softly in my ear. "Do you know when I knew I loved you? I mean, the first moment I realized I was head-over-heels, going-down-with-the-ship in love with you?"

I didn't know.

"Hmmm," I murmured."

"It was when…."

I was asleep before he told me.

Chapter Twenty

Chance was gone when I awoke in a tangle of blankets and bad dreams. A scar-faced douche had chased me on his Harley. A tattooed biker bitch wanted to clobber me with a whiskey bottle. I fought off the covers and sat up in bed. I mentally karate-chopped the bikers and wrestled-in a new day of awesome.

The coffee was hot when my bunny slippers shuffled to the kitchen. Savino had placed the newspaper and an apple-cinnamon muffin on the table. A sticky note on the fridge directed me to yogurt and a glass of orange juice. He left a few sweet, sexy notes around the house as well. Chance is an incurable romantic. It's a hard act to follow. I'm easily distracted with life and I suspect my romance gene has some holes in it.

I skipped my morning run. Inga was with Mama and I didn't feel like running alone. I drank more coffee, did a little yoga, and took a long, toasty shower. When I was ready to take on the world, I grabbed a jacket and my secret camera bag and zipped out the door. I skipped down the steps and stumbled on the last one. A man with no hair and a yo-yo leaned against my car. A buttery yellow Lexus blocked my driveway.

I smoothed my jacket, trying to look cool after almost tripping on my feet and wiping out on my face.

"Nicky," I said. "Once again you're blocking my way."

He had an expensive, white-capped smile. "Good morning, Ms. DeLuca."

I gave him my best smile. "Good-bye, Mr. Car Bomber."

He looked confused for a moment and then went straight to business. "I need a detective. I want to hire you."

"Make an appointment."

"I just did."

He wasn't being difficult or confrontational. Nick Provenza was a man who expected to get his own way. Because he usually did.

"Would you rather we speak in your office?" he said.

Being alone with a homicidal car bomber didn't seem like a good idea. Regretfully, my 9mm was tucked away in a drawer.

"I doubt there is that much to say. There are other qualified detectives in South Chicago you can contact."

The eyes that had been cold yesterday, smiled. "Are there so many gumshoes better than you?"

I shrugged. "No."

I wasn't bragging. DeLucas have been cops or crooks since anyone can remember. The men in my family have won medals and achieved some notoriety in law enforcement. When they get shot, it's usually not their fault. Besides the whole gene thing, the DeLucas train for this work from childhood. When my friends got Barbie dolls and kitchen playmate sets, I was learning to pick locks and Mirandize suspects. To be fair, Sophie and I had the Strawberry Shortcake Kitchen Set too. But I preferred climbing trees with my older brother Rocco. We were Starsky and Hutch and we shot people.

"Why do you need a private investigator?"

He blinked hard and his voice choked a little. "My book-keeper, Bernie Love, has apparently died."

He was good. I had to give him that. "Somehow, you always manage to seem surprised," I said dryly.

He let that go. "Bernie kept a ledger at his home of my business and personal accounts. It's irreplaceable. I want you to find it for me. I'm offering a generous reward."

"Are you asking me to break into Bernie's house?"

"It's not in his house. My guys were there."

"What makes you think I can find it?"

"Bernie was a hard man to get close to. There was one guy in the world he trusted. If that man doesn't have the ledger, he knows where it is."

"Why don't you ask Uncle Joey?"

"He doesn't like me much."

"I don't like you either."

"You don't know me." He sighed. "I'm offering you a simple business proposition. Did your uncle tell you about the ledger?"

"No."

I said it like a seasoned liar. I didn't blink. Or let a faint flush travel up my cheeks. I don't fib very often but I'm good at it. It my line of work, it's as elementary as tailing someone. I can bamboozle just about anyone I know. But I didn't fool Provenza.

He looked thoughtful. "Joey DeLuca isn't foolish enough to keep the ledger at his house. It would, quite reasonably, be the first place I'd look."

I shrugged and something flickered in his eyes. I wondered if I'd given something away.

"But he could give the ledger to someone he trusted."

His gaze on me deepened and it was hard to breathe. It was as if he was doing some lame Obi-Wan mind trick.

I stared back. When we were kids, my siblings and I would gaze into each other's eyes without blinking until somebody cracked. I could beat everyone I knew. Our eyes locked and I knew I had him. But Nick Provenza didn't back down. At the very last moment, I flinched. He gave a satisfied snort.

Provenza glanced past me to stare to my house. It was as if he knew the ledger was there and could almost see through the wall. When he looked at me again, his face softened.

"The ledger is rightfully mine," he said. "This is a nice place you have. Bring me the ledger and I'll pay off your mortgage."

He turned and ambled to his car. The driver opened the door for him.

Nick Provenza was a complicated man. Reckless, charming, deadly.

I watched them drive away. I didn't start the Silver Bullet until I checked under the carriage for explosives.

◇◇◇

I was waiting outside Animal Care and Control on Western when they opened their doors. I was on a mission to rescue Dixie, the black German shepherd whose human companion died adjusting his satellite dish.

Corey Corcino and Doug Schuchard were both ex-cops who'd found better hours, better pay, and less stress working for the police union. Last night I learned Corey's dog had been taken to the shelter. I imagined how frightened she must be. Dixie lost everything when Corey plummeted from their fourth-story window. Her world shattered with him. It was too late for Corey but Dixie deserved a second chance.

I also knew big, black dogs are the last to be adopted, and the first to be euthanized in shelters. Dixie's odds didn't look good where she was. I figured they'd improve tremendously if she stayed with me until she found a new family. In fact, I already had someone in mind.

The volunteer at the shelter was energetic and helpful. There were hundreds of dogs with sorrowful faces and I wanted to take them all. I told her what I'd heard about Dixie and she knew exactly who I was looking for. She brought me straight to Dixie's cage.

"Dixie has been with us four days," she said. "The vet examined her. She's about three years old, and she gets along well with dogs and cats. She's seems perfectly healthy, but she's just not eating. I think she's traumatized. Her owner died in a fall." She hesitated. "Did you know him?"

"No. But we had some mutual friends."

"A terrible thing to see yourself plunging to the ground headfirst. Knowing you're gonna be—"

I nudged her with an elbow. "The dog can hear you."

"Roadkill," she finished in a whisper.

The adoption process was quick and painless. It was the best sixty-five dollars I'd spent in a long time. I took Dixie to my car and opened the back door. She hopped inside and I scootched in next to her for a moment.

"You know Corey is gone. And someday, in the afterlife, you'll be together again. That's what I like to think." I rubbed her ears. "I'm gonna do what I can to make sure you have the best life possible."

Dixie's eyes sparkled and tail thumped against the backseat. I could tell she was totally getting this powwow. At least, that was my interpretation of Dog Language 101.

"First we'll walk in Oz Park. And then we'll stop by your condo. I want to see what kind of food you like. If you have toys or a blanket or something you want to keep, we'll take it with us."

The address I had for Corey and Dixie was a four-story walk-up on West Dickens, a stone's throw from Oz Park. The city park has statues of the Wizard of Oz characters. L. Frank Baum once lived not far from the park and Rocco's girls are huge fans. Sometimes I take the girls there and they play in Dorothy's playground. Then we go home and make popcorn and watch the movie.

I parked at the condo and we walked to the park. Dixie had been cramped in a cage for days and I let her walk off her stiffness before trying a tentative run. She had a graceful, athletic body and she ran like a deer. We ran for thirty minutes. I found a bench and sat beside her. She rested her head on my lap and looked at me with big brown eyes. My heart turned to marshmallow.

We walked back to the condo and I pressed the bell marked "Manager." No response. Dixie looked at me expectantly.

"Gotcha." I dragged out my lock picks and did my magic.

Dixie blew off the elevator and galloped up the stairs. Her condo, I remembered, was on the fourth floor. I wasn't sure about the number but Dixie led the way. It was a no brainer. The brass knocker on Unit 4W was a German shepherd head. The door mat pictured a black German shepherd and read: "Dixie's Digs."

"Honey, we're home," I said and let us in.

The condo was cozy—earth tone walls, hardwood floors, and heavy wood furniture. There was a guitar in a corner and a little

Buddha on the mantle. And there was a surfboard hanging from the ceiling. Corey had brought a bit of California with him. I would've liked the guy. I certainly adored his dog.

I followed Dixie to the kitchen. There was a half-filled coffee cup on the table and a small, forgotten dish of cottage cheese. I found an unopened can of chili on the stove beside a can opener and small pan. It appeared as if Corey was preparing his supper when he died. I wondered what he would have chosen if he'd known the meal would be his last. I'm guessing it wouldn't have been chili.

I gave Dixie fresh water and poured her a big bowl of Science Diet. She snarfed it up. I packed up her food and dishes, bed, blanket, her Frisbee and stuffed toys, her bones, winter coat, yellow raincoat and hat, dental chews, her *Dixie Girl* embroidered bath towel, her medical file with vet's name and emergency number, her AKC registration, her crate, and a few of her many photo albums. I made two trips to the car and when I returned the second time, a scribbled note attached to the refrigerator caught my eye. It said *Bernie Love* and a telephone number.

Cold fingers crawled down my spine. It was surprising enough that Bernie's number would be on anyone's refrigerator. Bernie had been a loner, a reclusive man with few friends or connections. In fact Joey said he was his *only* friend. Two strong, healthy guys, dead within days of each. An extraordinary coincidence?

I dragged out my cell and punched a number.

"Yello," Rocco said.

His voice was gravelly. My call woke him.

"Hey, Rocco. It's me."

"Hmmmph."

Oh yeah, he was still pissy.

"I wanted to give you the name of the guy in the park."

"You can cut the crap, Sis. I got it. Toby Smoak. And it sure didn't come from you."

I winced. "You swung by Mickey's after the birthday bash."

"Uncle Joey called me. The fire was out by the time I got there. Everybody knew who blew up the Ferrari. Shit, the bartender even knew. The goddam bartender. I'm the lead detective on this case, and I'm left out in the cold. I felt like a freakin' fool."

"Rocco, I'm sorry."

"Someone could've been killed. You know, if you'd given Toby's name at Tino's, Jackson and I would've picked him up. And Uncle Joey would still have his Ferrari."

"You're right. I should've given you the name. But it wouldn't have made a difference. You would've driven to North Park, and stared into the Chicago River."

"You don't know what I would've done. You know why? Because, you are not a real detective, Sis. A detective that works for a real police department has to follow protocol. You wouldn't last a day working for the CPD."

He had a point. You don't have to follow many rules when you run your own business. Plus, the pay is a hell of a lot better. "I'm at Corey Cancino's place in Lincoln Park."

He racked his brain. "The jumper?"

"Corey didn't jump. He fell. The running theory is he was fiddling with his satellite dish."

"Really? And there was a witness?"

"No. But somebody said he was having trouble with it lately."

"That's a new one."

"Corey wouldn't have left Dixie like that. Not without making arrangements for her."

"Who's Dixie?"

"The love of his life. She's coming with me to the fitting. I'll introduce you then."

"OK. So you're not alone."

"Nope."

"Keep it that way. Until we nail this prick."

"So, are you still pissed, or what."

"I'm pissed the perp is on the loose. But we'll find him."

"Not if I find him first," I muttered under my breath.

"Slow your roll, Sis. You listening to anything I said?"

"I'll be careful. I was calling to tell you Corey has a note on his fridge with Bernie's name and phone number."

"Huh. I didn't realize they knew each other."

"I didn't realize Bernie knew anybody."

"And now they're both dead. That's tough."

"That's hinky."

"It happens."

"So does lightening in a snow storm."

"Okay. What do you want me to do?"

"I'd like you to check Bernie's phone records for calls from Corey."

"I'll do it."

"Thanks, bro. I owe you one."

He grunted. "Just don't get yourself blown up."

I pocketed the phone, walked across the room, and opened the window. I studied the satellite dish for a moment. There weren't obvious dials or buttons to fiddle with. I couldn't imagine that anyone, even a trained technician, would adjust the settings on a dish while hanging out a window.

I closed the window again and jabbed a few buttons on the remote. The big screen TV was set to the Golf Channel. And the picture was perfect. I turned off the TV and wandered off, looking for Dixie.

I found her in Corey's bedroom, lying on the floor with her head on his slippers.

My eyes stung. I laid with her a long time. When we left the condo, we brought the slippers with us.

Chapter Twenty-one

When Mama walked into Agato's Formal Wear on Halstead to price the powder-blue tuxes in his store window, she didn't know she'd close the deal thirty-five years later. Papi Agato is older and a little stooped now but he's still there. He's provided tuxes for every Bridgeport school dance since the 1970s. He dressed my three brothers for their high school dances and weddings. And today he was fitting them with spiffy powder-blue tuxes for Mama's big church wedding.

What most people don't know about Agato is that he's a shameless hoarder. His front show room tastefully displays the newest trends in men's formal fashion. But his jam-packed back room and a shoddy warehouse fairly explode with every tux Agato ever rented. He stockpiles crates stuffed with meaningless receipts, former clients' measurements, and obsolete shipping orders. Agato's persistent difficulty parting with possessions is a fire hazard at the very least. On the bright side, his whacky affliction made Mama's eighties wedding dreams come true.

Agato was able to resurrect powder-blue tuxes with frilly powder-blue shirts for my brothers, Sophie's husband, Mama's papa, Papa's four brothers, some cousins, and Papa's ex-partner, Captain Bob. Powder-blue tuxes for everyone.

My brothers were having their final fitting this morning. I couldn't help myself. I had to see the testosterone-glutted DeLuca men in frilly powder-blue. I'd try really hard not to laugh.

I parked in a Police Only zone and displayed the Chicago Police Department placard I pilfered off Rocco last year. He's long replaced the permit but he's still trying to figure out where the one on my dash went. I told him he may not be the hotshot detective he thinks he is.

I opened the door and Rocco whined like I knew he would. "Dammit, Mama. I feel like a fairy in this girly shirt."

Inga charged the door howling. She ran circles around Dixie and me. Sometimes Inga's a nerd. Dixie was a little frosty at first but she warmed up after the customary butt sniffing.

Papa's eyes twinkled. "Your new dog is a beauty. Does this mean Inga lives with us now?"

I laughed. "You wish, Papa. This is Dixie. Uncle Joey's dog."

"I bet Linda doesn't know."

"That's OK. Uncle Joey doesn't know either."

Mama held Rocco's face in her hands and kissed each cheek. "You couldn't look more handsome."

Agato was straining to fit the ruffled blue tuxedo shirt across Michael's massive chest and monster-size arms. He pulled the fabric tight. There was no extra to spare.

Michael turned a bit, checking his reflection in the mirror. "I like this frilly shirt. I look like Tubbs."

"Me too." Vinnie tossed some Mike and Ikes in his mouth. And then he stopped. "Who's Tubbs?"

"Tubbs was a big television character from the eighties," Michael said. "He looked like us."

Michael thinks he's smarter than Vinnie. He isn't. The difference between them is Vinnie's just smart enough to keep his mouth shut when he doesn't know what he's talking about.

"John Travolta. Tubbs was played by John Travolta," Michael said.

Vinnie stood next to Michael and they studied their powder-blue reflections in the glass. They stood there like that, looking in the mirror, chomping down a few Mike and Ikes.

"Yep," Vinnie nodded finally. "We look like John Travolta."

"You kids would have loved the eighties," Mama said.

Papa grinned at Mama. "Hot pants. Remember your little white hot pants tight on your apple bottom…?"

Agato sighed wistfully. "Leisure suits. Tight fitting, low-rise bell-bottoms…"

I smiled. The beauty of hot pants was lost on the tailor.

Rocco gave me a copy of Bernie's calls. I kissed his cheek. "Thanks, Bro."

"I'll walk you to your car," Mama said unexpectedly.

I shrugged. "C'mon Inga," I said and the four of us stepped outside.

"Someone needs your help, Caterina," Mama said. "Both you and the FBI future father of my grandchildren."

For once I didn't argue. She chewed her bottom lip. She was worried.

"What's going on, Mama?"

"A Bridgeport man is missing. Mrs. Whitaker's neighbor."

"Ivy Whitaker? I thought you weren't friends anymore."

"She cheats at church Bingo."

"How is it even possible to cheat at Bingo?"

"What? You think she's so lucky to win every week?"

"You told Father Timothy, didn't you?"

"There may have been an anonymous complaint." Mama clicked her mouth. "Mrs. Whitaker's neighbor has disappeared."

"When?"

Mama shrugged. "No one knows for sure."

"And no one knows where he went?"

"Just Teddy. Teddy says Charlie went to Hollywood. Got a big movie deal. Had dinner with Meryl Streep."

"Is that what Charlie told him."

Mama made a dismissive sound. "Charlie didn't tell Teddy squat. Teddy had a vision. He's a psychic."

"A psychic." I massaged my temples.

"Mrs. Whitaker says Charlie likes gangster movies. And he listens to books on tape. He knows a lot of *The Godfather* by heart."

"What do you want me to do, Mama?"

"Pay attention, Caterina. I need to find Charlie."

"Uhm.."

She stuffed Mrs. Whitaker's address in my hand.

I opened my car door and told the dogs to get in. Dixie jumped in. Inga inched toward Mama. Mama looked pleased. She couldn't help herself.

"Inga, come," I said more firmly.

She didn't budge.

"We're on a big case, girl. We have work to do."

My partner sat there.

Mama gave a sheepish smile. "She has a play date today with the other granddogs. Sophia is having a birthday party for Boots at the dog park. She made an organic chicken-carrot cake with cream cheese frosting; no sugar, just the tiniest touch of raw honey."

I patted Inga's head. "Have fun at your party. You can come home tomorrow."

Mama smiled giddily. Inga is her favorite granddog. If she ever goes missing in the night, I'll know where to look.

"Your sister is amazing. Organizing this elaborate birthday party. Prizes. Decorations. Games." Mama laughed. "I don't know how she does it. And to think yesterday her kids were vomiting."

"They probably ate the dog cake."

Mama's face softened. "That's the kind of mama you'll be, Caterina. The best. Like your sister Sophie."

I clamped my jaw fiercely to block the words in my head from spewing out my mouth. I may not know a lot about God. But I know this. You talk that way to your mama, you're goin' to Confession.

Chapter Twenty-two

Mrs. Whitaker was waiting in the window when I pulled up to her home. The house was a sixties-era duplex. Her parents had lived in one half until they passed a few years ago. It was then that Ivy and her husband converted the duplex into a single, spacious residence. Undoubtedly, with her ill-gotten church bingo money.

We had coffee and prune kolaches on the sun-porch with a view of the garden. The kolaches might have been better than Mama's. But you could water-board the shit out of me and I'd still deny it to her face.

Mrs. Whitaker wrung her hands and stared at the house next door as if willing Charlie to appear in the window.

"I don't care what Ted says. Something terrible has happened to Charlie."

"Ted?"

"Charlie's neighbor on the other side. Ted's a quack. A fruit-loop. A..."

"Psychic?"

She snorted her disapproval. "Ted thinks Charlie's starring in a Hollywood movie and hanging out with Meryl Streep. Ha!"

"You think Charlie doesn't like Meryl Streep?"

"I think Charlie doesn't like people period. Certainly not enough to be famous."

"When did you see him last?"

"Wednesday morning. I told him my sister's husband isn't well and we'd be away a few days. We returned late Saturday night. If Charlie was home, I didn't notice."

"And the neighbors?"

"Charlie keeps to himself since his dog died."

Mrs. Whitaker went to the closet and dragged down a shoebox stuffed with photo-envelopes from Costco. I helped myself to another prune kolache and she searched through photographs until she found the one she was looking for. She passed it to me.

"This is Charlie and Spats. Charlie said he was a kid in a dog suit."

I studied the picture. Charlie appeared to be in his fifties with a tall, lean frame and with a full head of curly gray hair. Spats was a white bull terrier with black markings on his head.

"It's a great pic. May I borrow it?"

She nodded. "Spats was a clown. He was fun-loving and sweet. Charlie hasn't been himself since he lost him. He's more withdrawn."

I wondered if Charlie was depressed enough to commit suicide. I didn't ask though. We'd know soon enough.

"Did you contact the police to report Charlie missing?" I asked.

"I did better than that." She winked and tapped her head with a finger, signaling she was so damn smart. "I called your Mama."

I felt a headache coming on.

"Your mama said I did the right thing. She's a smart lady." She smiled and leaned forward, as if sharing a secret. "But not so lucky in Bingo."

"Mama says you're a bingo maniac."

"I pray to St. Cajetan. He's the patron saint of gamblers and the unemployed." She winked. "But he's a sucker for Bingo."

I laughed. "Mama says you keep an eye on Charlie's house for him when he's out of town. Do you have a key?"

"Yes. But I wouldn't feel right going inside."

I held out a hand. "You don't have to."

◇◇◇

I unlocked Charlie's door and got a whiff of lemon furniture polish. I exhaled a sigh of relief. No dead body smells. If Charlie offed himself, he didn't do it here. And his wallet was on the table. Wherever he went, he wasn't planning on spending money.

There was cold coffee in the pot. Half a glass of red wine on the table. And milk in the fridge. A goldfish swam circles in a bowl. I sprinkled fish-food in her bowl and made a quick search of the house. No sign of Charlie. And no clues to where he'd gone.

I returned the key to Mrs. Whitaker with the goldfish. Her forehead creased with worry.

"I have to say, I have a bad feeling about this," I said. "Charlie left in a hurry. He didn't take his wallet. Or his money. Or credit cards."

"But you'll find him," she said with undue confidence.

"I'll do my best."

Mrs. Whitaker squeezed my hand. "Pray to St. Anthony of Padua. That guy can find anybody."

When I walked back to my car, psychic Ted was waiting for me

"Ms. DeLuca?"

Maybe he was psychic after all. Or, more likely, Ivy told him I was coming.

"Hi, Ted. What can you tell me about Charlie?"

"Only what I hear from my guides. Hollywood. Movie deal. Probably a gangster movie." He laughed. "Charlie's a character, all right."

I gave him a card. "Call me if you hear from Charlie or think of something else. I told Mrs. Whitaker I'd try to find him."

Ted grinned broadly. "He's not coming back, you know. Once they get a taste of the bright lights, they never look back."

◇◇◇

I made a stop at the liquor store before Dixie and I zoomed to the Ninth precinct. We made it past the desk sergeant and were walking to the captain's office when the door to the men's room opened. Captain Bob stepped out, buckling the belt on his pants. Our eyes locked and his gaze moved to my hands. His lip curled.

No lemon crèmes.

"Hello, Bobby," I said.

Bob's face twitched and his gaze shot down the hall to his office. I've known Captain Bob my whole life and I could read his weasely mind. He intended to lock himself in his office. Or, more accurately, lock me out.

"*Seriously?*" I said.

Captain Bob charged the door and I bolted after him.

I had to admire his optimism. He has twenty-five years on me and a shameful number of lemon crèmes beneath his belt. To be fair, I wore running shoes and might have told Dixie to cut him off at the pass.

I was seated in his office examining my nails when Bob dragged through the door with the black shepherd. She was smiling.

"I think Dixie likes you," I said.

He parked himself at his desk, slightly out of breath. "Where's your beagle? Did this dog eat her?"

"Inga's at the mall helping Mama select beachwear for her honeymoon."

"You're her daughter. Isn't that your job?"

I shrugged. "She knows what Mama likes."

When I was a kid, Bob and Papa were partners on the Force. He's been part of the family ever since. He's like one of my uncles except he doesn't speak Italian and he wants to throw me in jail.

Bob's been present at every significant event in my life. He attended my Baptism, Confirmation, Graduation, and my Wedding. He was even at my Divorce party. But not cuz I invited him. A hysterical neighbor called the cops saying a man was on fire. It was an effigy of Johnnie Rizzo. I may have poured too much gasoline on his Armani wedding suit.

The captain looked at me squarely, projecting authority. "The answer is no."

"No, what?"

He sniffed pettily. "To whatever you want. Go away."

"You're mad about the lemon crèmes, aren't you. Maybe I brought something better."

He brightened.

I flashed my most winning smile and dragged Uncle Joey's bottle from my shoulder bag. I plopped it on his desk.

He gave a low whistle and shoved the bottle in a drawer so I couldn't take it back. Then he looked at me suspiciously.

"That set you back. What's it for."

"It's a bribe."

He shook his head. "It's a birthday present."

"Bribe."

"If it was a bribe, Caterina, I'd have to arrest you. But because it's my birthday, I'm saying 'thanks' and I don't owe you anything."

"I'm pretty sure it's a bribe."

Bob sighed and jerked the drawer back open. He poured himself two very fat fingers, brought the glass to his lips, and savored a sip.

"I know it's not your birthday, Captain, cuz if it was, you'd be a Sagittarian. You're not. You're a Taurus like me. We're practically soul mates."

I thrust out a fist and waited for a bump. I got a growl instead.

"You have a smart answer for everything, don't you."

I smiled. "Huh?"

His face relaxed and he almost smiled. "OK. The birthday present bought you five minutes." He looked at his watch. "Start talking."

"Captain Bob, two Bridgeport men have gone missing in the last several days. Bernie Love was killed Sunday night and his body was snatched."

He reddened slightly and he pulled a blue bottle of liquid antacid from his desk and gulped thirstily.

"My ulcer only screams when you're involved. Why is that?"

I shrugged. "Cuz we're soul mates."

He looked as if he was going to be sick.

"The second man disappeared sometime in the past week. Charlie Steele is fifty something and keeps pretty much to himself. In fact he's so reclusive, he can't hardly talk to people. No one's seen him for several days. One neighbor is concerned. She's one of Mama's church friends. Another nutso neighbor thinks he's gone to Hollywood to be a movie star. Were you aware he's missing?"

Bob grimaced and gulped more antacid. "Your Mama called me three times already to check on our progress with this guy. There is no progress. No investigation. There hasn't been a police report. I sent Tommy and Leo to talk to a neighbor. The neighbor told them about landing a big movie deal."

"Really? An introvert who can't talk to people?"

"Why not? They're all nuts in California." He switched drinks and slugged down the bourbon. "I suppose you have a better theory."

I smacked a fist on the desk. "Serial killer. Captain. Bridgeport could have one."

His jaw dropped.

I shrugged. "It's a theory."

"An insane theory." The captain looked at his watch. He finger-tapped vigorously as if it had stopped.

"Of course if Uncle Joey is right and Provenza proves to be Bernie's killer, the serial killer theory will be moot."

"Ya think?"

I ignored the sarcasm. "Rocco doesn't have a firm suspect. He's not convinced Provenza is our perp. And we know Bernie's murder wasn't a robbery."

"Are you going somewhere with this."

"I think we should at least consider the possibility that these disappearances are connected."

Bob stared at his watch. "This has got to be the longest four minutes and twenty seconds of my life."

"We make a good team, Captain. I suggest we check with other precincts for cases that may share similar facts. You know. Missing faces, missing persons, body snatchers."

"Times up!" Bob announced. He scooted out from around his desk, prepared to drag me out by my arm.

Dixie had been lying beside me on the floor. She leapt to her feet and gave a low, teeth-bared growl. Captain Bob put his hands us and took a step back.

I said, "He's OK, girl. Stand down."

Dixie relaxed and sniffed Bob.

He breathed again. "She's a good dog for you, Caterina. The way you piss people off."

"I have Inga."

"She's a beagle. She'd give you up for a ham sandwich."

I laughed. It was true. Inga's a food whore.

Bob followed Dixie and me to the door. I said, "If Steele left town voluntarily, it's the first time he neglected to set his lights on timer first. Maybe Leo and Tommy could check inside his house. We should know if he's playing the slots in Reno or if, like Bernie, he took a walk and disappeared."

"No."

"But—"

Bob gave me a little push and closed the door quickly before Dixie could react. He waved through the glass.

"Thanks for the birthday present. Next time, don't forget the cake."

I tromped to the car with Dixie, grumbling under my breath.

"I should have let you eat him, girl. He probably tastes like bacon and lemon crèmes."

Chapter Twenty-three

Joey was raking leaves when I dropped by his house. A brown Ford Focus was in the driveway. It was so not Uncle Joey.

"A rental?"

"Compliments of the little green gecko."

Dixie leaped from the car and scampered to Uncle Joey, tail wagging. He dropped the rake and knelt beside her.

"I remember you too, girl. Corey brought you by a few weeks ago." He looked at me. "How is she doing?"

"Missing her dad. Looking for a new one, Daddy."

"Linda doesn't do dogs."

"But you want a dog. And you love German Shepherds."

"I also love Linda. What are you gonna do?"

"Jewelry."

He laughed.

"When was the last time you saw Corey?" I asked.

"The day he was here. There was a problem with the union accounts at work. Some numbers weren't adding up. He wanted my advice."

"Why did he come to you?"

He smiled. "The same reason people come to you. They know you can keep a secret."

"Did you tell him to talk to Bernie."

"Damn, girl. How'd you know?"

"We stopped by Corey's condo for Dixie's things. I saw Bernie's number on his fridge. I was surprised they knew each other."

"They didn't. Bernie didn't know a lot of people. He liked it that way."

"Definitely not Italian." I picked up the rake and began moving leaves.

"I talked to Bernie. He agreed to look at the union books and I gave Corey his number."

I raked and Joey stroked Dixie's coal black fur. It was a moment before I spoke. "It was unsettling to see the note in the condo."

He let go of Dixie and looked at me. "Yeah?"

"I mean, Corey writes the name of a guy he's never met on a scrap of paper. And then suddenly, they're both dead. Within days of each other." I shivered as a chill ran down my spine. "It's creepy."

Joey came over and gave me a hug. Dixie trotted behind him and weaseled in on the hug.

"It doesn't mean anything, Caterina. It's life. Life will kick you in the ass."

My uncle's breath was a blend of coffee and good whiskey. He's not a big drinker but Bernie's death hit him hard. And Linda was in Vegas.

"Did Bernie figure out the problem with the union accounts," I asked.

"I don't know if Corey called him. Doug would know. He was Corey's boss and they were friends. They'd be working on this together."

I nodded.

"Why the curiosity?"

"I dunno. Something doesn't feel right."

"You're young, Cat, and you're still trying to make sense of the Universe. The truth is, and here's the spoiler alert, there's no sense to it. Two good guys died because the Universe sucks."

Joey pulled a stick from a pile of leaves and threw it for Dixie. She hurled after it.

"She's a beautiful girl," he said and shook his head regretfully. "And big. Really big. She would scare Linda."

I shrugged. "Probably at first. Until she gets to know her. Dixie would make a good companion on Linda's runs."

Linda is no bigger than a minute. She could use a big, bad-ass dog to run with.

"Linda says dogs drool, lick, snort, and fart."

"So do you. And you're still here. She'll get used to Dixie's farts too."

"You know Dixie would look good in my new Ferrari. Top down. Tongue out, catching the wind. He grinned. "I might have to thank Nicholas Provenza when I arrest his ass for killing Bernie."

Dixie's soulful brown eyes gazed at Uncle Joey. He patted his chest, inviting her to jump up on him. She did, holding on tight. I watched him melt like butter.

"I'm a sucker. Let's move Dixie's stuff into the garage."

My heart sang. "Possession is nine tenths of the law."

"I'll have to talk to Linda. But first I'll need to buy her something really expensive. What was it you suggested?"

"Jewelry."

He grinned. "Just another reason to thank Nick Provenza when I arrest him."

Chapter Twenty-four

I punched Doug Schuchard's number on my phone. When he answered, I heard laughter in the background.

"Sounds like a party," I said. "Am I interrupting?"

"No. It's Happy Hour. The party's at the next table. There's a whole office of happy here, celebrating something. I'm alone. Now that Corey's gone…" his voice caught, "…there's no one at work I want to drink with."

"Want some company?"

Doug gave his adolescent howl. "I want sex. But I'll start with company."

I bit my tongue and wondered, for the umpteenth time, why no one has ever knocked some sense into him.

"Where are you?"

"Louie's Grill and Tap."

"Order me garlic prawns and a Caesar salad. And Mac and Jack. I'm on my way."

Twenty minutes later, I pushed my way through the office party and found Doug in a booth near the back. He scooted over and thumped the seat beside him.

"I don't bite."

"This works," I said easily and sat across from him instead. He pushed my beer and appetizer across the table. I popped a buttery shrimp in my mouth.

"Thanks for ordering for me. I'm starved."

"Late lunch?"

"No lunch. Crazy day."

"What exactly does the lead detective at the Hot Pants Detective Agency do each day?"

He howled at his great joke.

I rolled my eyes. "Yeah. Like I never heard that one before."

He gulped a drink of beer and the goofy grin dissolved in a glut of tears. "Me and Corey used to come by here after work. I can't believe he's gone."

I blinked. It was like watching a Bi-Polar guy on fast forward. And then, just as quickly, the tears were gone. Doug blew into a napkin and tossed it on the seat beside him.

Doug was on a downhill spiral of grief, spinning out of control into crazy land.

"This is a hard time for you," I said. "Perhaps you could talk to someone about losing your friend. Maybe a, um, doctor."

"I'm fine. Keeping busy." He flashed a smile. "Did your brother nail the boss for offing Barney?"

"It's Bernie. Rocco's not convinced Provenza's good for it."

Doug's eyes popped. "Joey said it was all sewn up. Provenza's the guy."

I shrugged. "Rocco will figure it out. You can take that to the bank."

Doug switched to a whine. "It had to be Provenza. He blew up Joey's Ferrari. You and Tommy cudda been cooked. Roasted. Black as pigs on a spit."

I put my fork down. "You're ruining my appetite."

"I can finish that for you." He took my plate. "Hey, that reminds me. Where'd you guys go in Booker's car last night after the big bang?"

"Bernie's. His house was a mess. Provenza's guys tore the place apart looking for something. Joey emptied out the contents of Bernie's safe and we took it all with us."

Doug chewed my succulent shrimp and thought about that. "But what if Provenza hits Joey's house next. That would be the next logical place to look for—whatever."

I smiled. "You'd make a good PI."

"I'm an ex-cop. Still sneaky as hell."

He roared as if he'd said something hilarious. I hoped he wouldn't start bawling again.

"Joey thought of that. Junior's at college. Linda's in Vegas with her sister."

"And the box?"

"It's at my house."

"That's cool." He stabbed another prawn.

"Doug, I wanted to ask you about something. I saw a note on Corey's fridge—"

"Whoa. Back up, baby cakes. How did you get into Corey's apartment?"

"I'm a private jane. I'm licensed to pick locks."

He laughed. "Could you teach me?"

"Spend an hour on the Internet. YouTube is your friend."

I finished my Mac & Jack's and instantly, the server swept up the glass and offered another. I shook my head and she trotted away.

"Anyway," I continued, "Corey had Bernie's name and number on his fridge. Joey said he gave him Bernie's number because there was a question with the pension accounts."

"Keep your voice down," Doug whispered with a roar. "There would be a huge backlash if a rumor got out and cops started worrying about their pensions." He took a long pull of Corona. "Trust me. I'm the treasurer and the problem is fixed."

"So you knew about the problem."

"Of course I knew about it. I was the one who found the discrepancies. To be honest, I suspected a woman who retired early last year. She moved to Hawaii to be with her daughter. I was ready to go postal on her. But it was Corey's idea to get a discreet, independent audit by an outside party. It was a good call. I knew he got somebody. I didn't know who it was. I never met Barney."

"Bernie. So if he did check the books, you don't know what he learned."

Doug popped a prawn in his mouth. "I know somebody figured it out. Corey said the mystery was solved. The missing two hundred twenty-two thousand dollars was—"

I choked. "Two hundred *thousand* dollars?"

He laughed. "Plus twenty-two more. Corey said the auditor found the missing money in less than fifteen minutes and he was able to resolve the issue."

"Sounds like Bernie. Where was it?"

"In another special account set up for the education of children of fallen officers. The account was created in the sixties. There are a few fundraisers each year for those kids."

"So it was a bookkeeping buffaw."

"It makes sense how it happened. You remember those four cops who were gunned down in a coffee shop last year?"

"Of course. There was a huge public outcry. An astonishing amount of money came in for the families."

He nodded somberly. For a minute he was uncharacteristically serious. You would've thought he was all grown up.

"Those four officers had five underage children between them," he said. "Two hundred twenty-two thousand dollars was set aside to be deposited in an existing account exclusively for the education of those five kids. The auditor found the money in a general education fund that is shared by all children of fallen officers."

"That's a lot of money."

"Not if one of the five wants to be a doctor."

"Booker's kids have big dreams. He needs a pension like that to cover their education."

"Of course the downside is, you'd have to get shot." Doug gave a quirky smile. "College tuition. That's the second reason I don't have kids."

"What's the first?"

"I don't like them."

Chapter Twenty-five

I've known Doug for years. He's exhausting. He's one of those people who will suck the life juices out of you. It's how he's wired.

I left the bar feeling as if I'd been hit by a truck. My fuel light flashed on before I rounded the corner. I stopped for gas and a Snickers bar and headed home all pissy.

It was finally here. The Dinner from hell. The time had come when ex-hippie, anti-gun vegans would meet the gun-toting, bone-sucking carnivores. Papa would blab about slapping big juicy ribs on his monstrous Viking barbeque, boasting like a man returning from a great hunt. The Savinos, returning from an environmental conference in Norway, would declare that meat contributes to global warming. And pastures that feed cows could grow crops to feed the rest of the world.

At least Father Timothy would be there when the lions sat down with the lambs. I fully expected a bloodbath.

My six-month lucky streak of keeping the parents apart was over. The Mamas had found each other on Facebook. They were Besties.

God help me.

I was throwing out prayers to every Saint I could dredge up. Miracles could happen, right? I was totally planning on patting Mama down so she could not whip out my grandmother's wedding dress and toast a double wedding. The loaded M word hasn't come up between Chance and me. I don't know if it will.

But I do know Nonna DeLuca's wedding gown wouldn't hit my knees. And the waist would cut across my boobs. Nonna DeLuca is adorably short. She has a fierce spirit and top-heavy chest that can make her topple like a tree if she stands on her toes. She's like a busty hobbit.

My plan was to go home, take a soothing bubble bath, drink a bucket of wine, and stick my head in the oven. Then I'd curse myself for not investing in a gas range.

I parked in front of my house and did a double take. Fifteen minutes ago I left Doug at the bar, staring bleakly into his glass. And here he was, hunkered down on my steps.

This day kept getting better and better.

I tromped to the house and Doug spun a pair of sunglasses through his fingers. "Yoo hoo! You forgot something."

I removed the frames from my eyes. "I'm wearing my shades."

Doug frowned at the glasses in his hand. "Are you sure?"

"*Seriously?*"

I unlocked the door and punched the alarm code. Doug followed me inside.

"OK, Doug. Why are you here?"

"The glasses. I thought they were yours."

"No you didn't."

"They look like yours."

"Not even a little bit. Mine are Prada. Yours are Ray-Bans. You had them with you last night at Mickey's."

He gave a goofy grin. "You're a quick one, you are."

"What are you doing here, Doug?"

I glanced at my watch. I had a few hours before the dreaded dinner with the parents and Doug was cutting into my bubble bath time. His faced scrunched and his eyes darted back and forth as if conjuring up something convincing. The truth takes less effort.

"Uhhm…"

I checked my watch. "Doug, I don't have much time. I'm supposed to meet Chance's parents at seven. I'm hoping to drown in the tub first."

"Bwahahaha." He thought I was kidding. "Where are you going for dinner?"

"Mercaldo's Steak House."

He made yummy noises. "They got a juicy prime rib."

I made a face. "Savino's parents are vegetarians."

"Huh?"

"Don't ask. Was there something else?"

He blinked hard and his eyes got wet. "I guess I didn't want to be alone," he said awkwardly . "With Corey gone…"

"It might help to talk to someone. The union has grief counselors. There are small support groups."

He kicked a foot. "Strangers don't like me much. Not like you and Joey. You're my friends."

I felt a stab of guilt.

"And the Sunday night poker guys. They like me." He thought a moment and frowned. "Maybe not Max."

My head hurt. This was like having a conversation in a middle school lunchroom.

"Talk to Uncle Joey," I said. "He just lost a good friend too."

He belted a laugh and the happy Doug was back. The guy was an emotional rollercoaster. I wondered if he was having a breakdown.

"Hey, thanks a million, Cat. I feel much better."

"Uh, maybe you should see a doctor, Doug."

"Why?" he said defensively.

I shrugged. "I dunno. They've got good drugs. Counseling. A lobotomy?"

"I'm not loony tunes or nothin'. I'm just freaking out. It's totally understandable. Right?"

I rested a hand on his arm. "I'm only saying this because I care."

"Ahh. I'm totally getting it now." A lazy grin spread across Doug's face. "You want me."

"Huh?"

"Sorry babe. You're not repulsive or anything. I am pretty sure if we got caught, your old man would kill me. Him being

FBI and all. Or Max would. And they'd never find my body. No piece of ass is worth that."

I ripped my hand off his arm like I had been burned, and gaped like a goldfish.

He winked. "Gotta jam."

And he was gone.

◇◇◇

I took a long, hot soak in the tub with lavender oil to calm my nerves, and put on a sea mud mask to "plump" my face.

Dinner with four parents and a priest was *such* a bad idea. Frankly, I blamed Savino. I told him I was dead and couldn't possibly make it. What was it in the word *no* that was so hard to understand? The man was heartless, ruthless. I could see it all so clearly now.

I slid deeper into the steaming, fragrant water and fantasized about Puerto Rico with its pristine beaches and lushly forested mountains. There were dophins there. And sloths! I'd always wanted to see a sloth. Cute little devils. Now that Bernie had missed his flight, well, maybe there a beach-side *casa* complete with a scantily clad *cabana* boy just waiting for me....

Get a grip, DeLucky.

Damn that man's cobalt eyes. What was he doing in my fantasy?

I got out of the tub grumbling, towel dried my hair and started throwing every garment I owned onto the bed. What does one wear to a catastrophe? Silk or denim? Heels or flats? Sneakers? God knows I might need to make a run for it.

I heard a key working the front door and Chance let himself in. "Hey, Baby, I'm here."

I looked at the clock. The dreaded hour was forty-five minutes away.

Chance walked down the hall and rounded the corner to my bedroom. I stood there in Marie Jo white lace panties and bra, eyes wide in panic. His eyes traveled from my face down my body. He covered the space between us in two swift strides, lifting me up to twirl me around with a lingering kiss.

He pressed his forehead to mine. "You have no idea what you're wearing, do you?"

I stared miserably at the pile of clothes on the bed. "I've got nothing."

He laughed.

I feigned disappointment but it was a hard sell. "I guess you'll have to go to dinner without me."

"I suppose you're dead again?"

"Definitely."

He smiled. "My mother will hunt you down." He pressed a finger to my lips. "Stay."

He walked over to my lingerie drawer and pulled out a garter belt along with a pair of nude stockings with lace top. Shoving the clothes-mountain far enough to make room, he gently sat me down and began dressing me, his eyes and hands exploring every curve.

He knelt in front of me and expertly rolled each stocking in his hands to slide them up my legs and attach them to the garters, kissing the bare skin that peeked between panty and stocking. Then he went to the closet and returned with my *J. Renee* peep-toe pumps and slipped them onto each foot. Reaching behind me, he took up the Phillip Lim silk dress in emerald green.

"I love this color on you," he said, sliding it down carefully over my body and smoothing it to my curves with his strong hands, his eyes locked onto mine.

"Mmhmm."

The cobalt blues crinkled into a smile. "Why don't you brush your hair and we'll go. We can pick this back up later."

I wobbled to the bathroom and brushed my hair into a sleek curtain, hooking one side behind my ear. I added a quick sweep of mascara, blush, and lip smacker. For the finishing touch, I slipped on my diamond earrings. They were a gift from Uncle Joey last spring for my thirtieth birthday.

I walked back into the room on steadier legs. Chance hugged my wrap around me and held me a moment. His fingertips traveled lightly down the small of my back and he hummed softly in my ear. "My darling, you look wonderful tonight..."

Chapter Twenty-six

Chance parked down the street from Mercaldo's Steak House. I stepped outside and the aroma of grilled cow hit my nostrils. *Crap.* I'd begged Mama to choose a restaurant with more vegetarian options than a baked potato and side salad.

Chance dragged out his cell and answered a text. When he pocketed his phone again, he was smiling.

"Message from the 'rents, babe. We're doing Ethiopian instead."

"Yes!"

"My parents didn't know Mercaldo's was a steak restaurant until they got here. Dad suggested the Jebena Cafe across the street."

I flashed a smug smile. "Well, isn't Mama feeling foolish now."

"Maybe not. My mother blames you for not suggesting a vegetarian alternative."

My mouth opened and nothing came out.

He laughed. "I told her you had several ideas but Mama was stuck on Mercaldo's."

"What did she say?"

"She said I should quit picking on 'that sweet Italian woman'." We cracked up.

Savino touched my cheek. "You and I, we're good. Right?"

"We're good."

"So if my parents say more stupid stuff, ignore them."

"Deal. And if Mama throws a hobbit-sized wedding dress on the table with the dessert course, ignore it."

His brow shot up. "You'll explain later?"

"Not happenin'."

He hung an arm around my shoulder and we made our way toward the Ethiopian restaurant.

The light at the corner turned green and a big purple semi edged toward us. The lower gears were agonizingly slow and someone sat on a horn. A biker cut out of line. He hammered down, skirting the truck. His hand reached inside his leather jacket and a gold band shimmered beneath the city lights.

Time slowed to a crawl. The fine hairs on the back of my neck bristled. My heart beat wildly in my chest and I seemed to have swallowed my voice.

I reached for Chance and my heel caught a snag in the sidewalk. My knees crumpled under me. I plunged forward. A rain of bullets sprayed over my plummeting head, fanning my hair.

Someone screamed. It might have been me.

Chance hurled his body over mine and we crashed to the ground.

His voice broke. "DeLucky, are you hit?"

I shook my head and he tumbled off me. When I loosened my lips from the sidewalk and lifted my head, all that was left of the bike was a white ribbon of smoke.

I was mad. I wanted to kick some serious ass but I was shaking and my legs were jelly. It was the dreaded adrenaline crash.

Savino pulled me up and held me tight against him. I leaned into him a moment, my hand in his thick hair, feeling his strong arms around me.

Chance spoke in my ear. "Smoak?"

I nodded.

It was Smoak, all right. I smelled Alpo.

Down the block a door flung open and a wild man burst from Jebena's, wielding a pistol.

"Police!" Papa shouted.

Father Timothy was hot on his heels; the Last Rites ready to spill off his tongue.

Mama scuttled through the door next, a fist gripping her chest.

Mr. and Mrs. Savino brought up the rear. They looked a little shell-shocked in beads and Birkenstocks.

They weren't in Woodstock anymore.

Chance waved a reassuring hand. "Cat's OK. She wasn't hit."

They pushed through the crowd and Mrs. Savino's hand flew to her throat. "My god, Chancie! They were shooting at Cat?"

"It's true," Mama groaned. "My daughter's a snoop."

"Chancie?" I said.

Mrs. Savino threw an arm around Mama. "Poor dear," she cooed and glared at me.

I was a mess. My knees were scraped and bleeding. My stockings shredded. And my favorite dress ruined. The shoe that flew off my foot was missing a heel.

Father Timothy edged closer, smelling the grim reaper over my shoulder.

"Cat is consulting with the FBI on a case involving a homicide. It's classified." Chance spoke directly to his Mom.

"Bridgeport may have a serial killer," I blurted.

Savino's brow shot up.

"Too much?" I said.

"People shoot at Cat because she's a hero," Papa said rubbing his scarred bum.

Mrs. Savino chewed her lip worriedly. "They won't shoot when we have grandchildren, will they?"

I felt a headache coming on. Chance looked amused.

Mama giggled. "Wait until you see what I brought in my bag!"

Mr. Savino watched the women scoot back to the restaurant. He sighed deeply. "I need a drink."

I knew what he was saying. He wanted to drink in the bar with men who smoked cigars and would rather wrestle a snake than talk about weddings. But the bar was in the back of the café. To get there, they'd have to pass the women. Mama would reel them in.

"We'll never make it," Papa said.

Father Timothy grinned broadly and took off at a trot. "To the alley! I know the back way."

◇◇◇

The investigation with the cops didn't take as long as I had anticipated. Ettie Opsahl led the show. Ettie and I have a history. Suffice to say there's no love lost between us. Ettie mocks the Pants On Fire Detective Agency and totally dismisses my detective skills. I am pretty sure she's Captain Bob's nark. That, and her life is one long bad-hair day.

Ettie shrugged. "No one got the alleged shooter's license plate."

"Alleged? Look at this dress."

"I'm sorry, Ms. DeLuca." She wasn't. "We don't have much to work with without a plate or description."

"Work with this. The man behind the helmet is Toby Smoak."

Her mouth pinched. I swear a smile would crack her face. "Let me get this straight. It was dark. How much of his face did you see?"

"Enough."

"One witness described the rider as wearing a Darth Vader helmet. And yet you recognized him."

"I didn't have to see his face. I saw his Rolex."

"And he has a Harley," Chance said.

Officer Opsahl gave him a withering look.

Savino flashed his creds and introduced himself. "FBI. Special Agent Savino."

Ettie checked out the badge and identification. She rolled her eyes. Or maybe it was a minor seizure. Either way, she wasn't impressed. I'm guessing the FBI turned her down for general insanity, like my Cousin Frankie.

"Toby Smoak owns a Harley. He was in the park Sunday night with the dead body of Bernie Love," Chance said. "Cat is the only witness who can implicate him in Mr. Love's murder. She's a threat, and it stands to reason, he is trying to silence her."

Ettie yawned. "I was there Sunday. I saw Ms. DeLuca. What I didn't see was a body."

"You must know Captain Bob was called back a second time to process the murder scene."

"Still no body. The guy on the bike could be anyone."

"Anyone with a Harley, a Rolex, and a motive," Savino said dryly.

"You know, everyone isn't trying to kill me."

"Frankly, Ms. DeLuca," Detective Opsahl mumbled into her notebook, "I find that hard to believe."

Chapter Twenty-seven

I gave myself ten minutes in the restroom before joining the others at the table. I ditched the stockings and washed the blood and dirt off my legs and face. There wasn't much I could do about the dress. Frankly, I couldn't have cared less. I was lucky to be alive.

The server brought Red Lentils and vegetables cooked with spices. Gomen Kitfo, a chopped greens dish. Shero, highly seasoned chick peas, and Doro Wot for the meat eaters. Baskets of Injera, the delicious sponge-like sourdough bread were kept filled to sop up all the flavor of the dishes. I took pictures of Papa eating vegetables, and eating beans, and then getting gas. I posted them on Facebook.

The guys were pretty juiced after their stint at the bar. They didn't care what the women talked about. They were bleary-eyed and happy.

Mrs. Savino passed around pictures of a trip they took to New Zealand last summer where the Tolkien trilogy was filmed.

"People live in hobbit houses, built into the hills." Mr. Savino said. "It's like middle earth."

"Hobbit?" Mama's eyes lit. She reached for her bag. I steeled myself for Nonna DeLuca's wedding dress to dance across the table.

"You! You!" A shrill voice screeched behind me and Mama dropped her bag. I turned around. A crazy lady had stumbled from the bar. She was pointing at me.

I reluctantly pointed to myself. "Who, me?"

She shrieked. "You. Bitch. Ruined. My. Life."

I looked again. Crap. It was the liar-liar wife of my birdlike client, Jerry. Her big hairy bear of a lover snarled beside her.

"Gee, Cookie," I said. "I didn't recognize you with your clothes on."

She made crazed animal-like noises.

"Down, girl. What's going on?"

"Jerry kicked me out of my own house. He changed the locks."

"He can't do that," I said.

"Well he did. He says if I come around, he'll send your horrible, nasty photos to my parents."

"Ouch," I said.

Cookie groaned. "My father has a heart condition. It'll kill him."

I winced. "I'm sorry about your dad."

"He'll disown me. He won't leave me his money."

"*Seriously?* So what you really want is his money."

Her lip curled in a nasty sneer. "I'll get *your* money. I'll sue you for everything you've got."

"Wow. I guess those pictures will be in all the papers."

She lunged at me. Chance held her back and Yogi Bear charged him. A chair tipped over. Diners scattered.

Chance flapped his badge. "Federal agent. Stand down or you are under arrest."

"You ain't no cop," Yogi snickered.

He threw a quick and explosive jab but Chance has dancing feet. He dodged the blow and delivered a hammer fist to the side of his neck. Yogi's knees buckled and he shook his head, mixing up stars. Chance cuffed him and shoved him in a chair.

Cookie flung her arms wildly. She might be the worst fighter in the world.

Papa kicked his chair back and held her in a choke hold. "Now I've got something to say to you, missy. Don't. Mess. With. My. Little. Girl."

"Gee, Papa. That was sweet. Now if you'll let go of her for one moment—"

Papa dropped his hands. I reached into my bag and zapped the crap out of her. Cookie crumpled to the floor.

I blew the tip of my taser. I'd been saving that jolt for Toby Smoak but, what the hell.

Papa stepped aside and made a call on his cell phone. When he was done, he addressed Yogi Bear, handcuffed in the chair.

"My guys from the Ninth are on their way. You kids got maybe two minutes to disappear or spend the night in jail."

Yogi's eyes fired hate-darts. Savino removed the handcuffs and the big bear of a man lifted Cookie in his arms and carried her outside. He didn't look back.

Mr. Savino slapped the table and hooted. This was more fun than he'd had in a long time.

A deep chortle escaped Father Timothy's lips. He raised his glass. "The story's never this good when they tell it in the Confessional."

Mama made disapproving clicking sounds with her mouth. Mrs. Savino glared. I could've slapped them silly.

I knew what they were thinking. What transpired here tonight was not a good message to send to their grandchildren.

What grandchildren? I wondered if they realized the kids they talk about are like imaginary friends.

I knew one thing for sure. Chance would have to establish boundaries between his parents and us. I've already talked to my parents. They laughed their socks off.

"It's been a rough day, my Caterina," Papa said.

I pitched down my drink. Papa reached an arm around me and kissed my cheek.

I nodded. It happens sometimes. People shoot at me and I don't always piss them off. Occasionally a disgruntled cheater will confront me and make a scene. But on this day of all the days? The one day when we meet the parents? I mean, what are the odds?

I leaned close into Papa, and I wiped away the one lone tear that escaped. "Some days, it seems I just piss off the gods."

"Chancie" and I headed out while the parents and a tipsy priest decided on dessert. Papa walked with us to the car. He seemed tired and his limp was more pronounced. I hooked my arm in his and we walked at an easy pace. I felt a little sick when I saw the snag on the sidewalk that had caught my heel and saved my life . The shattered store window had been boarded up and the insurance company would've been called.

I have to be the luckiest or perhaps the unluckiest person I know. It's hard to tell.

When I was a kid, I was nearly struck down by a car that careened onto the sidewalk. Mama was a mess. She cried all the time and she wouldn't let me leave the house for a week. Papa talked to her. The priest talked to her. The school psychiatrist came to the house when she wouldn't let me go to school.

And then one day, Mama had a dream. She worked things out for herself after that. She said the dream told her that I am a Cat with nine lives. It's a little insane, I know. But she let me go to school after that.

I have to think if she's right, my luck is running out fast.

Papa helped me in the car and buckled me in. He kissed my cheek and shook Savino's hand.

"Get my girl home safe," he said.

I watched Papa limp back to the restaurant. He looked tired and a little old and it made my heart ache a little. I watched him from the window and Chance waited until he was gone. Then he reached over and grabbed my hand. He brought my fingers to his lips.

I turned to him and the deep burn in his cobalt blue eyes made something sizzle inside me. He took my face in his hands and kissed me slow and deep. When he let me go, I couldn't breathe.

Savino cranked the engine. "Let's go home and see if we can remember where we left off."

Chapter Twenty-eight

I awoke to a soft clatter of dishes and the glorious aroma of coffee wafting from the kitchen. It still gets me all tingly inside that my delicious G-man knows his way around a kitchen. DeLuca men can't load a dishwasher. My ex wouldn't take out the garbage. And if my twin brothers need a snack, there's still a good chance they'll call Mama first. She's not real popular with their wives.

I tugged on a robe, and swiped a toothbrush around my mouth. Then I finger-combed my hair, took two steps out the door, stopped and sniffed. The wonderful whiff of waffles greeted my nose. Yum. I took two steps back into the room.

This deserved some extra attention. So I dropped the robe on the bed and crossed to my dresser where the serious ammunition was. I slipped into a pink and white, satin and lace teddy and stuck on a couple twirly, silver tassel pasties. I made a low dive into the closet. I emerged in insanely tall silver rhinestone platforms, did a quick check in the full length mirror, and adjusted everything to the right place, and clomped down the hall to the kitchen where I fully expected some sugar before my coffee.

Savino's head was in the oven, checking to see if the ham was hot. It was a rear view but everything on that man is rock, hard, and gorgeous. Muscular back, wide at the chest, narrow at the hips, and a bum that can wow the shit out of a pair of jeans.

I moistened my mouth, and leaned my back against the door frame, raising a knee. That sexy pose you see in the magazines, was the one I was going for. I closed my eyes and held my breath. I was hoping I looked at least as tempting as the pig in the oven.

"Yowsa!" Max breathed.

My eyes popped.

"Max?? What the hell are you doing here!"

He made little circles with his pointy finger. "Can you do a little spin?"

I groaned and spun a teetering one-eighty on my stilts. I wobbled fiercely to my room. Max scooched behind me, whistling softly.

"Go away!" I said.

I scooped my robe off the bed and white knuckled it in front of me.

"No can do, Kitten. Savino called me. He doesn't want Smoak scattering lead around you again. He asked me to keep an eye on you."

"I'm pretty sure this isn't what he had in mind."

He grinned. "I'm a Seal, babe. We're thorough."

I made a mental note to kill Chance later. I'd happily choke Max now but my hands were a little busy with the robe.

"Go home, Max. I don't need a babysitter. I'm all grown up."

"So I noticed."

"Arrrgh!"

His expression became somber and his voice softened. "Seriously, Cat. Smoak is deranged. He does some scary shit. He blew up a Ferrari, for godsakes. Who does that?"

"What kind of monster kicks a beagle?"

"Exactly. Toby Smoak will regret that. I promise."

I nodded, surprisingly cheered.

"You are the one person who can place Smoak at the park with Bernie's body. Your testimony can send him to away for a very long time. He has his sights on you, Kitten. And he is going to do everything in his power to make sure you won't be able to testify."

Max was right, dammit. The cold, hard truth knocked some of the wind out of my sails. Maybe it wasn't a totally horrible idea to have Max around. He was, after all, easy on the eyes.

"I can take care of myself," I said with less conviction.

"I know that," he lied. "But I was actually on my way over when Savino called. He's not the only one who's worried about you. Tino insists you drive his bulletproof car. Joey's threatening to put a hit out on this asshole. And Rocco's ready to wring your neck."

"Rocco? Why?"

"Maybe because you wouldn't give him Smoak's name. Or his Chicago River address. Or the lead to the biker bar. Now, bullets are flying when you walk down the street, and, Rocco thinks you're still holding out on him." Max shrugged. "You've got to admit, there's one hell of a pattern here."

"I got nothin'." I hid my face in my hands. "Ah shit. My brother's gonna kill me."

"You might want to avoid him for a few hours, anyway."

"Ya think?" I gave myself a head slap. "Oh sure, I can bring Smoak in myself. Then Captain Bob would have to respect me and my agency. Yeah, right."

"So, what was the plan?"

"Plan?"

"You know. The master plan? First, you'd have to capture the guy, right? Then get him to the Ninth. How were you going to do that, exactly?"

"Uhm…"

"Cuz you didn't have a firearm on you. And I am betting he did."

"You don't know that."

"I know your Glock is almost always in your panty drawer. I'd be willing to bet it's there now."

"It's a safe bet I don't have it on me." I winked.

He smiled. "Get it, please, and carry it with you until we get this ass-wipe."

"I will have to get clothes on first, bossy."

He checked his watch. "It's early. We may be able to grab Toby Smoak before he crawls out from under his rock and deliver him to Captain Bob."

"I don't know where he is," I said miserably.

Max tapped his shirt pocket. "I do. Tino called in a favor."

"Yay!" I threw out a high five. "I'll show those bonehead cops. The Pants On Fire Detective Agency will get the respect we deserve."

Max left my hand hanging, and instead ruffled my hair. "That's never going to happen, Kitten. But it's adorable you think so."

"Well," I thought for a moment. "I'm glad Chance called you."

He gave a cheesy grin. "He clearly doesn't know how irresistible I am."

"Well I'm starving. Are those waffles I smell?"

"Waffles with blackberries, and whipping cream. Your favorite as I recall."

"Yum." I kissed his cheek. "You're irresistible and amazing."

"I'll pour coffee and we'll make our plans over breakfast." He lifted my chin with his thumb. "Oh, and get dressed, Kitten. You're distracting me."

◇◇◇

Tino's address for Toby Smoak was a well maintained two story clapboard with frilly, lace curtains. Not exactly the lowlife cockroach fest I'd expected from Rolex Man. Max pulled to the curb a few houses down and parked behind a brown Impala. The Impala's door opened and a bald African American man stepped out of his car and climbed into ours.

I passed back a hot coffee and breakfast sandwich to Ronnie that we had picked up on our way. Ronnie is a friend of Tino's. He's one of the guys who hang out in the back room. Sometimes customers hear hushed whispers, and that only stokes the rumors of the mysterious deli man's past. Once I walked back there and saw five guys hunched around a flurry of maps and diagrams. You'd think they were plotting a bank heist, but knowing Tino, I suspect something much more devious. Like, maybe he still works for the CIA.

The one thing I know for sure is Tino doesn't exist on a government salary. And he lives better than a man who sells sausages. Tino has oodles of money and he likes giving it away. Last summer an apartment fire in Bridgeport rendered several families homeless. The evening news did a story on an anonymous eye-popping donation that helped each of those families get back on their feet. Later a *Chicago Tribune* reporter traced the source of that money to Tino's door.

First Tino denied making the donation and when that didn't work, he tried explaining the meaning of "anonymous". The reporter was a cocky, arrogant sort who insisted on running the story. But the reporter's big mistake was insulting Tino's Ziti Al Forno. Ronnie and a couple friends approached the reporter on Tino's anonymous behalf. I don't know what was said but the donor story never made the papers. The *Trib* published, however, an endearing blurb about the "best deli in Chicagoland" and Tino's amazing ziti.

The day I walked into Tino's back room, Ronnie removed the papers in one grand sweep and Tino pulled a deck of cards out of thin air. He dropped them on the table.

"Care to join us, Caterina? We're playing cards."

"Of course you are."

I picked up the deck and dealt.

In the backseat, Ronnie gulped the coffee gratefully. His red, tired eyes looked as if they'd been propped open all night with toothpicks.

"Long night?" Max said.

"Let's say, it's good to see you. Smoak is in the yellow house on the right. It belongs to an aunt."

"Is she at home?"

"No. We think she's in Florida for the winter." .

"Good."

Ronnie cocked his head left. "The blue jeep across the street is Toby's ride. He got home around midnight and was a little lit. He could be sleeping it off."

"That's his Harley in front of the house," I said. "He was on it when he tried to fill me with lead last night."

"Damn," Ronnie shook his head. "You mean I could have just shot him, gone home and gotten some sleep. Instead I was watching his sorry ass all night."

"Anything else?" Max said.

Ronnie flipped through his notebook. "He had a visitor around 1:30. He didn't stay long. Half an hour or so."

"Thanks, man," Max said. "We'll take it from here."

Ronnie looked uncertainly at me and back at Max. "She going with you?"

"I got skills, Ronnie. This is what I'm trained for."

He choked on a laugh. "Honey, you're an overpaid dirty picture taker."

I heard my teeth grind. "Go home and get some sleep."

He blew me off. "Max, you and me. We go in there and get this guy. In and out."

Max shrugged. "Cat's a lot scarier than she looks. This is her case. I'm along for the ride."

"Shit." Ronnie shook his head as if dealing with the insane. "Take care of her, Max. Anything happens to Tony DeLuca's girl, Tino's gonna come for you."

I heard my teeth grind.

"And by that, I mean Tino's not comin'. He'll be sendin' me. Go home. We've got this handled."

Ronnie winked and took his coffee and breakfast with him. We watched the brown Impala drive away.

I exaggerated an eye roll. "What a bunch of macho crap. I was waiting for rulers to be whipped out, so certain body parts could be measured."

"Just don't get yourself shot." Max leaned down and checked his ankle holster. "I don't need to deal with the shitstorm that would follow."

"No one is getting shot today. Well, not us anyway." I gathered my hair and clipped it in a tight bun. "Here. Put these on." Then I pulled two pair of thick rimmed glasses and a big black leather Bible from my bag. I put on my glasses and Max did the same. We looked convincingly harmless.

Max grinned. "Is this a disguise?"

"Just a few props. We want the face shooter to come to the door without his gun. When he does, *voilà!*" I flipped open the hollowed out Bible and whipped out a taser. "Karma is a bitch."

"Or I can knock him out cold."

"I'm still gonna zap his ass."

We made our way up the porch and Max knuckle-rapped the door. Toby didn't answer. I pressed an ear to the door and listened.

"TV's on. Maybe he didn't hear you knock."

"Maybe he's ignoring us." Max removed the Bible-thumper specs, slid a hand in his coat and pulled out a 357 Magnum.

"Open it."

He stepped out of the way and I used my picks to turn the dead bolt and then the doorknob lock. After the final pin moved into place Max nudged me aside.

"Wait here, Kitten. I'm goin' in alone."

"Fat chance. Like you said, it's my case."

"I lied." He pulled me behind him. "Stay close. Get your piece out and cover my ass. Just don't shoot me."

I didn't drag out my Glock. This was all about Karma. I wanted this asshat alive. I took the stun gun and left the Bible on the porch.

Max opened the door and stepped inside. I was hot on his tail. He moved silently and deliberately into the living room, both hands extended, clenching the Magnum.

Judge Judy was on the television and a flurry of family photos were displayed on the coffee table. The room had the comforting scent of old women and gardenias. I felt a flicker of sadness for the aunt who'd almost certainly see her nephew return to prison for a long schlep.

The living room led to the dining room and kitchen that circled to a master bedroom. We crept up the stairs with the stealth of bandits, brandishing our weapons of choice, checking closets, and under every bed. We completed our search without shooting or tasing anyone and returned to the kitchen.

"I don't get it," Max said. "The guy had to slip out the back."

"Maybe he saw Ronnie parked outside and knew he was in trouble."

"I don't think so. It was dark and Smoak was drunk."

"OK. So a friend comes by and tells him about the brown Impala. Toby goes out back and they pick him up on the next block."

Max shrugged. "What are friends for?"

I snooped around the kitchen cupboards. Pork rinds and chips and a wide assortment of salty junk food. Toby ate like a teen on steroids.

The fridge was loaded with Pabst beer, stacks of Chinese takeout, and baby-back ribs. There was a bag of crusty White Castle burgers, a jar of dill pickles and some ketchup.

Max rummaged through mail, a kitchen catch-all drawer, and whatever else he could find that could connect Toby Smoak to Provenza. He came up empty.

"Sorry, Cat," he said. "Looks like the asshat's in the wind."

I was bummed. I wouldn't be strutting my stuff to Captain Bob after all.

I wandered to the mud porch off the kitchen. It was a small space with a box of mittens and gloves and a bag of rock salt for cold icy mornings. A stack of shelves leaned against an old stand up freezer that dominated the space.

I noted Toby had fled in a drunken frenzy without his Harley leather jacket and boots. I wandered to the freezer and pulled the door. It was stuck. I'm not easily discouraged where ice-cream dwells. I yanked harder. The freezer rocked and the door jerked open. A big frozen blob hurled at me, propelling me to the floor. My bloodcurdling scream was muffled by the paralyzing weight on my chest. I gaped with horror into his eyes. The fear in Toby Smoak' eyes was forever frozen on his knife-scarred face.

Max wrestled Toby Smoak's icy body off me. He pulled me up and held me against him. My Bible thumper glasses dangled from my nose.

"Are you OK?"

"Eeeuww!" I shuddered. "Dead guy germs on me. *Again*."

I was shaking and Max held me until the trembling stopped. Then he moved over to Smoak's body, knelt down, and jerked up one pants leg. And then the other. The second shin had an angry, red, beagle-sized bite. The wound was infected. Smoak should've had it looked at.

"That had to hurt," I said.

He gave a quirky smile. "Your partner nailed him. Her teeth put Smoak at the park with Bernie's body."

"Ted Bundy," I said smugly. "It would've been enough to convict him."

"For body snatching maybe. If we had a body."

I made a face and he laughed.

"You might want to call your brother," Max said.

I groaned. "I'd rather slip out the back door."

"It's daylight. We drove up in a Hummer. We're toting Bibles and wearing missionary glasses. Trust me, somebody noticed."

"Dammit."

He gave an apologetic smile. "Spoiler alert, Kitten. Rocco is gonna be pissed."

Chapter Twenty-nine

"Thank you, Captain Obvious." I dragged out my cell and punched Rocco's number.

"Yo, Cat."

"I got good news. And not so good news."

"Hit me."

"Tino got a tip on an address for Toby Smoak. He's in Bridgeport, house-sitting for a snowbird aunt. She's in Florida."

"Thanks for telling me first. Gimme an address. Jackson and I will arrest this asshole. If you wanna talk to him, I'll see what I can do."

"Not gonna happen."

"Huh?"

"That's my not so good news."

Rocco expelled air. "Dammit, Cat. You're there in the house now. Don't try to deny it."

"Trust me. I would if I could."

"I don't freakin' believe it. You screwed me again. Waja do to Smoak? Let him get away again?" He paused. "Ah shit, Cat. Tell me you didn't shoot him."

I took a deep breath. "Toby Smoak was in the freezer. He's hard and cold as a block of ice."

"Is he dead?"

Seriously? "Gee, I don't know, Rocco. Did a frozen hamburger ever talk back to you?"

Rocco muttered a word I hadn't heard him say since Mama washed his mouth out with soap. "How am I supposed to explain this debacle to Captain Bob."

"Maybe you won't have to. Not if you dash over here. Discover the body. You can say we followed you here."

"That is not going to fly." I could hear him tear his hair out. "Don't do anything, Cat. I'm ten minutes away."

Bang! Bang! Bang!

"Too late," Max said. "Somebody's at the door."

A voice bellowed. "Chicago Police! Open up!"

I groaned. "Hurry, Rocco. It's Ettie Opshahl. I think she's gonna arrest me."

"Don't say anything, Sis. I'm coming."

"You're ten minutes out."

"I'll make it in five."

Rocco is, hands down, my best friend.

He made it in four and a half. And it's a good thing. Ettie cranked my handcuffs so tight, I was pretty sure my fingers were turning blue.

Max brooded in stony silence. Ettie doesn't know the first thing about men. If she did, she'd know Max was one of the good guys. And if she had any sense, she wouldn't piss him off.

My brother and Jackson darted through the kitchen door out of breath. They got a view of our handcuffs. Jackson swallowed a smile. But Rocco's jaw tightened.

"What's going on here, Opsahl," Rocco demanded.

She tossed back her stringy dark hair. "A neighbor reported seeing two unknown persons in her neighbor's house. We discovered Ms. DeLuca here with the body of a man she claims made an attempt on her life last evening. It appears to be a classic case of tit for tat."

"Tit for tat?" I said. "What are you? Eighty?"

Rocco examined the body lodged between the open freezer door and the mudroom wall.

"This body is frozen," Rocco said.

"I'm not blind," she sniffed.

"You can't be suggesting Cat and Max killed Toby Smoak and shoved his body in the deep freeze."

She put her nose in the air. "They could easily have done the deed last night and returned today to… "

"To what? Hang out with the stiff?" Rocco said incredulously. Then he turned to me. "How did you and Max come to be inside the house?"

"I'm investigating the death of Bernie Love," I said breezily. "Toby Smoak is—er, *was*, a person of interest in Bernie's murder. This morning we received a tip that Smoak was staying at this address."

Max jumped in. "When we arrived, the door was open. We smelled gas and let ourselves in to render assistance. "

"I don't smell gas," Ettie said.

Jackson choked. "I do."

"And where was the body when you arrived."

"In the freezer," I said.

"Why did you open the freezer door?" Rocco said.

"I was looking for ice-cream." I shuddered involuntarily. "The body jumped on top of me."

Rocco said, "The homicide of Toby Smoak is part of an on-going investigation. My partner and I are taking over the crime scene."

"But…" Ettie sputtered.

Jackson unlocked our handcuffs and flashed a smile. "Thanks for your excellent work, Officer Opsahl. We'll take it from here."

"B-but…" she sputtered.

Rocco jerked his head toward the door and nodded a cool dismissal.

Her eyes raged. "Captain Bob will hear about this!"

I rubbed my wrists and flexed the blood back into my fingers. "Bite me."

Chapter Thirty

Toby's body was still thawing on the kitchen floor when Max and I climbed into his Hummer. I put my head back and breathed deeply. Rolex Man was dead. And so was his kill-list with my name etched on the top.

It occurred to me that I should perhaps feel a little sad for Smoak. And maybe I would later. But for now, when I thought to say a prayer for him, the word that came to mind was *Yahoo!*

I pulled a ziplock baggie from my pocket and studied a cigar through the plastic.

"A cigar?" Max said. "That's a new look for you."

"I found this on Toby's kitchen counter. I could swear I saw this same cigar somewhere recently. I'm racking my brain and I can't bring it up."

I leaned over and kissed Max's cheek. "Thanks, Max. You're off the hook. I no longer need a bodyguard."

"Anytime, Kitten. We'll have lunch at The Tapas Spoon before I drop you off."

I narrowed my eyes suspiciously. "Why Provenza's place?"

Max grinned. "I want to see the guy who whacked Bernie. Or maybe I want to thank him for taking out Toby."

"Only if you promise not to shoot him."

Max crossed his heart with a finger.

"Good," I said.

Max was still smiling.

"Or kill him with your bare hands," I added covering my bases.

"Spoilsport."

I wasn't hungry. I couldn't exorcise the image of Toby Smoak's horrified face falling on top of me. I would have preferred a shower with a loofah and insane amounts of soap until every last drop of hot water was spent. But Max wanted to check out Provenza and a shower could wait. Maybe he'd see something we missed.

Tapas Spoon offers thirty beers on tap. I let Max order. We had Bastille Beer with Bacon wrapped dates, Shrimp Skewers, Grilled Asparagus, Steak Sliders. We were on our second drinks when my cell phone rang. I dragged it out and flipped the lid open.

"Pants on Fire Detective Agency. We catch liars and cheats."

"Cat? Is that you? Thank God you're alive."

I frowned. "Doug Schuchard?"

"I heard you were dead. I bought flowers."

"I'm fine. My aura may have a few holes in it. Unfortunately, my favorite dress and killer heels didn't make it."

"The flowers are for them then. If you're at home I'll drop them off."

"I'm at Tapas Spoon with Max. We're having lunch."

"Hey, a guy's gotta eat. I'll see you there."

Click.

"That was Doug," I said. "He's on his way."

Max growled. "Why?"

"He thought I died."

"Doug's an asshole. I didn't make any promises about him." Max drained his beer. "Just putting it out there, babe."

Max lifted a hand and the server trotted over. "I'll take another beer. And I'd like a word with Nick, if he's available."

"He left about ten minutes ago. Would you like to leave a message?"

Max wrote a quick note, folded it, and she took it.

"You can read it," he said.

"I wouldn't do that," she said hastily.

"Go ahead. It's not a secret."

She opened the note and her eyes flashed fire. She ripped the note in tiny pieces and dropped them on his steak slider and stomped off.

"Whoa," I said. "What did you write?"

"I know you killed Bernie."

"You can tell the staff likes their boss. I wouldn't drink that next beer if I were you. Somebody's gonna spit in it."

Max shrugged. "Everybody's gonna spit in it."

A few minutes later Doug sailed through the door with a gorgeous spray of flowers where his face should be.

Max growled. "He was too damn close when he called. He's stalking you."

"Hardly. Doug's not the stalker type. I'm sayin' this as a professional stalker myself."

"I still don't like him."

"So don't buy him lunch." I lowered my voice to a whisper as the big flower head approached. "Doug just lost his best friend, Max. Play nice."

Max slapped a plastic grin on his face. "How's this."

"Perfect."

Doug held out the bouquet with a goofy smile.

"They're lovely, Doug. But not necessary. I'm fine."

"Keep 'em. Just in case. You never know when that Hell's Angel will strike again."

"Cheery thought," I said.

"Toby Smoak isn't going to be a problem," Max said. "It's handled."

Doug's gaze took in Max's intimidating size, the plastic smile, and cold, hard eyes. Doug jerked a finger across his neck, in a throat cutting gesture.

"You mean he's—"

"Pretty much," Max said.

"And you, uh, you whacked him?"

"I did."

Doug got all bug-eyed.

Max shrugged. "He pissed me off."

I laughed. "Stop."

Doug shifted uncomfortably in his seat. "So Toby's toast, huh?"

"It was more like, iced." Max said.

"I guess that means Cat's not gonna die."

"Not today," I said.

Doug sighed. "I suppose I could give the flowers to my mother."

The server came by with Max's beer and a fresh glare for both of us.

"Fat chance," I said. "Shut up and order."

"There you go, bud," Max said and nudged the glass over to Doug. "I bought you a beer."

Chapter Thirty-one

Max dropped me at the park and zoomed off in his Hummer to wherever hunky, ex-Special Forces guys go. Max is secretive about his professional life. I'm pretty sure he does covert, blue-cape ops for some secret government agency.

Max tends to disappear for unexplained periods of time, often returning with a tan. Last month he showed up with African trypanosomiasis, or sleeping sickness found only in the African Congo area. He swore he got the funk from a banana he bought at Whole Foods. Mama believed him. But I'm no fool. I surf the Internet.

Mama wrapped the sick guy in a blanket and brought him home with her. She flushed out his fever with chicken soup and shameless helpings of pastas. To an untrained eye, her actions appeared to be selfless acts of a good Catholic woman. But Mama doesn't fool me. The chicken soup and pasta were meant to super-charge his sperm count and purge some of the Danish from his blood. It's all part of her backup plan for future grandchildren.

Mama adores Max. If things don't work out between Chance and me, she fully intends to ambush him and drag us both to the altar. If she succeeds, I can promise you, one of us will be wearing Nonna DeLuca's wedding gown.

It was mid-afternoon and the Bridgeport park teemed with energy. The sky was blue and the autumn air crisp and clean.

Two old men fed the squirrels. Young mothers pushed strollers and toddlers scampered around the playground.

I made my way over to the bench where the young lovers had been kissing Sunday night. I sat and gazed over to the grove of maples where Inga identified Bernie's kill scene. Only a scattering of yellow and red leaves hung to the branches. It had been a rainy, stormy night the night Bernie was killed but it was a straight shot from my park bench. The young lovers would have had a perfect, unobstructed view of Bernie losing his face and Toby Smoak dragging his body into the bushes. If, that is, they came up for air.

I closed my eyes and sat there a while. I let the cool breeze nip my face and tried to not think about Rolex Man thawing out in the morgue. When I was ready, I walked across the park and placed Doug's flowers beneath the maples. I crossed myself and said a prayer.

"Rest in peace, Bernie Love."

◇◇◇

I showered and scrubbed myself silly with Dr. Bonner's Peppermint Soap as soon as I got home. This was beginning to become a bad habit. I watched the dead guy germs wash down the drain. My body tingled all over when I stepped from the shower.

I searched my closet for my soft fuzzy oversize peach sweater and charcoal jeans and sauntered to the kitchen to brew a cup of herbal tea when something caught my eye. It was the kitchen queen. The second drawer was slightly ajar. With a feeling of dread, I opened each drawer, and a chill went through me. An intruder had rummaged through my house when I was gone. I ran back to my room, grabbed my Glock, and slipped it behind my back. I looked through each room. The search had been invasive and thorough. Drawers and closets were slightly askew. Couch cushions and pillows not quite right.

A half-assed effort had been made to conceal the invasion. But when you live alone, you know how things are. For a moment, I couldn't breathe. I was shaken, for three good reasons.

First, my house alarm was on. My premium platinum alarm system may not discourage an outrageous, interfering family but it's as sound as Fort Knox against strangers.

Second. The one person I believed to be targeting me was laid out on a slab in the morgue. Unfortunately, Toby's club wasn't as exclusive as I thought. This hadn't been a burglary. The intruder bypassed jewelry, money, and a few very sweet bearer bonds from Uncle Joey. (I knew better than to ask where they came from.) He was after something specific and I was certain he hadn't found it. I was pretty sure he'd be back.

And third. This wasn't the work of Provenza's soldiers. I'd witnessed their MO firsthand. Those guys made holes in the walls. And they sure as hell don't even try to reset the throw pillows.

I poured more tea and was stirring in extra honey when the turn of a key in the lock made my blood run cold. The front door opened. I scooted behind the kitchen door, gun in hand. I couldn't breathe. I released the safety. I was armed and ready to shoot some dirtbag in the leg. Or arm. Or somewhere not fatal. Maybe I'm a freaking pacifist like Chance's Birkenstock parents. Or maybe I just hate going to Confession. Either way, I fully intended to beat the crap out of the guy with a rolling pin.

Before I could go all Rambo, Inga bounded down the hall and into the kitchen with Beau on her heels. She jumped on me, howling with joy.

"I stopped by your mama's with a *panna cotta al mango*," Cleo called, trailing behind the kids. "Mama said you were gonna pick up Inga. I thought I'd save you a trip."

She stepped into the kitchen. "Cat?"

Then she looked behind the door. I tried to tuck the gun back in my pants but it was stuck in my sweaty hands.

"My god, Cat. Are you OK?"

"No."

And that's when my emotions came crashing down. Flashes of Toby Smoak stuffed in the freezer like so much hamburger. The image of his terrified face crushing down on me had messed with my head all day. I didn't feel bad that Smoak couldn't shoot any more bullets at me. Or hurt anyone else. I guess I was bummed because his life was a wasted piece of crap. And all his chances were used up. And somebody out there probably loved him anyway.

Cleo took the gun from my hand, reset the safety, and placed it on the kitchen table. She'd been busy the last few days wrapping up a few cases for the Agency. Cleo didn't exactly fool me. I knew she was siding with Provenza's cook. I figured she was also working to prove Provenza didn't do it.

Cleo slapped two mango *panna cottas* on the table. Then she confiscated my teacup and poured a snifter of Brandy. She waited for me to drink it.

"Now," she said. "Tell me everything."

And I did.

That's when I remembered where I'd seen the other cigar. It was in Corey's condo, when I was gathering up Dixie's dog food and earthly possessions. There had been a half-smoked cigar in an ashtray. The label on the cigar-band promoted some Las Vegas casino. It looked a lot like the one I snatched at Toby's. But were they identical? There was only one way to find out.

Cleo opted to remain at the house to finish off the intruder should he return. The beagle and Tibetan terrier played backup. They could effectively take him with slobber.

"The bungler's coming back," she said, her eyes glazing over. "I'm ready for him."

"You do understand that firing at someone is the last option."

A laugh exploded from her mouth.

"Seriously, Cleo. When I was behind the kitchen door, my plan was to shoot his leg."

I thought her sides would split.

"It was a good plan," I said.

She composed herself and winked. "Yeah, right."

◇◇◇

My second romp in Corey's condo took less than ten minutes. I let myself in and walked straight to a small cherry table I remembered by the fateful window where Corey did his swan dive. I opened my purse and dragged out the small, plastic baggie with the cigar from Toby Smoak's house. I compared it to the half-smoked one in the ashtray.

The Palazzo Hotel and Casino. Vegas.

Bingo. I had a match.

A big toothy grin spread over my face. I scooted off to the kitchen for another baggie, crossing my fingers and hoping that Savino would get some DNA results for me. The odds of identical, somewhat unusual cigars in two homes where people died within days of each other were notable. But two cigars having been smoked by the same person could be evidence.

I found a nice little zip-lock and had turned back toward the living room when I felt an irritating itch nag the back of my mind. Something wasn't right. I walked back and looked around the kitchen. Nothing. I held my hand out and turned a slow circle. My outstretched finger moved like a radar beam. When it pointed to the refrigerator, it stopped.

The note Corey had slapped on the fridge with Bernie's name and number was gone. Vanished. Kaput! I made a quick check of the rest of the house. That short, scribbled page seemed to be the only thing taken. Everything else was just as I found it yesterday morning.

My radar finger also picked up a blood red lady slipper orchid in the window. It looked thirsty. I gave it a few ice-cubes and carried it to the condo across the hall. I knocked and a frail woman with snow white hair and baby blues answered the door.

"Ah, Corey's orchid," she exclaimed with a sad smile.

"I'm Cat DeLuca..."

"Eh?"

The woman was nearly deaf. We stood in the hallway and shouted at each other.

"My name is Cat. I wondered if you'd like to have something from Corey."

"How thoughtful. Thank-you very much." She took the plant and smelled the flower. "I know orchids have no scent but they look so fragrant. I can't help trying to coax one out."

I laughed. "I do the same thing."

"I don't care what that policeman says. Corey didn't fall from that window. He was pushed."

"What?" I choked. "You think he was murdered?"

"You're not deaf. You heard me. That boy didn't fall to his death trying to adjust a damn satellite dish. His TV was working fine that morning."

"I heard he'd been having trouble with it for a while."

"Poppycock. Besides, Corey was scared to death of heights. You couldn't get him to ride an elevator. I can tell you this. If Corey had a problem with his satellite dish, the cable guy would be hanging out his window. Sure as good heavens, it wouldn't be Corey."

"Did you tell the police."

"Of course I told them. One of their young men was here. When you're ninety-three years old, people pay you no mind. They think you're nuts."

"That's awful."

"Corey would never lock Dixie in the bathroom. He loved that dog."

"Are you saying Dixie was in the bathroom when Corey died?"

"That's what we're talking about, isn't it? She was locked in the bathroom like a—like a caged animal. Throwing herself against the door and howling to beat the band."

I was stunned.

"Mark my words, young lady. If you want to know who killed Corey, you ask Dixie."

Chapter Thirty-two

I picked up two hamburgers, a couple orders of fries, two chocolate shakes, and drove to the park.

A big yellow moon hung over the city. The two lovers who'd been here the night Bernie died were back. They were goo-goo eyed over each other.

I saw they were younger than I first thought as I approached them. Maybe thirteen. Fourteen. I wondered where their parents were. Or if they were raised by wolves.

I was only a few feet away when they looked up startled. They pulled away from each other. It was the same look I saw in Cookie's eyes in the mirror over the bed at the LaGrande Hotel.

"Nice flowers," I said. The girl hugged Doug's bouquet to her chest and giggled softly. The boy had found the flowers where I'd left them under the smattering of maple trees. She had to think he was terribly romantic. He seemed enormously pleased with himself as well. I expected Bernie would be pleased too.

"I brought you kids a burger," I said.

The boy hesitated, greedily eyeing the bag. "We ain't hungry," he said.

"Maybe later." I dropped it on the bench with an easy smile. "I saw you kids here Sunday night."

The boys eyes flashed fear. "We ain't seen nothin'."

"This is between you and me and the burgers in that bag. No cops. No names. I just want to know what you saw. Tell me and we'll never speak of it again."

"I told you no, lady. Are you deaf or something?"

The girl touched his leg, telling him not to be stupid. He sat back all sulky and she brought the bouquet up to her face, breathing the fragrance deeply.

"There was two of them," she said.

"Two?"

"Yeah."

That meant Toby had a partner besides Bernie's boss. We knew Provenza wasn't in the park that night. Dozens of guests support his alibi.

"The two dudes was following this guy with gangster shoes," the girl said.

I mentally slapped myself. I'm an idiot. I forgot about Bernie's black and white shoes.

"Maybe the dudes say somethin' cuz the guy turns around. And pop!"

The boy gave an involuntary shudder. "They iced him. Like that. We got the hell outta there."

"Is there anything you can tell me about the two guys you saw?" I said.

"They was white guys," the boy said. "One skinny. One…" he searched for a word, "round."

"The round guy pulled the trigger," she said. "Dude never seen it coming."

I decided there was some mercy in that.

"We booked. We come back, the body is gone."

I didn't say the body had been moved to the bushes, no longer an easy view from their bench.

"Thanks, guys."

I pulled out two Grants and gave them each one.

"One more thing. The guy they whacked. You ever see him before?"

The money in their hands gave them giddy grins on their faces. There were a lot of teeth involved.

"It could've been the guy that feeds the birds," the boy said.

"He's got a long black coat like that. And he ain't been around since that night."

She nodded sadly. "Snow's comin'. Who's gonna take care of the birds then?"

◇◇◇

I was a block from home when I received a text from Uncle Joey. With three pics.

First, Joey handcuffing Nick Provenza. One of them had a goofy grin. Second pic: Uncle Joey executing a search warrant of the Provenza home. And third, Nick in the backseat of a squad car.

The text read: *Gun with Toby Smoak's prints found in Provenza's restaurant. Likely used to kill Bernie Love.*

So, it was over. Nick Provenza had his bookkeeper killed after all. And he brought flowers to Bernie's dad's grave to say, what? *Oops? Sorry?*

Perhaps I should've felt better about the arrest but the DA would need some cold, hard evidence. There was no body. And Provenza was certain to lawyer up. Unless we found the lowlife friend who was with Toby in the park, Nick Provenza could get away with murder.

Mrs. Pickins' curtain moved when I pulled into the driveway. I waved and she ducked back from the window. The neighborhood snoop never sleeps.

I decided I wouldn't tell my assistant about Provenza's arrest tonight. Cleo believed Provenza was innocent. In her screwball mind, the flowers and candy on Bernie's dad's grave proved it. I figured Cleo Jones would find out soon enough.

And when she did, it wouldn't be pretty.

◇◇◇

I sat at my desk with the contents from Bernie's box around me. There were a number of ledgers and envelopes I didn't sort through. Bernie Love's passport and birth certificate, and a few other identifying papers were bundled together with a rubber band. What was glaringly missing was a second bundle of documents that established Bernie's new identity. That's the passport Bernie was taking to Costa Rica with him.

The ink on Bernie's will was still fresh; he'd revised it a week ago. A tidy list of assets included two life insurance policies for his sister in California. His monetary savings and stocks would go to the Rainsong Wildlife Sanctuary in Cost Rica. Bernie's Bridgeport house and a cabin on Lake Develen was willed to Uncle Joey.

I opened the drawer for a slip of paper and pen and I saw the picture of the missing Bridgeport man that Mama's church-bingo friend gave me. I took it out and studied it. His name was Charlie and the black and white dog he called Spatz was with him. I remembered Charlie loved old gangster movies. His neighbor said he went to Hollywood to make a few of his own.

Inga warmed my feet under the desk and I felt her soulful brown eyes on me. It was some time before I returned the photo to the drawer.

I looked at her and smiled. "I'm an idiot," I said.

I packed up the box that was Bernie's life and returned the contents to the secret space behind my pantry wall. Then I called Uncle Joey. He answered immediately, sounding cheered with alcohol. He was on speaker.

"Caterina! We're in the man-cave toasting Provenza's arrest."

"Atth-hole killed Barney!" Doug slurred in the background.

"Hey Cat. It's me!" a familiar voice said.

I laughed. "Congrats, Tommy. Uncle Joey gave you a coveted seat at his poker table."

"He earned it," Joey said. "Tommy put his career on the line when we broke into Bernie's the other night."

"Oh yes. Crime is a tight bond."

I heard Tino's deep chortle. "Hi, Tino," I said. "Is Max with you?"

"No. He's got a date with a woman he met at the gym. She teaches a belly dancing class."

Doug whooped like an adolescent boy.

"Come over," Uncle Joey said. "I'll buy you a drink."

"Another time, for sure," I said. "I was calling to say I'm kidnapping you. I'm going for a drive tomorrow and I'll be by to pick you up."

"Sorry, dear. I can't make it. I'm on the docket."

"You can. Captain Bob told you to take a few days off," I reminded him.

"He did, didn't he?" Joey is easily cheered by a few drinks.

"I need you to come because I found something that'll blow this case wide open."

"No blowing allowed. This case is closed. I arrested Provenza. I told him he bought me a four hundred grand car. If he didn't do it, I'm a dead man."

"This whole case is an illusion, Uncle Joey. It's not what it looks like."

"I suppose I could assume the new identity I got for Bernie. Live out my days in Costa Rica."

I laughed. "Call Captain Bob. Tell him I kidnapped you. "

"He'll want to arrest you."

"What's new?"

◇◇◇

I was in bed counting sheep, with an arm around Inga, when Savino called. He'd left several messages during the day but I hadn't picked them up. I was still a little pissy about Chance assigning Max to me without as much as a conversation. I was just pouty enough to expect my boyfriend to hang around when the bullets fly. Not send a surrogate hot guy.

I was emotionally exhausted and being a putz. I answered the phone on the fifth ring.

"Did you see I called earlier?" He was almost hollering.

"Yeah. I was handcuffed."

He laughed as if I'd said something funny. "Did you get my message?"

"No. Why are you yelling?"

"I'm in a helicopter."

"Oh no. You did not just say that." I heard the venom in my voice.

"I'm in Nevada. We have a situation here—I can't really talk about it."

"Of course you can't."

"I hate to leave you right now, DeLucky."

"Really? Cuz you sound chipper enough."

"I need to find this guy and bring him back. It was supposed to be a quick pick-up. In and out and home tonight. You wouldn't know I was gone. But the guy ran. I should be back in time for the wedding Saturday."

"Whatever."

"You're pissed."

"I'm tired, Savino. I've been shot at, nearly arrested, crushed by a frozen dead guy, and some dirtbag broke in my house."

"Dammit, Cat. I gave you Max. He's supposed to take care of you."

I didn't trust myself to answer that one.

He shouted over the engine's racket. "It's been a rough few days, babe. Things will look better in the morning."

"I can't hear you. You're cutting out."

"You're upset. I'll make it up to you. I promise."

"I didn't hear that at all."

Click.

I tossed the phone on the nightstand.

Cleo shook her pink-tipped head in the doorway.

"Unh, unh unh."

I made a face. "You overheard."

"No. I was eavesdropping." She sashayed in and plopped on the bed. "Gimme the scoop."

"Savino's in Nevada."

She shrugged. "He wouldn't have gone if he had a choice. Not with Smoak out there."

"So he says."

"I bet you're PMS-y. You've been a little bitchy lately."

"Shut up."

She laughed. "The guy's crazy about you. Last night he was ready to take a bullet for you."

I smiled. "I guess that counts for something."

"It's romantic as hell." She sighed, all dreamy and goofy. "I wonder what Frankie would do if someone was shooting at me."

My guess was, run like hell.

"You don't want to find out," I said.

Her eyes gleamed. "Yes, I do. We can test him."

"No we can't."

"We set up a drive-by. Frankie and I are strolling down the street when..." She made a gun with her hand. "Pop! Pop! Pop!"

Geesh!

"We might want to use blanks," she said.

"Ya think?"

I threw a pillow at her.

Chapter Thirty-three

A Cleo-sized wail woke me from a dreamless sleep. I jumped up, wrestled the 9mm from my panty drawer and charged down the hallway. My heart hammered in my chest. Cleo squawked again. I followed the sounds to the guest room, and blazed in, ready to blow a hole through my intruder. Cleo sobbed softy. She dragged a sweater and jeans from the closet, stripping and frantically pulling them on.

I set the weapon on the dresser and willed my heart back in my chest. "Uh, what's happening?"

"My sister's been in a terrible accident. She's at the hospital in Wheaton."

My heart wrenched for her. "I'm sorry, babe. Is that your sister, the nun?"

"No," she sobbed. "'It's my sister the h-h-h-ho."

Inga and Beau barked anxiously, picking up on Cleo's meltdown.

"I'll drive you," I said.

"No. I need to do this. I have to beg my sister to forgive me. She's probably at the m-m-morgue."

That unleashed a new fountain of tears.

Cleo tugged on socks and shoes. "She's my baby sister. Oh, why did I treat her so bad. Why was I so pissed off?"

Off the top of my head, it might be because she stole your money, your clothes, your dog, and your husband. But I kept that to myself.

"I really should drive you," I said and ducked into my room.

Her keys rattled and the door closed. I grabbed a robe and told the dogs to stay. I darted to the car after her.

"Be careful," I said. "And call me. If you need anything, I'll be there in a flash."

She peeled rubber, weaving erratically. Her taillights were all over the road. I watched her narrowly elude parked cars until she disappeared from view.

I turned back and the neighborhood snoop glared at me from her window. I waved and hurried to quiet the dogs before she called the cops.

I set the alarm and called Inga and Beau. They didn't come. The last time this happened, one of them had an accident on the carpet. I found them hiding under the bed.

"It's OK, kids," I said trotting down the hall. "Where are you?"

Their barks grew louder and more frantic. And then I got it. A shiver crawled down my spine and my legs faltered.

The dogs were locked in the bathroom. The bathroom on the other side of the house.

Holy crap.

My piece was in the guestroom. My phone was by my bed. And my taser was in the hollowed-out Bible in the trunk.

I would have to beat this jerk off with my bunny slippers.

I felt rather than heard him slither up behind me. I moved quickly and spun mightily, kicking up a foot with a killer move I learned from Jackie Chan. I was gonna feed this dirtbag his teeth.

And then something hard as kryptonite smacked my head. My flying bunny foot crashed in an explosion of brilliantly colored stars. Everything went black.

I don't know how long I was out. But a frenzied howling and scratching brought me back. I lay on the hallway floor mad as hell, feeling as if my head would explode.

I knew this much. If I was holding a gun, wouldn't be looking at this moron's legs.

The intruder was in my bedroom. I heard him banging drawers and tearing the place up. I was trapped. I couldn't make it to the front door without being seen. And if I ducked out the back door, the alarm would go off. He would chase me down before I made it to the gate.

I sprang to my feet and nearly passed out. The pain in my head was brutal. I moved silently to the kitchen, slipping into the pantry. I opened the secret space behind the wall with my jewelry, Bernie's box, and some dusty bottles of Prohibition moonshine.

I took a deep breath and sucked everything in. Then I climbed onto a shelf and folded like a pretzel, closing the door tight.

I hardly breathed. I heard the dirtbag for some time, throwing things and searching for me. I guess he finally decided I'd bailed cuz the alarm wailed. I let it scream and it wasn't until I heard the cops arrive that I stumbled out of the pantry.

My pretzel legs felt stiff and gumby at the same time. I let the dogs out of the bathroom.

And then I called Cleo.

I told her the ho was safe. The "accident" had been a ruse to get her out of the house. I said on the upside, she'd have a chance to make peace with her sister after all.

Cleo gave a smartass snort. "Peace?" she shrieked. "After all that snatch has put me through? Not gonna happen."

Yes, Cleo was just fine.

A paramedic examined the bump on my head. She cleaned away the blood and said I should have it looked at. I told her my neighbor was a doctor and she seemed satisfied. I didn't mention his doctorate was in marine biology.

The cops asked their questions. I said "no" a lot. No, I don't know why someone would target my house. No, I don't know what they were looking for. And no, I haven't pissed anyone off lately.

Okay, the last one was a lie. I'm always pissing somebody off. And the second one was a big, fat whopper too.

My intruder was after something in Bernie's box. Nothing else made sense. Maybe it was Provenza's guy. He seemed to think the ledger was here. But why send just one bully. I'd expected a small army.

My house was trashed. My head hurt. And I felt like crying. It was almost five a.m. and my merriest maid would still be sleeping. As God intended. I called her number anyway and left a message on her machine. She would come and work her magic. And when I came home tonight, I'd have my house back.

I sat on the couch with Beau and Inga. The cops buzzed around, checking doors and windows. A blue shirt with soft eyes came over and asked how I was doing. I said I was peachy.

I watched him step away and make a call. When he hung up, I checked my watch and walked to the kitchen to make coffee.

Rocco would be here in five minutes.

◇◇◇

Sleep was a lost cause. I settled instead for a cold shower and an early morning run. Rocco ran with us and made me promise to keep my gun with me. Max had said the same thing yesterday. If I'd listened to him, I wouldn't have this stabbing pain in my skull. And some freak would have a hole in his leg.

I packed the Silver Bullet with a large thermos of coffee and stuffed my surveillance cooler with sausages for Inga and Dixie. I threw together a picnic lunch with Cleo's Italian roasted chicken, Tino's antipasto salad, a big bunch of grapes, and a couple handfuls of tremiti olives. I packed a few bottles of wine and an extra glass in case we had company. And I didn't forget Mama's Tupperware with her pastries and creamy cannoli.

Uncle Joey was a little hung over when Inga and I showed up at his door. I lured him to my car with the promise of hot coffee and scones. He brought Dixie and his favorite Bruce Springsteen and Pink Floyd CDs. When I told him we had a long road trip ahead, he tracked back to the house for some Eagles, Queen, and Elton John. I figured by the time Mama and Papa get married Saturday, my hair would explode into a big, bouncy Farrah Fawcett 'do all on its own. I've tried to suggest to Uncle Joey how convenient it is to download his music. But he's like an old dog. I'm just grateful he's moved on from cassettes.

We took the 1-94 going north and crawled through snarled traffic until we hit the north suburbs and the road opened up. The sun was climbing higher and the sky was a periwinkle blue. Joey cranked up the music. He knows all the words. I knew a lot of them and faked the rest.

Joey gave me the play by play of slapping the cuffs on Nick Provenza.

He said he interrupted a small dinner party and some whacko cook assaulted him with a spiced, slow roast duck.

"Was this whacko cook's name Gabbie?"

"How did you know that?"

"Cleo and Gabbie are buds."

"Of course they are." Joey grunted. "Okay, Ms. Caterina, give it up. What are we doing here?"

I summoned my most innocent look. "What? We're having a picnic."

He answered with his grouchy look. "Last night you said you would blow this case wide open."

"Oh. That." I smiled. "I may have gotten a little carried away."

"Forget about it, Cat. It's done. We got our man." Joey stretched back in his seat, fingers linked behind his head. "The asshole killed Bernie and torched my Ferrari. He's goin' away for a long time."

"You should hope so. If he's not guilty, driving your new Ferrari around Bridgeport is gonna be awkward."

"Try suicidal. Nick Provenza is not a guy you want to owe a shitload of cash to. If by some miracle he's innocent, I'll be eyeing Bernie's place down in Costa Rica."

After an hour on the road, the big, blue Welcome to Wisconsin sign greeted us. The state sign is redundant. Wisconsin is all about cheese. The moment you cross into Wisconsin, massive CHEESE signs and tourist markets appear on both sides of the highway. Some signs even sparkle.

When you travel at a high rate of speed, the repetitive CHEESE CHEESE CHEESE can have a disturbing, hypnotic effect. You find yourself sucked into these roadside black-holes where the cheese is as lip smackingly delicious as John Hamm in spandex. It may be wrong but you can't help yourself. You just can't look away.

I filled Joey in about the cigars I found at Corey's condo and Toby Smoak's house. And about the old woman who lived across the hall from Corey. She was convinced he was pushed out of his window. I told about finding Toby in the freezer and how his frosty body crushed me against the wall.

And then I explained in great detail my uninvited guest last night, and how I escaped to hide in the pantry with the moonshine and Bernie's box. Joey blamed Provenza's soldiers for my head-bashing, and railed into a vicious rant. He was double-pissed that Savino was hovering over Nevada in an FBI chopper, trailing a fugitive.

Uncle Joey is a typical bossy, testosterone-gorged DeLuca male.

Despite my protests, he called Max and then they were both pissed. Max said he'd be there when I got home. And he'd stay with me until every last goon of Provenza's was, like Bernie, swimming with the fishes.

"I know a guy," Uncle Joey said to Max. "Call me when you got bait."

Joey hung up with a hard, satisfied smile. "That's a real man, Caterina.

Damn shame he's not Italian."

"Max is Danish. He eats lutefisk."

"'The Vikings were savages."

This from a man who had just called for rope, a cement block, and the long end of a pier.

I wondered if Max had made plans tonight with the belly dancer he met at the gym. And why her gyrating hips and the shimmering bauble in her navel irritated the hell out of me.

I got off the interstate at WI-50 and drove west on a mostly two-lane road that cuts through rolling hills and red-barn farms. Most fields had been harvested by now and the last few golden leaves were hanging on for dear life. The cool air smelled of sun and turned soil and a faint aroma of burning leaves.

I slowed down as we approached Lake Geneva. Lake Geneva is a small resort city on Geneva Lake and a favorite go-to place for anyone who wants a quick getaway weekend. Historically, the Chicago elite have come here to escape the oppressive heat and humidity of the city. They built huge estates all around the lake. Like the historic Wrigley Mansion. And the more contemporary Playboy mansion.

Today sex sells better than gum.

Sandwiched between the big money houses are an assortment of church and youth camps. For a slice of this prime real estate, you've gotta be filthy rich or nonprofit.

I parked and the four of us trolled the main street of town. Lake Geneva's a total tourist trap but I love it. The shops are so sweet they make your teeth hurt. There's an old fashion soda fountain, homemade fudge and gift shops on every corner. There are trendy art studios and high-end designer shops with $200 tees. There's something for everybody here.

I went with chocolate. I bought ribboned gift-boxes of homemade fudge for Mama and Maria and Cleo and my switched-at-birth sister, Sophie. And two super-sized boxes for the long suffering wives of Mama's twin boys. They'd be lucky if my piggy brothers didn't eat every piece.

Joey did diamonds. Aunt Linda was coming home tonight from Vegas. The new big, hairy, four-legged kid would be a total surprise. I followed my uncle into the Lake Geneva Jeweler and he picked out a Bulgari diva watch with enough gold and diamonds to work Linda's arm muscles.

I winced when I saw the price. "Geez," I said. "Linda really doesn't like dogs, does she?"

Uncle Joey looked a little sick. "She does now."

We passed by a deli and stopped for a warm loaf of sourdough bread for our picnic. And some Wisconsin dill havarti cheese.

On the left of town, the municipal park hugs the lake. We took the dogs for a walk. Dixie heeled like a Westminster champion. She's sleek and black as velvet and she moves with an elegance that wows just about everyone we meet. Beagles, on the other hand, are baying, nose-to-the-ground food whores who partner detective agencies and contaminate crime scenes.

"The last time I made this trip, I was with Bernie," Uncle Joey said. "He has a cabin somewhere around here. I'm not sure I could find it again."

I reached in my bag for the copy I'd made of Bernie's will and handed it to him.

"That's OK," I smiled. "I have the address."

Chapter Thirty-four

Bernie's cabin on Delavan Lake was half an hour from Lake Geneva. It's close enough to the fine restaurants, entertainment and beautiful people who make up Lake Geneva and far enough away for the fishing, and anonymity of Delavan Lake's cottage culture.

I programmed the GPS and it took us north, continuing on 50 until we hooked onto Delavan's South Shore Drive. We followed the water, eventually turning onto a forested dirt road and zigzagging our way toward the water. The structures surrounding the lake were mostly small summer homes on large plots of land. Most were closed for the winter. The warm days of summer had passed and kids were back in school.

Bernie's "cabin" was an engaging two-story log home, with a wraparound porch, on a densely wooded property. A boat was tied to a pier along a generous stretch of waterfront. Beside the house, a wood shed was stacked high with enough firewood to fend off the frigid, Wisconsin winter.

I swallowed a smile. "Gee, Uncle Joey. You and your new Ferrari could hide from Nick Provenza here."

He growled. "'That worked so well for Bernie."

I parked and dug out my trusty lock picking kit but Uncle Joey stopped me.

"Put it away. No one locks their doors around here."

In this part of the world, an intrusion by an unwelcome human posed less of a threat than the occasional uninvited bear or ill-tempered moose. After my harrowing escape to the pantry last night, I'd rather fend off Yogi or Bullwinkle.

We traipsed up to the cabin and breezed through the door. A red glow caught my eye and I moved across the room to a large, stone fireplace. A few lingering embers smoldered on the hearth.

I saw movement out of the corner of my eye and a figure stepped out from behind the door. His hands were steady and the weapon in them was designed to make big holes. I'd seen those eyes before in photographs. But without the dark, haunted circles and wary expression.

I laughed softly. "Hi, Bernie."

"You shouldn't have come," he said.

Joey gave an audible gasp. He blinked. Twice. I swear for a moment, he thought he'd seen a ghost.

His voice choked with emotion. "Bernie? What the hell..."

Bernie clenched the weapon in the two-fisted grasp of a man whose soft hands were made to create beautiful things. Like photography. And money.

"Don't come any closer," he warned. "I'll shoot."

Uncle Joey strode across the room and threw his arms around Bernie. "Shut up, you old fool."

◇◇◇

Dixie and Inga were off exploring the forest. They would check in frequently and then tear off, streaking through the woods again. The return trips were Dixie's idea. She'd lost one dad already and wasn't taking any chances. Beagles, however, are see ya later, nose-to-the-ground trackers. I knew how Bernie was about birds. I hoped to God my partner in crime wouldn't emerge from the woods with a mouthful of feathers.

Uncle Joey opened the wine and Bernie found a blue-and-white checkered cloth for the table. We ate our picnic on the deck with a spectacular view of the lake. The geese and ducks were showing off.

Bernie had appeared a little shell shocked when we arrived. Joey let the questions wait, letting him eat and drink a little wine before pressing him for answers. Bernie seemed ravenous.

I gave him my chicken and he had second helpings of the antipasti salad. I doubted he'd eaten much since the night he fled town, forgetting his pizza supper in the fridge.

When he'd devoured enough to pop a button, Bernie shoved his plate aside. I cleared the table and brought fresh coffee and a platter of Mama's pastries. He dug right in.

"What the hell happened back there?" Joey said. "I thought you were dead."

Bernie seemed at a loss for words. Maybe he didn't know where to start.

"Why were you in the park?" I asked.

He shrugged. "I had a few hours before my flight and I was starting to stress. I get that way when I fly. I hate to fly." Bernie's voice drifted off.

"So, you went for a walk to calm your nerves."

He nodded. "I knew almost from the beginning I was being followed. I can't explain it. They scared the hell out of me."

"They were scary guys," Joey said. "Cat talked to a couple kids at the park."

"I waited for my chance and I ducked behind a tree. They darted around until they picked up this other guy's scent. He was wearing a dark coat too. I guess they thought it was me."

"It was Charlie."

"Who the hell is Charlie?" Joey demanded.

"Some guy who liked gangster movies."

Bernie's face seemed to shift. "I pulled out my phone to call 911 but it happened too fast. Maybe the guy heard them coming. Because he turned around and...."The blood drained from his face. "They shot him in the head. Twice."

Joey filled his wine. Bernie gulped it down before continuing.

"They dragged him in the bushes. When they were gone, I ran over to see if..." His voice drifted off.

"Charlie was dead." Joey said it for him.

"His face was gone. I was in shock. I don't remember much until I got home."

"You switched wallets with Charlie," Joey said.

"Yes. I emptied his pockets and dumped everything from my pockets into his. Those men were brutal. They had followed me from my house. And they thought they'd killed me. I wanted to keep it that way. I didn't want them coming back."

"And the envelope you stuffed in Charlie's pocket?" I said.

"I wasn't thinking straight. I didn't really know what I was doing." Bernie looked embarrassed. "It's not much, Joey. A small thanks. I intended to give it to you at the airport."

"I don't want your money, Bernie. We're friends."

"I know. But I wanted you to have it. I knew the cops would get it to you."

Joey made a face. That wasn't exactly how Internal Affairs worked.

We sat in silence a few minutes while we concentrated on Mama's legendary cannoli.

"I've been watching the papers. There's been nothing about a body in the park."

"That's because there wasn't one," Uncle Joey said. "Those two asswipes came back and took it. We think they dumped Charlie's body in the lake."

Bernie stared at his hands. "That should've been me."

"This isn't on you," I said. "You should be at your beach house in Costa Rica. And Charlie should be watching gangster movies and living out his own sweet Bridgeport life."

Uncle Joey growled. "I got a place for those two guys. At the bottom of Lake Michigan with Charlie."

I noticed Joey didn't tell Bernie that Toby Smoak was in the Cook County Morgue.

Bernie leaned back in his chair and closed his eyes. There was a little powdered sugar around his mouth and he looked exhausted. Joey figured he'd had enough for a while. I glanced at my uncle. He looked spent as well.

"We're not done here but the last question can wait," Uncle Joey said. "We'll wrap this up later."

Bernie didn't open his eyes but his mouth flinched. He knew what that last question was. And he wasn't anxious to talk about it.

I cleared the dishes from the table. Joey followed me into the kitchen emptyhanded. I resisted the urge to say something. The DeLuca men are cops with blue-cape delusions. It's embedded in their DNA. They like to think they're saving the world. Or at least the good people of Bridgeport. But they can't possibly carry a few empty cups to the sink.

"Who the hell is Charlie?" Joey when said we were alone.

"A nice Bridgeport guy who's gone missing. I guess he didn't make it to Hollywood."

"Hollywood?"

"It's a long story. But last night I figured it out. That's when I knew it was Charlie—not Bernie—in the park. It was all because of the shoes." I smiled, all cocky now. "Charlie loved old mob movies. There was a gangster called Spats in Some Like It Hot. He wore those black-and-white spats shoes. Charlie even named his black-and-white dog Spats. And the guy in the park was wearing spats the night he was killed. It had to be Charlie."

"How did you know Bernie would be here?"

"I didn't. I knew he was alive. I just hoped he was here."

"You could've said something. I could have had a freaking heart attack when I saw him."

I laughed. "There were a few other things that didn't add up. Bernie's new ID and passport were missing. And his packed bags. A lottery ticket had been discarded in the trash after the shooting."

"It wasn't Bernie's lucky day."

I couldn't stop the cheesy grin.

Uncle Joey grinned too. "Good job. But it doesn't change anything with Provenza. He ordered the hit on Bernie. He blew up the Firedragon. And he bought me a spanking new one. Best of all, he won't be around to see me tear up Bridgeport in my new Ferrari."

"You can always send him a picture."

"I'll do that. Congratulations, Caterina. You did just what you said. You blew this case wide open."

I kissed my uncle's cheek. "You ain't seen nothin' yet."

◇◇◇

The guys walked down to the pier while I finished up the dishes. When I was done, I poured myself a cup of coffee and drank it on the deck. I watched the guys a while on the dock. Bernie had a fishing pole in his hands. Joey didn't try to fish. He can't sit still that long. I couldn't hear their conversation but the water carried the rhythmic hum of words and occasional spurts of laughter. The dogs darted out of the woods, ran down to the dock to deliver a few wet kisses, and galloped up to the woods again.

I walked out to the lawn and dragged a lounge chair into the sun. I lay down and closed my eyes. I guess I slept a while because when I looked at the water again, Bernie was holding up a line with four fish. He must've said something funny because Uncle Joey clutched his stomach and laughed.

My uncle called from the dock. "Caterina! Come down! Bring a six pack from the fridge."

Bernie mumbled something to Uncle Joey.

"And some chips from the cupboard," Uncle Joey shouted. "This guy is still hungry."

I trudged up to the log house, humming some catchy eighties tune from the CD's my uncle played in the car. I found a bottle opener in the kitchen and a six-pack of a Wisconsin Belgium Red beer. I tossed some salt and pepper potato chips and pretzels in a muslin bag and added the left over grapes.

I was bent at the waist with my head in the fridge when I heard a door open behind me and the sound of wary footsteps on the hardwood floor. When I spoke, I didn't recognize my voice. I could've been sucking on helium.

"Go away, Doug," I said. "You don't want to make things worse."

I turned around to Doug's wild-eyed stare. He'd lost it. Big time. I tried to focus on the crazy eyes and not look at the cannon in his hand. Doug was a big guy. But he was surprisingly dwarfed by a super-sized gun.

Doug's brow shot up. "You're not surprised to see me. How did you know?"

"I had a hunch. I hoped I was wrong."

He snorted. "And I thought you only chased panty-sniffing cheaters."

I felt my teeth grind. "The coincidences kept lining up. For the first time ever, you were late to the poker game Sunday night. That's because you were in the park with Toby Smoak. Only you, not Toby, were the face- shooter." Doug opened his mouth and I stopped him. "Don't bother. There were two witnesses."

"Are you finished gloating?"

"I'm just warming up. You told Toby Smoak where to find me the night I met the parents."

Doug gave a derisive scoff. "He was a terrible shot."

"Actually, he wasn't. I tripped and fell. The bullets brushed my hair."

"Maybe Toby wasn't such a dumbass after all."

"You lured Cleo out of my house last night and you cracked me over the head. Not cool, Doug. You're the only one who knew I had the box from Bernie's safe. You saw me punch in the code for my alarm. And you used to be a cop. You have all kinds of shady skills."

"I bet your head hurts like a sonofabitch."

"Not as much as the hole in your chest will when Uncle Joey finds you here. Shall I continue?"

"No."

"Yesterday you met Max and me at the Tapas Spoon. A few hours later a gun registered to your partner was found in the pub. You planted it there. And Provenza was arrested."

"You're hardly in a position to be a smartass. Or can't you see I've got a gun."

"I didn't want to stare. It's obvious you're compensating."

The gun twitched.

"Everything was going your way," I said. "But then I told Uncle Joey I was gonna blow this case wide open. You were terrified I knew the truth. So you put a tracker on my car and followed us here."

"You're not as smart as you think."

"Well you're definitely as stupid as I think." I sighed. "C'mon, Doug, if I figured it out, others will too. When you kill three people, you leave a trail."

His eyes got crazy again. With every word, he stabbed the air with his pistol. "Where. Is. Bernie's. Box. Tell me and I'll go."

I gave a harsh laugh. "I bet you made some sweet promises to Corey and Toby, too. It's over, psycho. Turn yourself in or take your chances and run. You were stupid enough to leave your DNA at two of the victims' homes. The FBI is processing your Las Vegas cigars as we speak."

That was a big fat lie.

Doug gulped and ran a hand through his hair. "Things got out of hand. I'm not a monster."

"You're a freakin' psychopath. And then Toby Smoak became a liability. The guy was a loose cannon. The cops were all over him. It was a matter of time until they picked him up. And you knew he'd sing like a canary."

Doug's eyes traveled down to the dock. "Who's that guy with Joey?"

"You really don't know, do you?"

Doug shrugged.

"It's Bernie Love."

The shock was palpable and the blood drained from Doug's face.

"Charlie Dalton. He's the poor sod you killed in the park. You went to kill Bernie Love and you didn't even know what he looked like. You're pathetic."

The wild eyes were back, darting back and forth, making a plan.

Knowing Bernie was alive, had sent Doug over the edge.

He grabbed me by the hair and dragged me toward the door that led to the deck. His body was pressed against me. I couldn't wrangle my Glock from behind my back.

"Call them," he snarled in my ear.

"Nope. You call them."

He jabbed the gun's hard steel nuzzle into my ribs. I may have flinched but I swallowed the gasp of pain. I wouldn't give him the satisfaction.

"What happened to you?" I said. "What did you do with all that money? Gamble it away?"

I felt him recoil.

"That's it, isn't it? You owe money to a loan shark. One of Toby Smoak's bosses, no doubt." I was buying time, making it up as I went. "So you made a deal with Smoak. He's gonna help you knock off Bernie. He thinks he's getting a shitload of cash from Bernie's house. And what do you get out of it? Oh, I know! Toby won't break your freaking legs."

I heard a noise at the backdoor. Uncle Joey and Bernie were coming for their beer. Doug aimed the compensating cannon at the door.

I screamed. "Joey, stay back! He's got a gun!"

My uncle didn't listen. He charged the room, gun drawn, but Doug pushed me in front of him and Joey didn't have a shot.

"Doug?" Uncle Joey's mouth dropped. "What the hell?"

I twisted violently. I kicked up my leg and totally nailed my Jackie Chan move this time. My foot connected with Doug's wrist and his weapon flew from his hand with an ear-splitting report. Time slowed and an ugly red stain clawed its way across Uncle Joey's shirt. His legs slowly folded beneath him.

I heard my voice scream, "No!"

Doug's gun skidded across the floor and Bernie stepped on it. Doug was momentarily thrown off kilter. Somehow my 9mm Glock was in my hand. I released the safety and fired at Doug's thigh. He yelped like a wounded animal and went down squawking. I stuffed the Glock in my back again.

From the corner of my eye a sleek, black streak hurled through the door. Dixie's feet lifted off the floor and the black shepherd cut through the air, charging Doug, teeth bared. Doug screamed with raw fear and scooted back against the wall on his bum. There was nowhere to hide. Dixie pounced on his chest, with her teeth at his neck. She snarled with a ferocity I couldn't have imagined from her. I was somewhat surprised she didn't rip his throat out.

Somehow, over Doug's whining and Dixie's squall and Inga's howl, I heard the voice of an old, deaf woman in my head. It was what Corey's friend across the hall had shouted in the hallway. "If you want to know who killed Corey Cancino, ask Dixie."

Bernie walked over to Doug and kicked him in the head. Doug quit screaming. He was out cold.

I rushed to Uncle Joey with a sob. He'd lost a lot of blood. Thankfully, the bullet had hit his left shoulder, missing his vital organs. Bernie rummaged up an ice pack and towel.

"I'm OK, Caterina." Joey tried to sound OK and failed miserably. "It hurts like hell but it's a clean wound. The bullet went straight through."

"At least it missed your heart," Bernie said.

"What heart?" Uncle Joeys' attempt at a smile was a grimace.

"I'll call this in." I dragged out my cell.

"Put the phone away," Bernie said. "You need to take Joey to the hospital now. There's one in Delavan. I'll help you get him to the car."

I looked from Uncle Joey to Bernie and back to Uncle Joey again. "But what about Doug? We have to call..."

Bernie flashed a smile that didn't reach his eyes. "Don't worry about Doug. I'll handle this."

Joey met his friend's gaze and then he turned to me. "Bernie's got this."

"Huh?" I said.

"Before you go, I'd like to answer that last question," Bernie said. "You wanted to know why I didn't call you."

Uncle Joey grumbled. "And why you waved that silly gun in our faces when we got here."

"Do you even know how to use that thing?" I said.

Joey's short laugh gave him a wince of pain. "Don't worry about Bernie, Cat."

Bernie spoke over his shoulder while grabbing clean towels, a blanket, and something from a drawer. "I was in shock when I

left the park and went home. The hit was risky and amateurish.
The guys were Neanderthals. Somebody wanted me dead that
night. I knew it wasn't my boss. He's not stupid."

Joey grimaced. Bad news for the Ferrari.

"I drove to your house. I wanted to tell you what happened
and have you take me to the airport."

"You were at my house? Why the hell didn't you come in?"

"Because he was there." Bernie crossed the room and kicked
Doug's bloody thigh. Doug was out cold and didn't feel it. "I
watched the man who tried to kill me in the park go into your
house. I'm sorry, man. I didn't know what to think."

"Christ," Joey said.

Bernie flipped Doug onto his stomach and looped plastic
flex-cuffs tight around his hands and ankles. I didn't even want
to know why a quiet bookkeeper from Chicago had those in
his desk drawer. In fact I didn't want to know anything from
here on out.

Bernie put the warm blanket around Uncle Joey. We helped
him to the car, sometimes stepping around Dixie who refused
to leave his side. The girls jumped in the back and I gave them
each a sausage.

I slid behind the wheel and Bernie closed the door. "Take
care of that shoulder. I'll keep in touch."

"But what about Doug…" I faltered.

"Caterina," Uncle Joey said. "Get me to the hospital before
I bleed out in your car."

Chapter Thirty-five

It was the day after Doug went batshit and shot Uncle Joey in the Great Cheese State. Uncle Joey's shoulder was mummy-wrapped and the five of us hunkered down in the man cave. Uncle Joey and Dixie, Chicago Police Superintendent Garry McCarthy, and me. And Captain Bob.

Boy, girl. Boy, girl. Weiner.

Garry McCarthy is Chicago's top cop. He has a mustache and his ride is a long stretch black limo. Few of Chicago's Finest get this close to their boss. Taking a bullet in the line of duty gets you a house call.

McCarthy had a dual purpose for being here. The second was inside the manila envelope on Uncle Joey's lap. The supe's gaze fixed on it. When he left, we all knew Corey's file would go with him.

I found the envelope in my Prohibition cupboard with the contents of Bernie's safe. The papers contained Bernie's audit of the pension accounts. Bernie had pointed an unwavering finger at union treasurer Doug Schuchard.

Doug had burrowed deeper in the funds than Corey imagined. The Chicago cops had taken a devastating hit. I knew when the scandal got out, every cop in Chicago would be pissed. The media would have a feeding frenzy.

McCarthy lit Uncle Joey's cigar. Then he lit his own and tossed the lighter to Captain Bob. The cigars were Cuban and

Joey had a nice box of them. The supe didn't seem to notice. Or more likely, he has his own box at home.

Garry McCarthy is one of the most powerful men in Chicago. But hanging out at Uncle Joey's, he was one of the boys. He smoked contraband cigars and drank the best whiskey that ever fell off the back of a truck. Uncle Joey was feeling no pain. The pain killers had kicked in. His eyes had a drug-happy glaze. If he took one more pill, he might just offer the supe a Ferrari.

Captain Bob squirmed in his chair as if his boxers had hemorrhoids.

His retirement was months away and he knew he was in trouble. He'd bungled this case. He'd pissed off the Pants On Fire Detective Agency. Now he was wondering what the odds were of me keeping my big mouth shut.

It didn't look good for him.

I had called the captain yesterday morning before breezing to Wisconsin with Joey.

"Good-morning, Captain Bob," I said.

"Good-bye," he said.

"Wait! I'm calling about the murder at the park. How's the investigation going?"

Captain Bob choked on a scoff. And probably a donut.

"I don't know how I can be clearer. There is no investigation, Caterina. We have no body, no suspect, no motive. No case. And one clearly unbalanced woman."

I fired a scoff back. "No case? This is the hottest story in Bridgeport. We're talking murder. And body snatchers. I was clobbered three times this week."

"I bet they were head shots."

I ignored that. "What about the bombed Ferrari? The parks imposter who hijacked the body was snuffed. And there are unanswered questions around Corey Corcino's death."

He exhaled. "I didn't believe the satellite story either. The guy was a jumper."

I shook my head incredulously. "My favorite silk dress is

ruined. Do you honestly think I'm fabricating these bumps and bruises?"

"I do. Give the woman an Emmy."

I heard my teeth grind. "Nobody can make up a mess like this, Bobby. If I could come up with this crap, I wouldn't dangle from hotel windows and stalk cheaters for a living. I'd write a flipping novel."

A haze of cigar smoke hovered over the man cave. The temperature was cool enough but sweat beaded on Captain Bob's brow. His facial twitch was working into a spasm. I had reported a murder and he blew me off. The evidence had been there but Bob refused to look at it. He could only hope that his boss wouldn't find out.

The faceless body in the park was one piece to a puzzle that led to another. Rocco, and Jackson, and Uncle Joey, and a couple ex-spies, and the church bingo lady, and even Cleo flashing her hoohah over Provenza's fence, uncovered others. When the pieces all came together, they made a perfect picture of Doug Schuchard's murderous, lying ass.

Captain Bob looked as if he was gonna be sick.

The head honcho was here. He wanted to know how one man managed to murder three people, shoot one of his officers, and rape the police pension fund while chugging beers with the Ninth Precinct at Mickey's.

It was a fair question.

"Cat cracked this case open when she discovered a body in the park," Bob said trying to schmooze me.

I threw him a look. I'm not easily schmoozed.

"The credit goes to my partner," I said. "Inga found the body. A two-bit crook who worked with Doug Schuchard stole the body. His name was Toby Smoak. He became one of Doug's victims."

"This isn't the first time the Ninth Precinct and Cat's Pants on Fire Detective Agency teamed up," Uncle Joey said proudly.

"What is it now, Bob? Three, four cases?" I smiled at the top cop. "Bob and I kick ass. We make a mean team. With my partner, Inga, of course."

Bob slugged down his drink and choked.

I slapped his back. "Supe, this man is an inspiration. It's a win-win when we combine our resources. Isn't that right, Bobby?"

Joey swallowed a gulp of laughter.

"Intriguing," McCarthy said. "I'd like to hear more. And I wouldn't mind meeting your partner, Inga."

I smiled. "Her big brown eyes will blow you away."

Bob had the look of a man searching for a lifeboat on a sinking ship.

McCarthy's head bobbed up and down. "Robert, you're lucky to have this woman on your team. She is going places. If you're smart, you'll bring her over to the Ninth and pin a badge on her."

I gave a giddy laugh. "Gee. Would I be able to work with this man?" I threw an arm around Bob's shoulder. "Just think, Captain. I could be by your side twelve, sixteen hours a day."

"But I'm retiring," he protested, his face turning beet red.

"Nonsense. You're in your prime." The Chicago Police Superintendent fingered his mustache and winked. "Your retirement isn't written in stone. Is it, Bob?"

◇◇◇

The supe downed a last swallow of hijacked whiskey and put on his coat.

Uncle Joey handed over the manila envelope that Corey had given Bernie. Corey's simple gesture had triggered an insanity in Doug Schuchard that would cost three men their lives.

Garry McCarthy shook Joey's good hand. "The people of Chicago thank you for your service. When you're up for it, we'll have an award ceremony. The press will be there."

"Cool," Joey said. "Maybe I'll finally impress my Harvard son."

"Harvard?" McCarthy smiled. "Smart kid."

Joey shrugged. "The boy doesn't know a damn thing about football."

The supe laughed and dropped his cigar in the ashtray to burn out.

Captain Bob drained his glass. "We're gonna find the bastard, Superintendent. I can promise you that."

"Good luck with that," Uncle Joey said as solemnly as he could, considering he couldn't hide the silly grin plastered on his face.

"I'm assigning my best detectives to finding this guy," the captain said. "I'll be in contact with the FBI and Interpol later today."

"Interpol?" I said. It sounded like overkill.

"You can bet Doug Schuchard is on a tropical island by now," Bob blabbed smugly. "Sucking down piña coladas and living high off union funds."

"Maybe," I said.

But I doubted it.

McCarthy folded his arms across his chest. He had something to say. And he expected pushback.

"I met with the mayor this morning," he said.

"I bet that went well," Joey deadpanned.

"The mayor is, as I am, deeply disturbed that one of our own would gouge the police pension accounts. The morale of the men and women who serve under our watch is at stake here. As is the public trust in elected officials. And a grueling, national embarrassment."

"A helluva year for an election," Uncle Joey chuckled. "I smell a cover-up."

"The mayor prefers 'containment,'" McCarthy said.

"Politics," Bob spat.

"To be fair, the mayor is facing a tough reelection," I said. "A scandal like this could kick his legs out from under him. It's not fair. It's Doug's bullshit."

"I didn't vote for the guy the first time," Bob grouched.

McCarthy's uncompromising gaze made the circle. His eyes bored into each of us. "What I'm about to say doesn't leave this room. Do you agree?"

Joey giggled and swallowed another pain pill.

I finger-crossed my heart.

"O crap," Captain Bob said.

"The situation has been addressed. There is no scandal," McCarthy said quietly. "The mayor assures me by the time I leave here, all missing funds will have been deposited to the pension accounts."

Bob blurted a horrible, choking sound. I slapped his back.

"Robert, I appreciate your fine work," McCarthy said. "As of now, my team will be taking over the investigation of Doug Schuchard and Toby Smoak. All case files are to be turned over to my office immediately."

Captain Bob stammered.

"I understand a few other people are aware of the hacked pension accounts."

"Ex-spies," I said. "They're trained to keep secrets under torture."

Captain Bob's face twitched. "With all due respect, it isn't right, sir. You're saying the city is funneling funds around to cover the police pension losses? Isn't that morally reprehensible? I mean, *how* can that even be possible?"

"What can I say?" McCarthy smiled broadly. "This is Chicago."

◇◇◇

I stayed with Aunt Linda and Uncle Joey and Dixie that day. Friends dropped by with flowers and gifts and a startling variety of casseroles.

My parents brought Mama's Italian sausage and spinach cannelloni, a Tupperware of cannoli, and half a lemon layer cake. For once, Mama didn't worry about Linda purging her cannoli.

Mama looked at Joey and bit her lip worriedly. "Uncle Joey is in terrible pain."

Joey grinned through an oxycodone blur.

"Perhaps we should call off the wedding," she said.

We all felt Papa stiffen. Even Dixie perked her ears.

Papa's quiet voice sounded almost dangerous. "Isabella DeLuca. You and I are getting married tomorrow. My brother, Joey, will be there. I'll carry him into the church and hold him up through the service if necessary."

He lightly slapped Mama's bottom and she blushed, pleased. Papa was not gonna spend one additional night in the guest room.

"That is so sweet," Linda sighed. She held a creamy cannoli to her lips and for once Mama didn't flinch.

Uncle Joey just laughed.

Chapter Thirty-six

Mama and Papa had a big, joyful wedding.

The house was packed. The sweet smell of flowers filled the chapel and the organ played the great hits of the eighties. Papa stood tall in his white Miami Vice suit. He didn't look at all like Don Johnson to anyone but Mama.

Papa's hand rubbed his bum where he'd taken a bullet for the people of Chicago. Sort of.

Uncle Joey touched his left shoulder. He was Papa's best man and he was a little pale after losing so much blood yesterday. His arm was in a sling and the powder-blue tux draped over his left side.

The two brothers were Chicago's Finest. They each took a bullet. And they were both heroes. From now on when Papa rides in the Bridgeport parades, Uncle Joey will ride next to him.

Aunt Linda sat near the front between Maria and the twins' long suffering wives. She's a stunning woman. And she rocked the Bulgari gold and diamond watch.

I called Linda last night from the hospital in Delavan. She was frantic by the time we finally made it home. Her eyes were a mess of red. Not unlike Uncle Joey's shirt. When a big, black dog jumped out of the car, she jumped back and with an ear shattering squeal.

But once Uncle Joey explained how Dixie had saved his life, there was nothing more to say. Dixie was welcomed into the family.

Cleo waved at me. She was rockin' the Cyndi Lauper look, sitting next to a cocky Indiana Jones. The whip would be on Frankie's lap. Or perhaps Cleo's.

There was a soft whimper from the front of the church and Nonna Deluca sobbed into a white hanky. Nonna lives with Uncle Rudy and Aunt Fran now. Her memory isn't what it used to be. Sometimes my grandmother needs to be reminded that her bra isn't worn over her dress.

"I thought they were married," she wailed. "What about the children?"

Aunt Fran whispered something in her ear and popped a pill in her mouth. Uncle Rudy dragged a silver flask from his pocket and poured something down her throat that made her choke a little. And then smile. She was happy after that.

I glanced around the church for some eye candy. Savino isn't hard to pick out in a crowd. He's tall, drop dead gorgeous, and definitely M.I.A.

"I'm gonna kill him," I muttered through my bright smile.

Sophie gave a little snicker. She keeps her husband on a tight leash.

She's like Mama but scarier.

Chance had called three times that morning to assure me he'd make it to the wedding. The last time I spoke with him, I was getting my hair and make-up done. Uncle Joey had called in a favor to a famous Chicago make-up artist he'd let off once. The guy's whole team was there. The Delucas never looked so good.

I steeled myself for the kind of big hair a can of lacquer can pull off.

But the stylist was a man of compassion. He turned my long, dark hair into a funky Cher. I told him Sophie adores the fried, processed, chemically-treated, big-eighties hair. She looked like a rock star on steroids.

"I won't miss the wedding, babe," Chance said the last time he called. "You have my word."

"Uh huh."

"I'll be getting dressed on the plane."

"Whatever."

"I knew I probably wouldn't make it back to my place before the ceremony so I picked up something to wear down here. I'm coming as Magnum P.I. You know, Tom Selleck. He was cool, back in the day."

This could work, I thought to myself. Magnum was hot.

"Uh, where are you, Savino? Cuz I'm pretty sure I hear a helicopter."

"'Nevada. But I won't let you down, Babe. Don't worry."

"Bite me."

Click.

Mama's two sisters played matrons of honor. They were having so much fun with Mama's wedding, they were planning a second goround for themselves. Their husbands weren't speaking to either of my parents.

The twins squirmed a bit in their tuxes and I could tell they wanted to scratch something. My brother Michael had a small red smudge on the side of his mouth. To the inexperienced eye, it appeared to be lipstick. But I knew better. It was Hot Tamales. His pocket rattled a bit when he walked. He had a box of candy in his pocket. Vinnie's, I guessed, would be Mike and Ike's.

Rocco looked surprisingly at ease in his powder-blue ruffled shirt. The stylist had sexed up his hair and for once, every shirt button was fastened.

Maria smiled at him with her big, brown, doe eyes. They could've been the only ones in the room.

My sister Sophia was in her glory. She loves romance and weddings and kids. It was nice to see her without a baby attached to her breast.

Sophie's boobs weren't happy though. It had to be past feeding time because the girls seemed to grow before my eyes. There had to be an extra pint of milk in each one. A soft gasp escaped my sister's lips and her eyes widened. She'd sprung a leak. My God, they were going to explode.

Sophie adjusted her shawl to cover her chest. The men didn't get it. A few women smiled.

The organ trumpeted those first notes of the wedding march. Dom da da da, Dom da da da. Dom da and the congregation rose to its feet. The back doors of the chapel swung open and there was Mama.

She was breathtaking. Mama is a beautiful woman in her own right. I don't always notice it so much. When her mouth is moving you have to duck for cover. And Mama's mouth is always moving.

She wore a dress little girls dream of. Her strapless white gown had bling. It was embellished with crystals and beading and the long cathedral train floated when she walked. Her bouquet was a romantic mix of orchids and roses.

I knew Mama had plans for that bouquet. She intended to throw it directly at my face. She'd like to flower-punch me until I heard wedding bells. But if I knew Cleo, she was certain to run interference.

Papa's face melted into a blubbering display of tenderness and love. We were a soggy-eyed lot up there. Except, of course, for the twins. They wanted to escape. They were like kids at a grown-up event.

Nonno Rispoli stood in the doorway with Mama. His thick, snow-white hair was stunning against the powder-blue tux. My grandfather had waited a long time to walk his little girl down the aisle.

Nonno smiled into Mama's eyes. "It would have been nice to do this before you had children."

Mama laughed softly. "It would have been nice to do this when Tony could still remember his vows."

She took her father's arm and they made the long walk down the aisle together.

◇◇◇

Father Timothy gave the opening wedding prayer, occasionally dragging a hand down over his mouth. It appeared to be a thoughtful pose but I knew he was wiping a silly grin from his face. And it wasn't just the sacramental wine.

In a few short hours, the newlyweds would be off to a world far away where satellite reception was sketchy, at best. Father Timothy was thinking Mama would be weeks without cell service. The priest was practically giddy. I know I was.

Joey Jr., my cousin Ginny and her fiance Roger, and Aunt Mimi's twelve-year-old daughter performed a string quartet of *Ave Maria*. Ginny carried the slow, haunting melody on her violin and Mama said it gave her goose bumps. A cantankerous great uncle read scripture and a pimple-faced cousin recited a poem she wrote. Sophie's oldest boy wore one white glove and slugged a few notes on the piano. He played, according to the wedding program, Michael Jackson's "It's The Falling In Love." The performance sounded, I thought, Freddie Kruger-ish but my sister beamed as if her boy was a prodigy. Mama and Papa eyes got watery. It was the DeLuca Family Amateur Hour. It was perfect.

"May we have the rings?" Father Timothy announced.

The rear doors of the church swept open and an explosion of grandchildren burst into the sanctuary. Girls in leg warmers, boys in alligator shirts. There were umpteen of them, ages one through ten.

"The children," Nonna DeLuca wailed, "look at all the poor, bastard children."

Aunt Fran pinched her and when her mouth opened, Uncle Rudy was there with the flask.

Rocco and Maria's oldest daughter carried the sacred ring pillow in her outstretched hands. Her face pinched with concentration as she carefully balanced the rings on the pillow's smooth surface. The other kids carried wedding baskets with rose petals. They were to follow the ring-bearer, scattering petals for the bride and groom's grand exit. The youngest wandered aimlessly. Michael and Vinnie's kids ate their flowers.

Mama began planning her wedding day when she was twelve. She stitched a pillow for the ring-bearer, embroidering two interwoven gold bands with a heart and floral border. My grandmother stitched handmade Italian lace around the edge of the pillow. When she was finished, she made Mama promise she'd marry a doctor.

Rocco's daughter led the way down the aisle and the munchkins trotted behind her. For maybe ten seconds. And then one of Sophie's devil children screamed, "Ninja warriors!"

The ninjas ran wild. All hell broke loose.

Rose petals flew everywhere. She brandished her basket like a sword, taking out a toddler and an old man's cane resting against the pew. Strangers' attempts to console the toddler were met with bloodcurdling screams.

Rocco's ring-bearing daughter was a superstar. The world crashed all around but her steadfast eyes pored over the rings on Mama's embroidered pillow.

I held my breath. Almost there, almost there.

And then Ninja girl saw Grandma in her magical, white gown.

"'Nonna!" she cried and tossed her basket on the floor. The grandchildren zoomed up the sanctuary steps to hover around Mama and Papa.

The ring-bearer's careful progress went all to hell when she tripped over Ninja girl's basket. The crowd gave a collective gasp. Her arms flailed and she narrowly dodged kissing the carpet. The embroidered pillow took flight and the rings rocketed up the steps. Mama's ring dropped at Father Timothy's feet. Papa's ring crash-landed deep inside a heating vent.

Rocco's daughter's face crumbled like she wanted to cry. Rocco gave her a hug and set the embroidered ring pillow back in her hands. He placed Mama's ring on the pillow with the ring from his finger. She smiled and took her place beside Papa and Uncle Joey.

The grandchildren looked uncertain, as if wondering if they'd done something wrong. Papa and Mama's eyes locked for a moment. Then they threw their heads back and laughed.

And so Mama was married to Papa, thirty-five years after he asked her. When Father Timothy said, "You may kiss the bride", umpteen grandkids leaned in too. Papa and Mama had more than enough kisses to go around.

◇◇◇

People poured from the church showering rice on the bride and groom. It was an assault of big hair, parachute pants, off-shoulder shirts and glitter make-up. Papa's Buick was parked on the curb. Tin cans trailed from the bumper and the twins had smeared Just Married in shaving cream on the windows.

The wedding reception would be at the Old Neighborhood Italian American Club on 30th and Shields. There would be dancing and dinner and a seven-tier Italian wedding cake. Happily for guests, there was an open bar, compliments of cousin Ginny and her computer nerd soul mate, Roger.

I have bragging rights for bringing Ginny and Roger together. Roger is a big, generous, teddy bear of a guy and he's BFF with Bill Gates. Roger elevates the DeLuca social status a lot. Before Roger was one of us, we DeLucas didn't know many famous people.

My great grandfather had some questionable history with Al Capone. I know Frankie met Scotty Pippen once while working security for a Bulls event. Before the evening was over, Scotty told Frankie to quit stalking him. And Uncle Joey had drinks with Rod Blagojevich a few times before he went to the slammer.

Mama's friends lined up outside the church to take selfies with the bride. Uncle Joey and Papa hung out by the car, each with a hand gingerly placed over a battle wound. It was an inspirational photo op. A shoulder and bum pic. Many guests captured the image on their cell phones.

You get a lot of notoriety in Bridgeport when you're shot. There's an aura of mystery and immortality that surrounds a person who takes a bullet and lives to brag about it. I'm not saying the good people of Bridgeport want to be shot. I'm just saying they're glad for someone else when it happens to them.

If you're a Chicago cop and you get shot, there's an added bonus. You get medals and a plushy ride in the Bridgeport parades. Local businesses give you free ice-cream and donuts for life. And neighbors will bring you dinners and homemade pies for months. I expect my Uncle Joey will think he's died and gone to heaven.

Papa opened the car door and tried to prod Mama inside. "To the Italian Club!" he shouted. "Let the party begin."

"Not yet." She gave his hand a playful slap. "Caterina has to catch the bouquet."

"God, yes," Papa breathed.

There was a sympathetic murmur of agreement among the guests.

"*Seriously?*" I said.

"Cat needs all the help she can get," my switched at birth sister sang.

She was nursing Chiara; a pink receiving blanket covered the baby's head. Sophie's devil children clung to her skirt.

Mama called the single women together. "Let's see which lucky lady gets married next."

A whole bunch of giggling women crammed the church steps. Uncle Joey's partner, Booker, pushed his daughters into the mix. He was worried about paying for their college education. Maybe his strategy was to marry them off first and let someone else save the Oregon frog.

I tromped up to the very top of the church steps, hoping Mama couldn't throw that far.

On the ground below me, some smart ass guy sang a few lyrics from an old Sonny and Cher tune.

"I've got you, Babe. I've got you, Babe."

I'd heard a rash of Cher's greatest hits since the stylist did my hair.

I hung my head over the rail and Max grinned up at me. He wore tight stonewashed jeans, a black and neon shirt, and a leather jacket. His hair had an eighties' feathered, blow dry thing going. He was all hunky-gorgeous.

"Damn," I said.

"Caterina!" Mama shouted. "Are you ready?"

I took my place again. Mama was warming up her arm. I smiled to myself. She was radiant. And she hadn't grabbed her chest all day.

"Stop the bouquet!" Cleo screeched. "Wait for me!

Cyndi Lauper and Indiana Jones rounded the corner at a gallop. Cleo mounted the church steps, clawing her way through a swarm of women. She knew where Mama was aiming the bouquet and she jostled in next to me at the top.

Her eyes had a dark, frenzied shine. "Back off, girlfriend. I've got this bouquet."

I stared. She was serious. "You understand this is for fun, don't you? Catching a bunch of flowers doesn't mean you're getting married."

"Shut up."

I shrugged. I knew it didn't matter who caught the bouquet. The next wedding will be Roger and Ginny's.

Cleo waved her arms in the air and bellowed. "Send 'em here, Mama!"

Mama crossed herself and looked hard at me. She wound up her arm and pitched the bouquet into the air.

"Catch it, Caterina!" Mama called.

"Grab it, Cleo!" Indiana Jones yelled.

The flowers, hurled high in the air, whirling and soaring straight for my face. I'm taller than Cleo and I reached out my arms and the blossoms brushed my fingertips. Papa cheered. Mama gave a sob of joy. And Cleo made a diving tackle for the bouquet.

She leaped into the air and heaved her body to the side, pushing me away with one hand and grappling for the flowers with the other. I was knocked off kilter. I tried to correct myself but time seemed to suspend and for a moment, I hung in the air with the flowers. The only movement I saw was Cleo's body at full throttle. I felt myself plunge over the railing and a sick sensation of gravity grabbing me. Everything slowed to a crawl and I thought curiously of Corey and his long descent from his condo window to the street below. This fall was far less dramatic and couldn't seriously hurt me. But it could mess up my ankle.

"Max!" I screamed.

On my way down Cyndi Lauper caught the flowers. I heard her screech. "I got it!" And then, "Cat? Cat? What the—"

Powerful arms reached for me and pulled me into him. I buried my face in his chest and he smelled smokin' hot.

I felt his breath on my neck and something quivered inside me.

"Whew!" I said awkwardly. "Thanks, Max."

I lifted my head and looked into Magnum's curiously cobalt blue eyes.

I blinked. Yes. It was Magnum P.I.

In spite of myself, I smiled.

He nudged Max aside. "I'll take it from here," Savino said.

Chapter Thirty-seven

I remember the Canadian geese were flying over the lake when I told Bernie that Cleo and I followed Provenza to Candy Andy's grave. I said Nick brought flowers and tootsie rolls. And that he got all choked up when he thought somebody whacked Bernie in the park.

Bernie was quiet a long time after that. I guess he figured his boss wasn't trying to kill him after all.

Maybe that's why he went to see Nick when he returned to Chi-Town.

Or maybe he was just pissed because Provenza's guys trashed his house, looking for the ledger.

When Bernie walked into Tapas, Nick passed out cold and bonked his head on a table. After the paramedics revived him and assured him Bernie wasn't a ghost, Provenza grabbed his bookkeeper and kissed him on each cheek. That's what Italian men do. And it's just another reason why Bernie Love prefers birds to people.

That night, Nick brought Bernie home to dinner. When Provenza's cook, Gabby, saw him, she hit her head on the floor.

In the end, Cleo was spot on about Provenza being one of the good guys. I felt like a putz.

I'm not privy to the details. What I know is this. Bernie agreed to oversee Provenza's books for a few more years. On a limited basis from Costa Rica. Provenza will hire a bookkeeper for the daily grunt work of running the business. Bernie will manage the overseas accounts, a little friendly money-laundering, and investments. He says that's the fun stuff anyway.

That was Bernie's end of the bargain. Provenza promised to smile when Joey tears up Bridgeport in a Ferrari that cost him almost half a million dollars.

◇◇◇

Bernie met with Captain Bob in his office. Bernie said his wallet had been stolen before he left town for a week. He didn't appreciate the cops raiding his house and wrapping it in crime scene tape. He told Bob he wants his hard drive back. And that someone said Cousin Frankie ate his pizza.

These days Charles Dalton and his black and white spats, are the buzz of Bridgeport. The disappearance of a quiet man known only by a few neighbors would have passed quietly if it hadn't been for Charlie's "psychic" neighbor, Ted. Ted believes Charlie is alive and well in California. I didn't have the heart to tell him that his friend lost his face a few blocks from home.

Last month Ted wrote a blurb for the Bridgeport Blog called: "It's Never Too Late to Shoot for the Stars."

The piece recounts the story of a fifty-something man who walks out of his old Bridgeport life and into the bright lights of Hollywood. In Ted's delusional world, Charlie is the paparazzis' hottest new photo-op.

Since Ted's article appeared, a baffling number of residents say they were besties with Bridgeport' s dazzling new star. They say they had breakfast with him at Connie's Restaurant or ribs and beer at Schaller's Pump. Some claim they watched a Godfather marathon with Charlie. That's nine whole hours with the Corleones and a huge tub of popcorn.

I've got my own dysfunctional Italian family. Now that's what I call a marathon. Give me a freaking medal.

Charlie has become something of an urban legend around here.

Jackalope Coffee serves a Charlie Chicken Pita with star shaped veggies. And residents report seeing Charlie in movies and on cable TV.

He's rumored to be dating Christie Brinkley on the down-low. A blizzard is brewing north of Chicago but we're hoping to escape the city before it buries us. This Christmas I'm dreaming of the white sandy beaches of Costa Rica. Bernie bought tickets for Uncle Joey's family, Cleo and Frankie, and Chance and me to spend the holidays with him. I'm packing light. A few gifts, a couple bikinis, some cool summer dresses, and a light White Sox jacket for evenings. Oh, and the teddy I picked up when I was stalking Cookie Allen at the love store. Chance hasn't seen it yet. But the twirly, silver tassel pasties gave Max major eye-poppage.

I might just wrap myself in mistletoe.

To receive a free catalog of Poisoned Pen Press titles, please provide your name and address through one of the following ways:

Phone: 1-800-421-3976
Facsimile: 1-480-949-1707
Email: info@poisonedpenpress.com
Website: www.poisonedpenpress.com

Poisoned Pen Press
6962 E. First Ave. Ste 103
Scottsdale, AZ 85251